# Praise for Jenny Frame

## *The Duchess and the Dreamer*

"We thoroughly enjoyed the whole romance-the-disbelieving-duchess with gallantry, unwavering care, and grand gestures. Since this is very firmly in the butch-femme zone, it appealed to that part of our traditionally-conditioned-typecasting mindset that all the wooing and work is done by Evan without throwing even a small fit at any point. We liked the fact that Clementine has layers and depth. She has her own personal and personality hurdles that make her behaviour understandable and create the right opportunities for Evan to play the romantic knight convincingly…We definitely recommend this one to anyone looking for a feel-good mushy romance."—*Best Lesfic Reviews*

"There are a whole range of things I like about Jenny Frame's aristocratic heroines: they have plausible histories to account for them holding titles in their own right; they're in touch with reality and not necessarily super-rich, certainly not through inheritance; and they find themselves paired with perfectly contrasting co-heroines…Clementine and Evan are excellently depicted, and I love the butch:femme dynamic they have going on, as well as their individual abilities to stick to their principles but also to compromise with each other when necessary." —*The Good, The Bad and The Unread*

## *Still Not Over You*

"*Still Not Over You* is a wonderful second-chance romance anthology that makes you believe in love again. And you would certainly be missing out if you have not read *My Forever Girl*, because it truly is everything."—*SymRoute*

## *Someone to Love*

"One of the author's best works to date—both Trent and Wendy were so well developed they came alive. I could really picture them and they jumped off the pages. They had fantastic chemistry, and their sexual dynamic was deliciously well written. The supporting characters and the storyline about Alice's trauma was also sensitively written and well handled."—*Melina Bickard, Librarian, Waterloo Library (UK)*

### *Wooing the Farmer*

"This book, like all of Jenny Frame's, is just one major swoon."—*Les Rêveur*

"The chemistry between the two MCs had us hooked right away. We also absolutely loved the seemingly ditzy femme with an ambition of steel but really a vulnerable girl. The sex scenes are great. Definitely recommended."—*Reviewer@large*

"This is the book we Axedale fanatics have been waiting for…Jenny Frame writes the most amazing characters and this whole series is a masterpiece. But where she excels is in writing butch lesbians. Every time I read a Jenny Frame book I think it's the best ever, but time and again she surprises me. She has surpassed herself with *Wooing the Farmer*."—*Kitty Kat's Book Review Blog*

### *Royal Court*

"The author creates two very relatable characters…Quincy's quietude and mental torture are offset by Holly's openness and lust for life. Holly's determination and tenacity in trying to reach Quincy are total wish-fulfilment of a person like that. The chemistry and attraction is excellently built."—*Best Lesbian Erotica*

"[A] butch/femme romance that packs a punch."—*Les Rêveur*

*Royal Court* "was a fun, light-hearted book with a very endearing romance."—*Leanne Chew, Librarian, Parnell Library (Auckland, NZ)*

"There were unbelievably hot sex scenes as I have come to expect and look forward to in Jenny Frame's books. Passions slowly rise until you feel the characters may burst!…Royal Court is wonderful and I highly recommend it."—*Kitty Kat's Book Review Blog*

### *Charming the Vicar*

"Chances are, you've never read or become captivated by a romance like *Charming the Vicar*. While books featuring people of the cloth aren't unusual, Bridget is no ordinary vicar—a lesbian with a history of kink…Surrounded by mostly supportive villagers, Bridget and Finn balance love and faith in a story that affirms both can exist for anyone, regardless of sexual identity."—*RT Book Reviews*

"The sex scenes were some of the sexiest, most intimate and quite frankly, sensual I have read in a while. Jenny Frame had me hooked and I reread a few scenes because I felt like I needed to experience the intense intimacy between Finn and Bridget again. The devotion they showed to one another during these sex scenes but also in the intimate moments was gripping and for lack of a better word, carnal."—*Les Rêveur*

"The sexual chemistry between [Finn and Bridge] is unbelievably hot. It is sexy, lustful and with more than a hint of kink. The scenes between them are highly erotic—and not just the sex scenes. The tension is ramped up so well that I felt the characters would explode if they did not get relief!…An excellent book set in the most wonderful village—a place I hope to return to very soon!"—*Kitty Kat's Book Reviews*

"This is Frame's best character work to date. They are layered and flawed and yet relatable…Frame really pushed herself with *Charming the Vicar* and it totally paid off…I also appreciate that even though she regularly writes butch/femme characters, no two pairings are the same."—*The Lesbian Review*

### *Unexpected*

Jenny Frame "has this beautiful way of writing a phenomenally hot scene while incorporating the love and tenderness between the couple."—*Les Rêveur*

"If you enjoy contemporary romances, *Unexpected* is a great choice. The character work is excellent, the plotting and pacing are well done, and it's just a sweet, warm read…Definitely pick this book up when you're looking for your next comfort read, because it's sure to put a smile on your face by the time you get to that happy ending."—*Curve*

"*Unexpected* by Jenny Frame is a charming butch/femme romance that is perfect for anyone who wants to feel the magic of overcoming adversity and finding true love. I love the way Jenny Frame writes. I have yet to discover an author who writes like her. Her voice is strong and unique and gives a freshness to the lesbian fiction sector."
—*The Lesbian Review*

Visit us at www.boldstrokesbooks.com

# Sweet Suprise

*by*

Jenny Frame

2021

**SWEET SURPRISE**



**ISBN 13: 978-1-63679-001-5**

This Trade Paperback Original Is Published By
Bold Strokes Books, Inc.
P.O. Box 249
Valley Falls, NY 12185

First Edition: November 2021



---

**Credits**
Editor: Ruth Sternglantz
Production Design: Stacia Seaman
Cover Design by Jeanine Henning

## Acknowledgments

Thank you to all the BSB staff for their tireless hard work.

Thank you to Ruth for always helping my books be the best they can be, and thanks to my family for their support and encouragement.

Lou and Barney, thank you for always accepting me and my weirdness, and reminding me we are all a little weird.

To my darlin' Lou,
I love being weird with you!

# PROLOGUE

I knew I shouldn't have done this," Flora Buchanan repeated over and over as she escaped from the suffocation of the large sandstone building in the Glasgow city centre. Panic propelled her faster and faster as she tried to get to the safety of her car. The car was parked across the street next to the casino. At half past nine at night, the city was dark and foreboding.

The town was full of noise, laughter, and merriment that winter evening. Most people would be enjoying the cosmopolitan atmosphere of modern Glasgow, but to Flora, every noise jarred her inside, and every laugh made her heart pound with fear.

Living with OCD and social anxiety was hard enough during the day, but at night it was ten times worse, the noise and the visual stimulation sending Flora into panic mode. It shouldn't have come to this. Flora had one rule that she stuck by—never go out at night. The people, the lights, sights, and sounds were too much for her.

That rule had always kept her safe and secure, but as her OCD was getting progressively worse, a friend had persuaded her to go along to a support group, which of course only met at night.

The tension, the pressure, the pain of having to go through this was defeating the purpose of being at a support group. As soon as it came to an end, Flora bolted from the building, while the others stayed behind for a coffee and a chat.

The thought of coffee and a *chat* sent fear racing through Flora, so she was happy to get out of there. She arrived at her car and started to rummage through her handbag. It was always the same. She never seemed to be able to fish out her keys quickly.

Every time Flora thought she was close to the fob, she was disappointed. Finally, her fingers touched the cold metal of keys, and she tried to get them out. Worryingly she started to hear men's voices coming towards her. Flora looked up and saw a large group of drunk men getting ever closer.

This was one of her worst nightmares: night-time, a group of men where drink had been consumed, and she was about to be in the middle of them. She got her keys and was just about to press the button to open the car when she dropped them, and the loud group of men were upon her.

"Awrite, darlin'," one of the men said, "where you rushing off to?"

❖

"This has got to be answered."

Laura Sharkey—Mack—sat on the corner of her cousin Nikki's desk at the casino while Nikki briefed her people. Mack was wearing jeans and a short sleeved shirt.

Mack was not formal, not that she needed to be, while her cousin Nikki, the head of the Sharkey clan and business empire, was beautiful in her feminine designer power suits. Mack had no need to fit in with that corporate world. The streets were her playground.

Nikki continued, "No one sells drugs in a Sharkey territory, but to sell them outside my child's secondary school, when he was warned time and again for his actions? Mack and I will go ourselves."

"Are you sure, Nikki? You don't need to get your hands dirty," Eddie, one of her guards, said.

"It's beyond that now. My little girl is at home crying her heart out because her best friend Charlotte is dead, and now he is going to wish he was dead."

"I don't understand how he got Charlotte to try drugs," Mack said.

"We'll find out."

Most people underestimated Nikki Sharkey, mostly because of her feminine appearance, but while you were assuming she was no threat, Nicki would have a gun against your head, or despatch a punch across your face. She was an alpha personality from the tips of her high-heeled shoes to the ends of her beautifully styled hair.

Mack, on the other hand, was a butch whose idea of hell was wearing a suit, but they complemented each other, in every way. It's what made them the perfect team.

Plus Nikki trusted Mack implicitly, which was essential when you ran a business empire that sometimes operated on the fringes of the law.

"Don't worry, Murdo," Mack told one of Nikki's closest lieutenants. "I'll make sure she's safe."

"You don't have to worry about me. Is he waiting for us where I asked?"

"Yes, we picked him up a few hours ago," Murdo said.

Mack turned her head around to look at the banks of TV monitors that surveyed the blackjack tables, the poker tables, and the slot machines. Mack liked when they met at the casino—it was full of life and sounds, laughter, and sometimes tears, as the full gamut of human emotions were played out down on the casino floor. Then one of the outdoor cameras caught her eye. It surveyed the area around the.corner from the casino's front door.

Mack watched a rowdy group of men surrounding a woman who had her hands over her ears. They were pawing at her, and then they started to pull her away from the car into the dark. Mack was on her way in moments. She pointed at two of her burly workmates and said, "You two, with me."

They made their way downstairs as quickly as they could. The two bouncers at the door to the casino joined them, and they hurried around the building, then heard muffled screams from the alley behind the casino.

Anger and rage filled her chest when she saw the defenceless woman up against the wall, one of the men's hands across her mouth. Some of the men ran when they saw the big men Mack had brought, which left three who hadn't seen them approach.

Mack grabbed the ringleader and shouted, "Get your hands off her." The bouncers and her other guards got hold of the men. "Deal with them," Mack instructed, while she pulled the trembling, shaking woman into her arms.

Mack walked back around the corner with the woman and guided her to the side of the car. "It's okay. You're safe now—you're safe with me."

The woman clung to her like she was clinging to a rock in a storm. The woman flinched as they heard the men shout out after some punches and kicks were no doubt meted out.

"I promise you'll be safe. We'll call the police and report these men. They won't bother you again."

One of the bouncers came around the corner and said, "What do you want us to do with this scum?"

"Hang on." Mack relaxed her grip on the trembling woman. It was only when she did that, that she realized how much she liked the feeling of the woman in her arms. "I'm just going to talk to my man over here, but I'll be right back. I'll take care of you."

Mack walked over to her man and heard a car door open and shut behind her. She turned around quickly and saw the terrified woman about to pull away in her car. "Don't—wait," she called out.

But it was too late. The woman without a name was gone in an instant.

## CHAPTER ONE

Mack zipped up her holdall and placed it on her bunk. This was her last morning in prison and hopefully the start of a new life.

"Please, Mack."

Mack's most recent cellmate, Kelly, was sitting on the bed, trying to control a tremor in her hands.

"No, you know I don't have anything to do with drugs," Mack said.

"You're a Sharkey. You can get anything in here—phones, drink, drugs, anything."

Mack had been listening to this broken record for days and was getting fed up with it.

She went to put on her jacket, but before she could, Kelly jumped up and grabbed her by the T-shirt.

"Are you listening to me?"

Mack quickly grabbed her by the neck, gained control, and pushed Kelly up against the wall. "Don't ever touch me," Mack snarled.

Kelly looked terrified. "Sorry, sorry."

"What does that mean?" Mack pointed to the underside of her forearm, where she sported a big shark tooth tattoo.

"You're a part of the Sharkey family," Kelly spluttered.

"Aye, and being a Sharkey means following the family code. We don't take drugs, we don't sell drugs, we don't allow them in Sharkey territories, and we sure as fuck don't supply them to addicted prisoners." Mack let go of her and said, "You've got an opportunity here—you've not got long to go in your sentence. Get to the docs in here, and get on a rehab program. Okay?"

The cell door opened and a prison guard said, "It's time, Sharkey."

Mack gave Kelly a soft punch to the arm. "Good luck, okay?"

Kelly nodded.

Mack put her jacket on and lifted her bag to follow the prison officer out.

As they passed through the main part of the jail, other prisoners shouted and whooped as she passed. She was popular amongst the women, not just because of the name Sharkey, but because she was genuinely liked and helped people where she could.

When the final paperwork was dealt with, the officer took her out the front door and towards the main gate.

"You won't be coming back here, will you, Sharkey?"

Mack Sharkey glanced to the prison officer beside her as they walked towards the prison gate.

"Me? Nah. It's the quiet life for me from now on, Officer Davis."

Davis chuckled as she opened the gate. "When has a Sharkey ever lived a quiet life?"

"I'm a changed woman."

"I'm sure. Good luck then."

Before she knew it, Mack was standing out of the prison on the pavement. The day was chilly, but the sun was bright in the sky. Mack looked up and took in a big gulp of fresh air. She'd been dreaming of this moment ever since she'd been sentenced a year and a half ago, and the time had finally come.

Mack started walking, enjoying the freedom already. There were so many things she was looking forward to, the main one being seeing her true love again, but having a shower and sleeping in her own bed were right up there.

As she walked along the road, a blacked-out Land Rover pulled up beside her. The front passenger window opened slowly and a big beefy looking man glowered at her.

"Get in the car."

Instead of being frightened, Mack burst into laughter and said, "You need to work on that menacing persona, Murdo."

Murdo screwed up his face. "It works on most people."

"Well, most people don't know you burst into tears if one of your tropical fish dies."

Murdo jumped out of the car and grinned ear to ear before pulling Mack into a bear hug. "It's so good to have you back."

"It's good to be back. Now get me away from this place," Mack said.

Murdo opened the door for Mack, and before she slipped in, he said, "Mack? What you did—well, I just want you to know that we've all got big respect for you, man."

"You've got to be willing to take one for the team, Murdo. It's the golden rule."

"Aye, you're no wrong."

Growing up as a Sharkey was a very particular experience and one that instilled great family loyalty, and those that worked with them had to get their heads around that fact, or they didn't last long.

She sat in the back, and the younger driver of the car held out his hand to shake hers. "Mack, you're a legend."

Mack laughed. "Thanks, Jamsey, but I don't think I've reached legend status yet."

But as self-deprecating as she was, Mack knew that serving time for her cousin Nikki, the head of the Sharkey family, had elevated her status to one of ultimate respect.

"I know you've probably got some other things you'd like to do, but Mr. Thomas asked me to drive to the HQ."

HQ was the Sharkey family home on a large piece of land in the leafy outskirts of Glasgow. Thomas, her uncle, lived there with her aunt Christine, and next door Mack's mum had her own house.

In all those long months in prison, it gave Mack comfort to know that her mum was safe, right next door to her aunt and uncle.

"That's okay, I want to see ma wee Ma and the love of my life."

Murdo and Jamsey laughed. Everyone in their family knew who the love of her life was, but those on the outside would never believe it.

The car drove off and travelled through the Glasgow streets. The sights and sounds of daily life were something that she had dreamed of, while cooped up in her prison cell. One thing was for sure—she wasn't going back.

When she'd taken the blame for her cousin, both Nikki and Nikki's father, her uncle Thomas, promised her she could take a step back from the business and follow her dream to have a quieter life. Although when it came to family, Mack knew she would do anything for them, if it came to it.

The urban city gave way to the leafier suburbs, and before long they were driving through the gated entrance to the expansive Sharkey property.

They pulled up to a large modern home. Just next door was her mum's house, built by Uncle Thomas. Mack saw her mum standing on the porch of her aunt and uncle's house. She was waving frantically and smiling ear to ear. Mack got out the car almost before it stopped, and her mum ran into her arms.

She lifted her mum up and spun her around. Her mum kissed her all over her face. "I missed you so much."

Mack set her mum's feet back to the ground. Mary Sharkey was a petite woman, and even though Mack didn't have many memories of her dad, she thanked God that she took her height from him.

"I missed you too, Ma—are you okay?"

"I'm fine now you're home." Her mum cupped her cheeks with her hands. "We're so proud of what you did, but I don't want you going back to jail."

"I won't. A quiet life is all I want now."

"And maybe meet a nice wee lassie?" her mum said hopefully.

"Give me a chance, Ma. I've only been out of prison for two minutes."

It was her mother's dearest wish that she settle down, but Mack had never wanted a long-term girlfriend. She loved women but had never been in love. And the women she had met weren't who she wanted to bring home to Mum. She doubted she would ever get that far with a woman.

"Well, just remember—I want a grandchild just like Isla." Isla was her eleven-year-old niece, and adored by the family.

"Yes, maybe one day," Mack replied.

Her mother clapped her hands together and said, "My baby's home."

Mack glanced to the car behind her and caught Murdo and Jamsey grinning.

She felt her cheeks go hot. "Ma, don't call me that in front of the boys."

Her mum looped her arm through hers and led her to the door. "Everyone's waiting for you."

She opened the door, and in the large hallway her aunt and uncle and Isla were waiting. There was a *Welcome Home* sign, and balloons everywhere. Her family shouted, "Welcome home!" Then they pulled some party poppers, shooting streamers in the air.

"Wow, thanks." Mack hurried over to them. She hugged her aunt, the matriarch of the Sharkey family, and as fearsome to outsiders as her uncle Thomas had ever been.

"We're so glad to have you home, Mack. Your mum has missed you so much."

"Thanks for looking after her for me, Aunt Chrissy."

Uncle Thomas grasped her and patted her back. "You were missed." Then he cupped her cheek and said, "You and I will talk later, but we are so proud of you."

"Thanks, Uncle Thomas."

That statement made Mack so happy. Uncle Thomas had been her father figure since her mother left her dad when she was very young, and she looked up to him so much. Mack didn't share his love of business and figures like Nikki did, but his unshakable loyalty and kindness to his family was something she always sought to emulate.

Mack then turned to her quiet little niece, who was smiling broadly. She held out her arms and used a particularly Scottish term of endearment for a small child. "Come here, wee barra."

Isla jumped into Mack's arms and squeezed her tightly. Isla had a special relationship with Mack. Nikki adored her daughter and lavished as much time on her as running the Sharkey family would allow, but Mack gave her something different. She made her laugh and feel light-hearted. Mack was the silly one, the childlike one, who loved nothing more than playing with Isla.

"I missed you, Mack."

"You too, we've got so much to catch up on." Mack gave her a big kiss. "Where's your mum?"

"She sends her apologies, but she still has some business to be finished in Paris. She'll catch up with you in a couple of days," Thomas said.

Her mother said, "But there's someone else who's dying to see you."

"My baby?" Mack said excitedly.

Her mum signalled to Isla, who smiled and ran off to open the kitchen.

A small dachshund came running out, wearing a cute little jumper and a bow tie. Mack fell to her knees and held her arms out. The dog stopped for a second, not expecting to see Mack, but when he realized who it was, he shot over to her at top speed and nearly bowled her over.

"Dexter! I missed you so much."

Dexter was quite simply the love of her life. Nobody expected the big and feared Mack Sharkey to have a dachshund, but those on the outside didn't know the true loving softie that she could be.

Her little pal went everywhere with her, and it had broken her heart to leave him for so long.

"I love you too, Dex."

Dexter was so hyper—he went from licking her face off, to zoomies, to jumping on her lap. Eventually she got him to calm down enough to hug him. "Have you been a good boy, Dexie?"

"He has," her mother replied.

Uncle Thomas then said, "Apart from when he ran off with my glasses and chewed them up."

Aunt Chrissy gently smacked him in the stomach. His wife was the only one who could get away with that. "You shouldn't have left them where Dexter could get them."

"Sorry, Uncle Thomas."

"I needed new ones anyway."

Her mum had her arm around Isla. "Isy's been helping take care of him for me, haven't you, Isy?"

Isla walked over and knelt down next to Mack and stroked Dexter. "I took him out for lots of walks every day, Mack."

"Thanks, wee barra."

Mack lifted Dexter above her face and looked into his cute little eyes. "I'm not leaving you again, Dex."

❖

After the best lunch she'd had in a year and a half, Mack retreated to her uncle's office. He poured out two drinks while Mack sat with Dexter in her lap. Thomas handed her a glass of brandy and smiled at the little dog.

"He's happy now."

"He won't leave my side. I think he's frightened I'll disappear again."

Thomas took a seat behind his desk. "Isy's loved taking care of him. I think she'll want one of her own, but Nikki isn't too keen on a dog in her apartment. Your mother and Chrissy think that a therapy dog would be just what Isy needs."

"A trained therapy dog sounds like a brilliant idea. How has Isy been? No better?"

Thomas took a sip of his drink and sighed. "No, she's a sensitive little soul, not like you and Nikki when you were young. The anxiety and panic attacks only seem to be getting worse."

"Is her therapist not helping?"

Thomas shook his head. “She’s on to her third one in six months. The best that money can buy, but she won’t open up and talk to them.”

Anger filled Mack as she thought about the pain Isy was living through. She had always been a quiet little girl, but she’d enjoyed life. Since she’d watched her best friend die from a drugs overdose, Isy had become anxiety ridden and suffered panic attacks. The fun-loving little girl was changed forever.

“I just don’t understand it,” Mack said. “Why would Kevin Drury take a chance selling in a Sharkey territory, and at a school where your granddaughter is a pupil? He must have known that we would come after him, just for selling, never mind anything else.”

“I’ve thought about it a lot. The sixth years, I’m sure, have a few who like to dabble in drugs, but Isy’s friend Elizabeth? They’re only eleven. There was definitely force involved. Isy told her mum that a woman asked who Isla Sharkey was, Elizabeth said she was as a joke, and Kevin Drury grabbed her.”

“Why didn’t you tell me?” Mack was furious. “A hit on our wee girl?”

“Because you would have stewed with frustration and anger, locked up in that prison. We needed you out on time, not adding time to your sentence. The worst thing is we can’t touch that little fuck now. Not without bringing suspicion on to the family. We need to play this right, so no one can touch us.”

“His time will come, Uncle Thomas, but who put Kevin up to it? The McDades?”

“Frankie McDade hasn’t got the balls for a direct hit on our family. He’s old and soft. If it was his son in charge, maybe, but Nikki has people working on it. A little drugged-up fuck like Kevin Drury has a lot of enemies. They will talk. Now, on to a much happier subject—your new start in life.”

Mack smiled, and Dexter snuggled his little head into her neck.

Thomas leaned forward and said seriously, “You’ve been extremely loyal to your family, and we all greatly appreciate what you have done. I can’t imagine what state Isy would be in if Nikki had been put in jail.”

"It wasn't even a second thought, Uncle Thomas. Nikki had to be kept out of this. For the business, and for Isy's sake."

"You are a Sharkey through and through, Mack. But this is your time now. We promised you a quiet life and one fulfilling your dreams."

Mack had trained as a barber as a teenager and was a natural, but over the years her job in the family had taken up too much of her time to allow her to achieve her dream of her own barbershop.

After Mack took the blame and jail time for her cousin Nikki when the police came upon them handing out some justice to the man who'd targeted Isla and her friend, Mack was promised that she could take a step back from the family business and set up her own barbers. The Sharkeys owned commercial property all over Glasgow and the surrounding areas, and when a lease came available in Mack's preferred spot, Nikki and Thomas earmarked it for her.

Thomas opened his desk drawer and pulled out a bunch of keys. "Everything's been done to your specification, and these are yours." He pushed the keys across the desk.

Mack went to take them but hesitated. She looked up at Thomas and said, "You know my first priority is the family, and I'll always do anything you need."

"We know that. Just enjoy your new life, okay?"

Mack grasped the keys and looked at her adoring little dog. "Are you ready to start a new chapter, Dex?" Dexter barked and licked her nose. "I suppose that's a yes, then?"

# CHAPTER TWO

Flora Buchanan turned her car engine off and picked up her bag. It was six thirty in the morning, and she was ready for another day's work. Her traditional family sweet shop had been started by her grandfather and passed down to her. Sweet Surprise, as it was called, had now become a Glasgow institution, and well-loved by young and old alike.

She parked her car in one of the twenty-four-hour staffed car parks. It was expensive, but that gave Flora the peace of mind to know that there were real security guards nearby and not just a camera.

She picked up her bag from the passenger seat and then turned the driver's mirror so that she could look at herself. Most women used the mirror for checking their make-up, but not Flora. She rubbed the tip of her nose, tapped her fingers three times on her chest, and was just about to finish her little ritual when another car pulled up noisily beside her.

Flora sighed, knowing she'd have to start all over again. The older she got, the more mentally tiring her OCD was becoming. It dominated her day, but it was just who she was, and Flora couldn't see any hope or way out of it. It was just something she had to do to keep some level of control in her life.

She waited for the person in the next car to get out and leave their car and began again. She ended her ritual by tapping the steering wheel three times. Now she could start her day.

Flora made her way down the car park stairs to the street. Even this early, the Glasgow streets had people coming and going on their way to work. Flora looked down and let her strawberry-blond hair form a barrier between her and the people she passed. The last thing she wanted to do was to make eye contact with someone.

She turned a corner onto the street where her shop was located. Flora loved the spot where her little shop sat. The grand Victorian buildings housed one of the more affluent shopping areas in the town, and quite an eclectic bunch too.

At the very bottom of the street was the Armani shop, some expensive coffee shops, food shops, and delis, plus across the road a large Victorian building was the home of a gay nightclub, split over two levels. She had often watched the patrons and imagined what it would be like to go in there.

Flora felt she was gay. She knew she wasn't attracted to men, but a few times over the years she had seen a masculine-presenting woman who made her stomach flip, and one in particular one whose memory she didn't like to dwell on.

She imagined walking into the bar across the road and exploring her sexuality but knew that was all it would be. Her imagination.

Flora slowed her pace as she neared the shop next door to her own. It had been boarded up for a year with no sign of life, but a week ago, she had noticed people coming and going, and a refurbishment started. What was new this morning was the elaborate signage above the boarded-up windows.

Mack the Knife? Interesting, thought Flora.

Flora unlocked the shutters over her shop, Sweet Surprise, unlocked the door, and quickly disabled the alarm as she entered the shop.

She looked with pride around her shop. On the back walls were rows and rows of old-fashioned sweets in jars. It was a sweet shop from a bygone era, and even after a refit last year, Flora only had enhanced the Victorian features. She had retro sweet posters on some of the walls and old-style glass jars, not the plastic ones the sweet manufacturing companies used.

There were no fridges full of drinks—if you wanted one, you

had to ask and either she or her co-worker Sandra would get it from the back. Once Flora put her jacket and bag into the staff area out the back, she came out to start her morning routine.

The shelves had a wooden ladder attached, on wheels, so they could get to the jars higher up, in safety. Every morning and evening Flora straightened every jar in the shop and made sure they were in the correct order. Back when she was still a teenager, Flora managed to convince her grandfather that the jars should be kept in her own sensible order.

One of Flora's obsessive compulsions was displaying sweets in colour order, just as she ate them. Of course most of the sweet jars contained mixed gums, jellies, and boiled sweets, and those jars disturbed her OCD brain.

The best she could do to feel calm about it was to keep the mixed-colour jars together on one wall of the shop, which Flora called the Corner of Chaos, then the chocolate ones together, and the toffee, all in groups, until she got to her own Corner of Calm.

There all the single colours were shelved, like the strawberry bonbons, the cola cubes, the lemon sherbets, and many more, but still in a strict order of colour of Flora's devising, cold colours to hot.

Organization like that kept her as comfortable as possible. All her rituals and routines were trying to achieve that, but in reality they added to her stress as they took over her life.

Flora sighed as she looked up at the many jars on the wall. Having straightened up the jars last night, so the labels were perfectly centred, logically Flora knew they wouldn't have moved since then, but that didn't stop the compulsion to check again.

As Flora climbed up the ladder to the shelves, she thought about how tired she was of this. Tired of checking every little thing, and the constant anxiety. This was exhausting, and she was sick of it.

❖

The day before the opening of Mack the Knife, Mack was supervising the last few fixtures and fittings being installed in her shop. Four workmen were installing the ornate gold mirrors above each customer stall.

Everything was just how she had dreamed her new barbershop would be, and she had her family to thank for that. In those long months in jail, Mack had planned for a Victorian steampunk style shop—traditional, with a twist.

The couches, fixtures, and fittings looked to be straight out of a gentlemen's club, and steampunk artwork and Victorian posters on the wall set the tone. In one corner a hatstand sat, with top hats and bowler hats casually hanging on it. On the coffee table at the waiting area, a display of smoking pipes and cigars added to the period feel of the place.

In another corner of the room sat the most important part of the shop, Dexter's bed. After being apart for so long, she knew they both were going to love spending every day together. At the moment Dexter was hiding under his blanket. He wasn't too happy with all the banging and noise going on.

Her old friend and new co-worker Liam came out from the back and held up his hands. "Well? What do you think?"

Liam was wearing a waistcoat over a T-shirt with a shark tooth printed on it, and a Victorian butcher's apron. They'd both agreed that, along with designer jeans and boots, this would be their uniform.

"Looking good, big man," Mack said.

Liam and Mack had trained as barbers together and been friends ever since. When Mack asked him to help run her new business, he had jumped at the chance. Liam was a big bear of a man, with a hipster beard and the requisite ponytail, but a gentle giant, one of the kindest men she knew.

"Not too bad yourself," Liam said.

Mack looked at her own waistcoat and pulled it to straighten it out. She loved the smart casual style. It just fit her, somehow, and the whole steampunk vibe fit her and her shop. Mack loved dressing up.

When Mack and her cousin Nikki used to play as children, Mack would always put on her uncle's clothes and wear his aftershave.

Now she could have fun dressing up every day and doing something she loved.

Mack patted the back pocket of her jeans, where she kept her cutthroat razor. She always carried her razor. It was her weapon of choice, and in fact she was known for it in the criminal underworld she sometimes had to wield it in. Some people called her The Barber because of that, and she struck fear into those who had to be persuaded to talk or behave.

Just as the workmen were bringing out the last mirror to put up, one of them lost their grip, and the mirror came crashing to the floor, shattering glass everywhere. Dexter jumped in fright and ran.

"Dexter?" Mack called after him, but it was too late—he had already shot out the door. "Fuck!"

Mack ran out of the shop after him. Once on the pavement, she looked both ways and saw nothing. Panic was filling her—traffic was heavy, and if Dexter ran onto the road, he'd be a goner.

Which way should she look first? Mack picked right and jogged a few steps, but her attention was drawn to the sweet shop next door to hers. A woman's laughter drew her to the door, and she saw a woman with blond hair facing away from her with Dexter up in her arms, his little head resting on her shoulder.

Relief swept through Mack, and she hurried into the shop. "You got my Dexter. Thank you so much for rescuing him."

The woman turned slowly, and Mack got the surprise of her life. "You?" It was the woman she had saved from the gang of drunk men.

The woman gasped and her face went white as a sheet.

They stared at each other silently. Mack's heart pounded, as the memories of that night flooded back. An older woman from behind the counter came up to them and said, "Do you know each other?"

Before Mack could speak, the woman thrust Dexter at her and ran through to the back of the shop.

"Yes, no—" Mack couldn't think straight. The woman that she saved that fateful night, before she and Nikki went to deal with their little drug pusher problem, had haunted her thoughts. When Mack had looked into her eyes, she'd seen a lost soul, and felt a need that she didn't quite understand.

But she never expected to see her again, especially not next door to her barber's.

"Yes, we met, but I didn't get her name. Can you ask if I can speak to her?"

"I'll try, but I don't know if she will. She's quite…reserved."

When the older woman walked into the back of the shop, Mack remembered to breathe. Her heart was thumping in her chest.

"It's her, Dex."

Mack didn't know anything about this woman or her life, but she wanted to know, she *had* to know. She kissed Dexter and said, "Don't you run off again. You could get hurt."

She heard someone come through the beaded curtain that led to the back of the shop. Mack looked up, hoping to see her mystery woman, but instead she saw her older co-worker.

"I'm sorry, she's not able to talk right now. Can I take a message?"

Mack was disappointed. "It's okay. Just tell her I wanted to say hello and ask how she was. I've opened a barbershop next door—"

"Oh, you're the new owner? I'm Sandra, by the way."

"I'm Mack and this is Dexter. What's your friend's name?" Mack said.

Sandra hesitated for a second and said, "Flora."

"Can you tell Flora that I'm grateful for her rescuing my little Dexter, and if she ever wants to talk, just pop in next door. I'd love to speak to her."

"I will do, but as I say, she's shy."

Mack nodded and walked out of the shop. She inhaled a large lungful of air. This was insane and the coincidence of all time. The woman she'd saved on the night her life changed was right next door to her but didn't want to talk to her.

"Flora." Mack tried out her name.

It seemed fate had brought them together, just as it did that night outside the casino. Why was she so hesitant to talk to her? It felt like Flora was frightened of her, but Mack had helped her.

Perhaps it was seeing her brought the whole horrible night back to her? Mack hoped so, anyway. The last thing she wanted was for Flora to be frightened of *her*. She turned back to the shop window, hoping that her mystery woman had come out from the back of the shop, but there was no sign.

She turned when she heard Liam shout, "You got Dexter, Mack?"

Mack turned and walked back to her shop door. "Aye, the sweet shop lady had him."

"That's going to be dangerous," Liam said.

"What do you mean?"

"A sweet shop a few paces away from work." Liam smiled and patted his stomach. "Ma belly is going to grow bigger and bigger. I'll need to spend every night in the gym."

"You're not wrong," Mack said.

Liam walked back into the barber's, and Mack looked to the sweet shop. "I don't know about you, Dex, but I feel we're going to be eating more sweets too."

Flora was a mystery she wanted to solve.

❖

Flora's heart was beating fast as she held her hands over her ears and her eyes tightly closed, trying to block out the conversation in the shop. She got the fright of her life when she saw her rescuer from the night she couldn't forget.

She'd never told anyone about what happened, preferring to push the memories right down, deep inside, and pretend that it didn't happen to her. But of course the truth found its way out through her OCD behaviours and rituals of control.

When she saw her rescuer, everything she felt that night—fear, panic, loss of control—surged through her anxiety-ridden body. She tried to control her breathing as much as she could, but seeing her rescuer suddenly there in front of her knocked the wind right out of her.

Flora jumped when she felt a touch on her shoulder. It was Sandra.

"Flo, are you okay? Who was that? Did she upset you?"

Sandra was always so protective of her. Sandra had worked for Sweet Surprise since the last few years before Flora's grandad died. Flora didn't have friends in the way other people did, but Sandra was as close a friend as she could get.

Sandra understood her anxieties to a degree, the way Flora needed help in the shop dealing with customers, and that meant the world to her, but she'd never shown anyone, not even Sandra, who she truly was.

"No, no. I—she tried to help me one day when I was struggling with a panic attack, and it just all came back to me."

It wasn't a lie. Flora did have a panic attack—it was just a bigger meltdown than she'd ever had in her life.

"That's okay then. Her name's Mack. She's opened the barber-shop next door," Sandra said.

Flora's stomach dropped. She rubbed the tip of her nose and tapped her collarbone as discreetly as possible, trying to soothe her panic.

"Are you sure you're okay? She seemed nice enough."

Flora's mouth went dry, and she pulled her oversized cardigan tightly around her in a hug. She heard the ding of the shop door.

"I'm fine. Could you get that customer for me?"

"I will do. Take your time, Flo."

When Sandra walked away, Flora closed her eyes. *I'm going to have to see her every day. I'm going to remember every day.*

❖

Mack locked up, and then Liam pulled down the shutters on Mack the Knife, while she held on to Dexter.

"Everything's looking spot on, Mack," Liam said.

"Aye, we're all set. I can't wait to get started."

"You headed home now?"

"No, Nikki's back from France. She asked me to meet her for a drink at The Deep."

Liam stroked Dexter and said, "I'll see you both in the morning then. Night, mate."

"Have a good yin."

Mack looked both ways and crossed the street towards the club. It was only three in the afternoon, so the club would be gearing up for the evening. She was glad about that. Mack used to love her visits to the Sharkey bars and clubs.

As well as The Deep across from her barbershop, there was a pub just around the corner from the shop called The Reef, and several others in the Greater Glasgow area. Throughout her twenties and early thirties Mack enjoyed the atmosphere and the women who she met there, but now, and especially after her time in jail, that wasn't attractive any more. This was her chance to make a life that would fulfil some needs that became apparent every night as she lay in the dark in her cell.

Mack closed her eyes and imagined a life like the one her aunt and uncle had. A loving family home with someone to love her. But bringing that life she imagined into reality was a harder conundrum to solve.

Finding someone to trust, to bring into the Sharkey family, was so difficult. So difficult that she'd never even tried. Her aunt and uncle had managed that, but her mum hadn't, and she'd brought her up herself. Nikki too had never settled down, not that she ever seemed to want to.

Nikki was happy with being a family, just her and Isy, with the occasional short-term playmates. That wasn't enough for Mack, but it might just have to be. She couldn't risk bringing harm to her family. They might have been running legitimate businesses for a few decades now, but they did run on the edges of the law at times, as Mack's time in jail was testament to.

So she couldn't be too careful.

Now across the street, Mack was just a few yards away from The Deep, but something made her look across the road to the sweet shop. She saw her new neighbour, Flora, watching, but before Mack could wave or make any acknowledgement of her, Flora put her head down and hurried out of sight.

"Why is she running from me, Dex?"

Something in this woman's eyes made Mack determined to know more. Mack knew fear when she saw it. She'd seen it in the eyes of many with whom she'd dealt over the years, but Mack hated to see the innocent so frightened, especially a woman. If Flora was frightened of her, then Mack had to do something about that.

She walked up to the door of the club and entered. There were no bouncers and no ticket office staff on, as it was so early. Dexter barked and wriggled in her arms.

"Okay, okay, wee man. Off you go." Dexter knew his way around the club, so she put him down, and he trotted off around the corner.

It was so strange to be back here after so long away. The Deep had three floors, each with a different vibe. The ground floor had a relaxed pub vibe, usually a meeting point for friends and those that wanted to chat. The first floor DJ played classic and cheesy pop, the second catered for the high energy dance crowd. Both The Deep and The Reef were very safe places for those in the LGBTQ+ community. A lot of people would go to The Reef earlier in the evening, then make their way around to the club, knowing they were perfectly safe in this little corner of Glasgow.

Mack walked around the corner and saw the club's head of security, Jay Douglas—a woman who was known to the regulars as The Amazon—crouched down, rubbing Dexter's tummy. Jay was a former MMA fighter, who trained like she was still competing. "Ma wee dog's found some attention already?"

Jay looked up and grinned from ear to ear. "Mack." She stood up and held out her hand to Mack, then pulled her into a hug. "So good to have you back, mate."

"Good to see you, Jay. How's things been?" Mack asked.

"Aye, ticking over well. You were well missed, especially at poker night. I missed taking money off you," Jay joked.

"At least you had Nikki's money to take. How's Annie?"

"Aye, she's doing great. The Reef is keeping her busy. Nikki's in the main bar—let's have a pint and catch up soon, okay?"

"Yep, will do."

Dexter ran ahead of her again, and she followed him into a large open bar area with tables and a small stage at the back of the room. She spotted Nikki sitting at one of the booths over in the corner.

Mack laughed when she saw Dexter forcing kisses upon her cousin, while Nikki was trying to keep him from covering her face with those kisses. Her cousin didn't dislike dogs completely, in fact she knew how much her daughter Isla loved Dexter, but her perfect make-up and expensive designer skirts and blouses didn't mix well with dog hair.

"Dex, down," Mack said.

Nikki heard her voice and looked up quickly. She put Dexter on the floor and stood up as Mack walked towards her.

"Look who the cat dragged in," Nikki said.

Mack had always been in touch with her masculine side, with her build, dress sense, and attitude, but no one could doubt that Nikki was the Sharkey leader. She exuded power from her alpha femme personality and could control and enthral most adversaries, both business and criminal, with a look, the tapping of her painted fingernails, or simply crossing her legs.

Nikki held open her arms and Mack hugged her tightly. "It's so good to see you, Mack. I've missed you so much."

"You too, Nikki."

Nikki pulled back and joked, "Maybe I won't have to trip over this dog and find dog hair everywhere."

Mack laughed and they both sat down. "I heard my wee barra has really enjoyed looking after my Dexter."

Nikki rolled her eyes. "I know. That's all I hear about from Isy, Mum, and Dad."

"I know a good breeder." Mack smiled.

"I'm quite sure. I'll think about it." Nikki let out a breath. "I'm really sorry I wasn't back from my business trip in time to welcome you home."

"Don't worry about it."

"I can't tell you how much I've missed you, Mack. What you did—"

Mack held up her hand. "Stop. We've been over this more than enough times. I did what I did for you, for the family, for what was best for us of all. I love you, Nikki, and the business and Isy needed you outside of prison."

"I'll never forget what you did. Never. Let's have a drink." Nikki raised her hand and caught the attention of someone at the bar.

In seconds a young butch woman hurried over with an order pad and pen. Nikki sat back and slowly crossed her legs, gave the woman a smile, and said in a honeyed voice, "Thank you for coming so quickly."

The young woman dropped her pen on the table and became extremely flustered. "Sorry, Ms. Sharkey, what can I get you?"

Mack covered her laughter by picking up Dexter and placing him on the seat beside her.

Nikki picked up the pen and handed it to the young woman with a devastating smile. "Oops. Here you go, and call me Nikki. Mack, this is Lee—Lee, this is my cousin Mack."

"Awrite, good to meet you, pal," Mack said and shook her hand.

"You too."

Mack could feel the tremor in Lee's hand and saw her gulp hard. She was both terrified and tantalized, as Nikki tended to make people.

"Could you be a wee darling and bring us some drinks?"

"What would you like, Ms. Shar—sorry, Nikki?"

"Glass of white wine for me, and Mack?"

"Pint of lager, thanks, and a bowl of water for ma wee pal here."

"Right away," Lee said.

As she scuttled away, Mack watched with amusement as Nikki's eyes followed the denim covered behind. Nikki loved women, but especially androgenous or masculine-presenting women.

"Another one under your thrall, big cousin?" Mack joked.

Only then did Nikki look back to her and gave her a glare. "Shut up. She is gorgeous, though. It's just her first week."

"You've got her shaking in her boots already." Dexter was wriggling and trying to get down. "Okay, trouble. Go and run about."

"No accidents on the club floor," Nikki warned.

"He'll tell me if he needs to go out. Don't worry."

Just at that, Lee came back with the tray of drinks. She set down Mack's pint and handed Nikki her glass of wine, extremely carefully.

"Thank you, Lee. I was just telling my cousin how well you were doing on your first week."

"Yeah? Really?" Lee blushed and put down Dexter's bowl of water.

"Absolutely. Excellent work," Nikki said. "Off you go then."

Lee ruffled Dexter's ears, then stood.

"Could you keep an eye on him, Lee," Mack said, "in case he wanders off?"

"No problem."

Once she left, Mack shook her head and laughed. "Seriously, is she why you're in here instead of meeting me at the office?"

"Don't be ridiculous. She's probably ten years too young for me. Just having a little fun. Besides, I've been stuck in offices for all of my business trip, and back at home, it's more relaxing to work here."

"And fun?" Mack asked.

Nikki laughed. "Yes, you are right. Anyway, I want to get home to Isy on time for dinner tonight. In the office there are always more emails, more files coming across my desk."

"I'll let you off then."

Nikki took a sip of wine and said, "So how is the new shop looking?"

"Perfect. We're ready to open tomorrow. I can't thank you and Uncle Thomas enough for making this happen."

Nikki reached forward. "We owe you more than we could

repay, Mack. This time is for you. Take a step back, and enjoy what you want to do with your life."

Mack leaned forward and looked at Nikki seriously. "You know I will be there if you need me, at a moment's notice. I would go through it all again if it was needed by our family."

"I know that. You're a Sharkey and always will be. I don't anticipate any problems. Things have been very quiet since our last dealings with Mr. Drury, but I have plans for him. I'm just letting things settle."

"Uncle Thomas said Isy's not any better."

A painful look crossed Nikki's face. "No, her anxiety is terrible. The last therapist said she has PTSD. Sometimes I don't know what to say to her. I haven't been around anyone with mental health issues before. It's not the way you and I are wired. Stress is like water off a duck's back to us. So I'm having to learn every day how to talk to her, how to help her, but I'm worried about her."

"I'm here to help. I'll do whatever I can to help," Mack said.

"I know. It's not just Isy. I've missed having my best friend with me. There's no one I can talk to like you. Which is why I want you to lie low and enjoy your new start. I want you on the outside with me."

Mack had an unshakeable bond with Nikki. They were more like sisters than cousins and had been brought up as such. "I love you, Nikki, and I'd do anything for you."

"I know that."

Mack turned when she heard Dexter bark. She laughed when she saw Lee playing with Dexter around the stage area.

"He's made a friend," Nikki said.

Mack's mysterious new neighbour popped into her mind. She needed to find a way of showing Flora that she didn't need to be scared of her.

"Nik, do you remember when we met at the casino before going to deal with Drury?"

"Uh-huh. It's etched on my memory."

"Before we left, I saw a woman being attacked, and I ran down with some of the boys to help her."

Nikki tapped her fingernails on the stem of her wine glass. “Vaguely. My mind was clouded with anger that night.”

“I helped her, and the boys gave the men a doing, but the woman ran away.”

“Yes, I remember you telling me that. Why?”

Mack’s stomach twisted as she thought about that incident. She felt it any time she thought about the woman, who she now knew as Flora.

“My new neighbour, at the shop? It’s her.”

Nikki furrowed her eyebrows and said, “What? Really?”

“Absolutely. The sweet shop next door. It’s her. Dexter ran out of my shop door, and when I chased after him, he’d gone next door and was up in Flora’s arms.”

“Flora? Nice old-fashioned girl’s name. What did she say?”

“Nothing. She handed me Dexter and ran through to the back of the shop. She looked terrified,” Mack said.

“Does she know who you are? Maybe she saw your face in the media at the time of the trial.”

Mack shook her head. “I don’t think it’s that. Her co-worker didn’t know who I was and said that Flora was extremely shy. But there’s shy and shy—she was terrified. I don’t want a woman scared of me, especially when she went through such a traumatic event.”

“Maybe that’s what’s wrong. You suddenly turning up in her life triggers the panic and pain she experienced that night,” Nikki said.

“That’s brilliant. You could be right.”

Nikki lifted her glass to Mack and said, “I’m learning a lot about the effects of trauma with Isy. Believe me.”

Mack’s mind was racing. That made perfect sense. Now she just needed to fix the problem.

“What do I do to change that, so she won’t be frightened of the memory of me that night? You’re an expert with women.”

“Not this kind. The women I meet are generally impressed that I’m a Sharkey. But if you can’t tell her in person that you aren’t a threat, write her a note.”

“A note? What kind thing would I say?”

Nikki sighed heavily and replied, "I don't know—maybe introduce yourself, and promise that you won't talk about that night if she doesn't want to."

Mack was strangely filled with hope and excitement. "You're a genius. I could kiss you."

"Please don't. Why does this matter so much to you?"

Mack clasped her hands in front of her tightly. "I don't know. That night, the look of fear and confusion in her eyes—I remembered it for the whole time I was in prison. I wanted to take it away, and now she's turned up on my doorstep. I just need her not to be frightened of me. Is the sweet shop a Sharkey rental property? Most of the street is."

"I'll try to find out."

She heard Dexter yelp and saw him jump up and down at her feet. "Oops. I think he needs to go outside."

"I don't want any accidents on my floor, Dexter."

"He won't. He's a good boy."

Mack scooped up Dexter and hurried towards the club's back fire door.

"He better not."

# CHAPTER THREE

Flora pulled her car into her driveway after another long day at the shop. She couldn't wait to get behind her front door and shut out the world. Painful and terrifying memories had returned to her today.

She let go of the steering wheel and performed her car OCD ritual, rubbing her nose and tapping. Her condition and stress were much worse today. When she saw her rescuer this morning, her fear had skyrocketed.

Get inside, Flora told herself. She would be safe inside.

Flora got out of the car and moved quickly to her front door. The large sandstone lower flat, in the leafy west end, once belonged to her grandfather. The building used to be one big mansion house, now separated into flats.

She hurried up to her door and got in quickly. As soon as she shut the door, Flora snibbed a chain and clicked two other locks. Once that was done, she let out a big sigh of relief. She had made it to the safety of her cocoon, and no one was getting in.

It was a very desirable area, and Flora could make a tidy profit and buy something much cosier, but she couldn't bear the thought of going through the whole house selling business. She could not deal with the social anxiety it would bring. So she was stuck here, making the best of things, as she always did.

The flat had a drawing room, three bedrooms, a bathroom, a

living room, and a kitchen, but Flora really only lived in the kitchen and her bedroom. Flora made her way to the kitchen, which served as her kitchen, dining room, and living room, as she had a table and TV in here. She closed the kitchen door and felt warm and safe at last. Flora hung her coat up and rubbed the tip of her nose in a self-soothing action.

She was safe here, but her heart was still racing. Today she had come face to face with someone who took her right back to the most terrifying night of her life. Flora covered her ears with her hands and tried to regulate her heart rate.

"I need a distraction," Flora said out loud.

Flora hurried over to the kitchen table and grasped the TV remote. She pointed it at the TV on the wall, and her favourite channel came on. An episode of *The Simpsons* was playing, and she started to relax a bit.

Routine and everything being the same brought calm to Flora's world, and the same set of shows ran every night at dinnertime. If they were changed around for any reason, Flora was anxious and uneasy. She knew watching was just another self-soothing action, and after today she needed it.

She walked over to the kitchen area and switched on the oven for her dinner. But her visions of her saviour from that fateful night ran through her mind. Flora leaned against the countertop. Why next to her shop? Surely coincidences like that didn't happen?

Flora did feel bad for running away from the woman. Sandra said her name was Mack. This Mack had only come to her aid, saved her from what might have been… She didn't want to think what. It wasn't her fault that Flora felt such anxiety and fear at seeing her.

She opened her fridge and brought out the ingredients to make a stir-fry. Before she began to chop the vegetables, she tapped the chopping board three times. The compulsion was definitely stronger today. Flora hated it, but her mental health dominated her day, especially on days like today when fear coursed through her veins.

Flora started by cutting and preparing her ingredients and trying not to let her mind wander, but just as she was about to throw her vegetables in the wok, she heard shouts from her neighbours above, and then the booming of music.

Although this was a quiet and respectable area, the flat upstairs was rented out by a property company, and the two young male students who occupied the flat, probably paid for by Mummy and Daddy, tormented her with loud music, parties, and lewd shouting from the windows sometimes.

It had gotten worse after she complained to the management company. The men sensed her vulnerability. Their shouts and laughter brought on a panic attack. She threw her knife in the sink, left the vegetables where they were, and hurried through to her bedroom.

She got her earphones and put on her calming YouTube videos and jumped under her duvet. In her mind Flora played through the night she was attacked, while trying to find comfort in the safety of her small cocoon.

The face of the woman in her shop—Mack—and her sweet little dog kept circling around her mind. When that small sausage dog ran into her shop, it made her laugh out loud, which wasn't a common occurrence. She didn't know his name, but he was so friendly, giving her kisses, without even knowing who she was. Then *she* walked in.

Flora came out from under her quilt and sat up against the headboard. The earphones kept away the sounds of upstairs. Her thoughts about her new neighbour made the panic attack ease. Flora was desperate to know more, to find out who this Mack was, while knowing that she never would have the courage to talk to her.

*But what if she talks to you?*

Every day, she was going to be next door, walking past the shop, on her way to and from work. Mack was going to talk to Flora again, and if she did, Mack would no doubt talk about the last time they met.

"I can't. I just can't."

❖

Dexter lay on his back, paws in the air, sleeping and content with a full belly. He was happy after demolishing the bowl of fresh chicken, vegetables, and brown rice that his grandma made for him and sent Mack home with a week's supply.

Mack sat on her couch beside him, watching TV, and was just about dig into an Indian meal she had delivered. The taste of a real Indian curry was one thing Mack fantasized about in prison, and now she was close to overdosing on them.

She tickled Dexter's tummy, then picked up her bowl of curry. She took a bite. "Hmm, so fucking good."

A mindless game show played on the TV in Mack's modern apartment building, sitting on the River Clyde, which ran through the city of Glasgow.

Just then she was interrupted by a video call. It was Nikki. She accepted the call and saw Nikki with Isla beside her on the couch.

"Hi, Mack," Isy said.

"Hiya, wee barra," Mack said.

Dexter was suddenly awake at the sound of Isla's voice and poked his nose on the screen.

"It's your favourite girl, Dex," Mack said.

Isla waved and smiled brightly. "Hi, Dex. I miss you."

Nikki rolled her eyes, and Mack smiled. Every one in their family was constantly trying to persuade Nikki to let Isla have a dog.

"Evening, Mack, Mr. Dexter," Nikki said formally. "I've got some info on your new neighbour."

"Great. What did you find out?"

"I asked my PA to look at our records. Apparently, Dad tried to buy the property years ago, when he was running the business. The present occupier's grandfather owned the shop. It's the only one on Waterford Street that we don't own for leasing."

"Uncle Thomas didn't give him an offer he couldn't refuse, then?" Mack asked.

Nikki smiled. "No. I called Dad, and he said it was Granny's favourite sweet shop, and Dad became friendly with the man, so he was happy just to leave the property as it was."

"Thanks for that," Mack said, "maybe I can introduce myself."

"You're welcome. Oh, Isy wants you to cut her hair," Nikki added.

"Any time, wee barra. Just text me, Nik, when you want it done."

After she hung up, Mack thought: The only shop in the street not belonging to a Sharkey. Mack had to know her better.

## Chapter Four

Flora was late. She never got much sleep last night as her upstairs neighbours decided to have an all-night party. Flora looked at her watch. *I'm so late.*

Sandra would be at the shop any time. Just as she rounded the corner of Waterford Street, she saw her new neighbour, Mack, lifting the shutters on her barbershop. She quickly retreated back around the corner. Flora didn't want to walk past her in case she tried to engage her in conversation.

She watched until she saw Mack go inside her shop, then hurriedly rounded the corner and headed to Sweet Surprise. As she neared Mack the Knife the barber, she let her hair fall down on her face and pulled the collar of the jacket up as far over her face as she could, so Mack couldn't catch her eye.

Flora made it to the shop and opened up quickly. As she went through the door, she noticed a white envelope on the doormat. She picked it up and saw it was handwritten: *To Flora.*

This was intriguing. Flora locked the door behind her and went through to the back of the shop. Once she'd dispensed with her jacket, Flora opened up the letter.

*Dear Flora,*

*My name is Mack Sharkey, and I'm your new next-door neighbour. First of all, thanks for rescuing my little boy Dexter yesterday. He is everything to me.*

Wow. Flora felt a warmth expand in her chest, and the corners of her mouth rose in a smile. Mack looked like a tough, no-nonsense butch, not someone you would expect to have a sausage dog she treated like a baby. Certainly, when they'd met that fateful night, her looks, confidence, and tone of voice conveyed a really tough person who wasn't afraid of anything.

The letter continued:

> *I had no idea you owned the shop next door to mine, or that I would ever see you again. I understand that I might remind you of a night you'd rather forget. I'd love to say hello and buy some of my favourite blue raspberry fizz bombs, and I won't ever bring up that night unless you do. You never need to be scared of me.*

Flora was quite shocked. How did Mack know meeting face to face would be difficult for her?

She felt an unusual flutter of excitement and then hurried out into the shop. Flora went straight over to a large jar on the wall filled with blue raspberry fizz bombs and touched the jar.

Flora chuckled, thinking about Mack's choice of sweet. Blue raspberry fizz bombs left you with a blue tongue for quite a while—that was half the reason the kids liked them. Adults didn't usually go for them. Mack must not take herself too seriously.

She lifted the jar from the wall. She'd take them to her and say hello. She froze with the jar half on, half off the shelf. Flora's initial burst of excitement and enthusiasm was waning, and the reality of her social anxiety hit her.

"I can't do this."

Flora put the sweets back and hurried back to the shop to get ready for her day, anger at her own inadequacies coursing through her.

❖

Mack's first morning had been busy. A few of her old friends took the first appointments as soon as she was open for business. Mack opened a tub of face cream, scooped some into her hand, and worked it over the face of her customer and pal, Ewan Campbell.

He owned a gym in the town centre, in a Sharkey property. They all used the gym—Mack, Jay, Nikki, and the Sharkey staff. They were all good mates, and even before she had her own shop, Mack cut his hair, just as she did for her other friends.

"It's good to have you back, Mack. My hair's not been the same without you, ma man," Ewan said.

Ewan had a short choppy hairstyle with a close-cut beard. She had shaved his beard into a good shape, cut his hair, and was now beginning a massage of his face. Mack loved the tradition in other parts of the world, like Turkey, Greece, and India, of giving a massage along with a haircut. It made the whole experience more special, pampering, and relaxing.

Above the mirror in front of them was a camera, mounted on the wall. She'd always liked to post how-to videos on YouTube, demonstrating different styles, long before she ever had a shop.

She'd noticed her subscriber list growing rapidly, and she became aware that people with no real interest in cutting hair were watching the channel for relaxation purposes. It was a fun YouTube channel, and now with her own shop she could do it more professionally.

Mack wiped her hands on a towel and began to massage Ewan's shoulders and back. "You've been bulking up, bud," Mack said.

"Yeah, I've been working on it. You coming back to the gym soon?"

"Aye, will be—I feel stronger than ever. There wasn't much else to do in the big house I was staying at but to work hard in the gym." Mack winked at Ewan. She didn't want the customer Liam was working on to know she was referring to jail.

"That's true. Any problems when you were there?" Ewan asked.

Mack eased Ewan forward and worked her way down his back. "Nae bother." While in jail, she got no trouble from anyone because of who she was. She generally didn't get involved in any of the petty squabbles in there, unless there was bullying going on.

She massaged his back for a minute or so and then moved on to his arms and hands. "How was that?"

Ewan rolled his neck from one side to another. "Amazing, man."

All that was left to do was put some wax through his hair. Mack then held up a mirror so he could see the back of his sharp style.

"Brilliant—cheers, mate."

"Glad you like it." Mack washed her hands, then went to the till. Ewan paid and booked in for the next week.

"Thanks, bud," Mack said.

"I'll see you at the gym, Mack. Cheers."

Once he was gone, she started to clear up her station. Mack was enjoying this simple life so far. It wasn't for the money—as a Sharkey family member, Mack had received a share of the family business since she was eighteen—but it was rewarding, enjoyable work. Something that had always been a pastime was now her everyday job.

Once everything was cleared up, Mack grabbed her coat and said to Liam, "I'm just going to head to the bank. Keep your eye on Dexter. I won't be long."

Liam looked up from shaving his customer. "Aye, nae bother."

It was now late afternoon after a busy day. "You be good, Dex." Dexter barked in reply. "Good boy."

When she left the shop she saw a long line of loud schoolchildren emerging from the door of Flora's sweet shop.

When she walked past the shop window, she saw some teenage boys inside, throwing bags of sweets and chocolate bars around. Flora was behind the counter looking extremely distressed. Mack immediately pushed past the line at the door and into the shop. The children were laughing at the two older boys who were throwing around the chocolate bars.

"Hey! You two, put that down or pay for it."

The laughter and chatter in the shop stopped. One of the two boys said, "Who the fuck do you think you're talking to?" He brazenly opened one of the bars and took a bite.

Mack strode over to him, never once looking away from his eyes. "I'm Mack Sharkey, and I'm talking to you, ya wee dick." Mack pulled up the sleeve of her jacket slightly and exposed the tattoo of a shark tooth on her forearm.

The cocky, confident boy looked down at it and then dropped his chocolate bar on the floor.

Mack quite calmly said, "Now go and pay for your items at the till and apologize for causing trouble."

The boy nodded and walked over to the counter, as good as gold. Meanwhile Mack said to the rest of the kids, "Line up quietly if you want to buy something, or leave."

They did as they were told, and Mack stood with her arms folded at the other end of the counter. Flora looked over at her, and Mack smiled and winked.

Flora smiled back and then got to work serving the children. Mack watched her work quickly, climbing the ladder for the jars of sweets and weighing out the right amounts in little paper bags.

Mack observed Flora as she worked. Flora was a pretty woman but appeared as if she was totally unaware of that fact. She dressed a lot older than her age, with a big oversized cardigan covering up her body, and her thick hair roughly pulled back into a ponytail.

She clearly didn't have a lot of confidence, and Mack wanted to know why.

It didn't take long until the line of children was gone, and Flora had put the last amount of money in the till. She looked up at her and said in a croaky voice, "Thank you."

"Nae bother. Any time you need anything, me and my pal Liam are right next door. Don't hesitate."

"Thank you. Um…" Flora gulped and appeared to be struggling with what to say next.

But was she just nervous and scared with her, or with most people? Mack really hoped it wasn't just with her.

"I'll leave you to it then."

Just as she started to move, Flora said, "Sandra—my friend. She's usually with me at all the busy times, but she had a hospital appointment today."

"Oh, okay. Well, like I said, you ever need any backup, or someone's getting out of hand, we're just next door. I'll always help you if I can."

Flora rubbed the tip of her nose like a little frightened mouse. She had to find out if she was the cause. After saying goodbye, Mack went to the coffee shop and ordered a couple of drinks for her and Liam.

"It'll just be a minute," the barista said. "You're from the new barber's across the street, aren't you?"

"Aye, that's me. I'm Mack."

"Susie."

Susie extended her hand to shake Mack's. Her touch lingered on Mack's hand. "So there's an actual Mack of Mack the Knife?"

"Yep. That's me. It's a really nice street."

"Yeah. It's a prime territory for the higher-end businesses like ours. The customers from the designer shops on the next street up all come down this way. You'll do really well, I'm sure."

Little did Susie know that she knew exactly how prime a spot this was for her business, as the Sharkeys owned the land, including the one this coffee shop stood on.

"What about the sweet shop, Sweet Surprise? What's it like?"

"Hmm." Susie scrunched up her eyes. "It a nice enough traditional sweet shop, but it attracts a lot of kids. I've had them in here trying to steal things. Plus the owner is a bit of a weirdo."

Mack's defensive hackles immediately rose, and anger rolled around her stomach at that description of Flora, but she played along to get the information she wanted. "Oh? How?"

"She never talks or looks at any of us other business owners. She's, like, a mute. Flora, that's her name, is the actual owner of Sweet Surprise, but any business meetings we have locally, she sends Sandra, her other staff member. If you pass her in the street, she puts her head down, so she doesn't have to say hello. As I say, weirdo."

As annoyed as it made Mack to hear someone talk about Flora that way, without any knowledge of what she had been through, she was so happy to hear that it wasn't just her Flora had difficulty talking to. Flora wasn't frightened of her, as Mack had feared.

Susie's workmate brought over her two coffees, and Mack said firmly to Susie as she picked them up, "It not good to judge other people when you don't know anything about their life."

Susie's face fell and Mack walked out.

❖

"I'm so sorry I wasn't here, Flo," Sandra said as she took off her coat the next morning.

"It's okay. You can't be here all the time," Flora said. "You do enough for me as it is. Your hospital appointment was important. You can't be babysitting me all the time."

"It's not babysitting. I'm only too happy to help you. You know that."

Flora smiled. She was so lucky to have Sandra. Having grown up with her, she knew and understood, to some extent, that Flora had difficulties with the public-facing side of the business. She manned the till, attended local business meetings, and handled any other face-to-face duties that were difficult for Flora.

"Really, it was fine. Mack from next door came in and had a word with the boys, and whatever she said worked. They said sorry and lined up to pay, as good as gold."

"I'm glad she was there."

Flora was too. The rest of the day yesterday, she kept thinking about what happened in the shop. Usually she tortured herself over what she should have done or said, but this time, Mack swept into her thoughts and banished the tortured what-ifs, just as she had done yesterday, and the first time Flora met her.

Mack hadn't swept in and threatened violence. She just had a quiet confidence that exuded power and made all the kids behave. The image of Mack standing at the end of the counter, arms folded and silent, just monitoring the kids, made her heart flutter and a surge of excitement rush through her. And when Mack winked at her? Her stomach twisted and turned in a pleasant way.

She'd always found confidence attractive, since she had none, and Mack exuded the stuff without even trying. How amazing would it be to feel that way, just for a second?

"Flo?"

Flora didn't notice that she had been lost in her thoughts. "Sorry?"

"Is there anything you'd like me to do first?"

"Would you mind doing me a favour?" Flora asked.

"Anything, what do you need?"

"If I make up some sweets, would you take them next door, just to say thank you?"

Sandra smiled. It was out of character for her to try to make a connection with someone, and Sandra was probably pleased and surprised.

"That's a nice idea. Aye, what are you going to give her?"

"She mentioned that she loved raspberry fizz bombs," Flora said.

"Fizz bombs? Interesting choice for an adult."

Flora laughed. "It is, isn't it?"

Sandra looked at her strangely.

"What is it?" Flora asked.

"You seem—I don't know, happier, lighter today."

"Do I?" Flora hadn't noticed until that moment that she was. She was distracted and not doing her OCD rituals quite as much. Of course as soon as she acknowledged that in her own head, the urge to do them came roaring back.

Flora always tried to be as discreet as possible around Sandra, but she was sure she had noticed over the years. Thankfully, Sandra never brought it up.

"I better get the sweets together." Flora turned away and picked up two of the glass gift jars. As well as normal bags of sweets and boxes of chocolates, Sweet Surprise supplied nice glass jars that customers could fill with sweets of their choice as a gift. She filled up the jar with fizz bombs and then took out a bag from under the till. On her way to work, Flora had picked up a few bags of dog treats.

"Dog treats?" Sandra said.

"Yes, for Mack's little dachshund, Dexter. She mentioned him when she was here."

Flora only fibbed slightly. She didn't want to let Sandra know about the note Mack sent her, because then she would have to explain how she first met Mack, and Flora had never told anyone about that night. Not the therapist she had at the time, no one.

It felt like if she didn't tell anyone, if she didn't acknowledge it and what might have been if Mack and her friends hadn't arrived, then it hadn't really happened.

"Can you help me package this?"

"Yes. Hang on."

Sandra cut a length of clear plastic at the wrapping station, and Flora brought the jar and dog treats over.

"I wanted to give her workmate Liam some sweets too, but I've never spoken to him."

Sandra started to package up the gift and tie the bow around it. "You're normally good at matching the sweet to the person. Have you seen him?"

"Just once or twice when passing." Flora tapped her chin once or twice and said, "I have an idea."

❖

Mack was finishing checking the week's appointments on the computer. Word of mouth was making business pick up already.

She went and sat on one of the barber chairs and patted her lap. "Dex? Come on, ma boy."

Dexter ran at breakneck speed and jumped on her lap. "There's my good boy."

She ruffled his ears and he kissed her on the lips. Liam walked over with a couple of bottles of water and smiled.

"He's one happy wee dog."

Mack laughed. "I'm making up for lost time. I hated being apart from ma wee pal."

Dexter settled on her lap, and she took the water from Liam. "Thanks, mate. Did you talk to your wee cousin about a job here?"

"Aye, he's really keen. He leaves school this week and would like to get working as soon as possible."

In their first week, they'd only booked in a few of the regulars they'd both cut hair for over the years, but next week would start to be full on, and they'd need at least one person at the start as an assistant, and someone Mack could trust.

"Perfect, well, tell him the job's his, and we'll train him up as a barber if that's what he'd like," Mack said.

Liam took a swig of his water and said, "Did you find out anything about our new neighbour from the other shop? I asked at the cafe and they said she was, in their words, an oddball."

Mack didn't like that. "The manager of the coffee shop described her as a weirdo. Not a nice thing to say. She's just quiet and shy, as far as I can tell."

She didn't want to tell Liam about their first encounter, a year and a half ago. That was Flora's story to tell, if she wanted to.

"People can be so judgy, can't they? I think the rest of the shop owners are up their own arses, if you ask me, just because they're in a fancy city centre location."

Mack smiled. "And yet working class Sharkeys own the land beneath their feet."

They were interrupted by a knock at the shop door. It was Sandra from Sweet Surprise.

Mack put Dexter on the floor and went over to open the door. "Come in."

"I hope I'm not disturbing you," Sandra said.

"Nah. We're finished for the day. Sandra, this is Liam, my friend and the other barber here."

"Nice to meet you, Liam. Flo wanted me to bring these over to you both, to thank you for yesterday."

"She didn't need to do that. If ever me or Liam can help in any way, we will."

Liam agreed. "Aye, of course we will."

"Well, I'm almost always with Flora at the busy times, but I had a hospital appointment yesterday, and when the schoolkids arrive, there's always a few chancers causing trouble." Sandra handed Mack the beautifully packaged jars of sweets and dog treats.

"Fizz bombs and treats for you, Dex. That's really kind of her."

Sandra then handed a package to Liam. "Flora wasn't sure what your favourite sweet would be, but she thought you might like these."

Liam looked in the package and said, "Yes! Yellow-bellied snakes. Aww, man, that takes me back to being a wee boy. Tell Flora that was a great choice, and thanks."

"Yeah, this is great. She didn't have to do that."

"Flora felt she did, and it's not often she reaches out to people, if you know what I mean," Sandra said.

It was more than shyness that Flora was troubled with—Mack was sure of that. Sandra was trying to tell her that making connections with others wasn't normal for Flora, and her experience with the other shopkeepers was testament to that.

Mack hadn't even spoken to Flora properly yet, but she already felt protective, just as she had the night they first met. She wanted to know Flora but didn't want to push it. This was a first step for Flora, in response to Mack's note, and if she wanted to know more of the puzzle that was Flora, she'd need to take it slow and carefully.

Her first instinct was to go next door and thank Flora herself, have a chat and get to know her, but she resisted. Instead, she waited until closing time. They shut early today, since they had no more clients, and after the shutters were down and Liam walked away, she walked next door and looked through the sweet shop window.

At first Flora didn't look up, but when she did, Mack made Dexter wave his little paw. Flora gave her a big genuine smile, which made Mack's heart thud. It was such a beautiful smile. Being who she was, one of the closest members of the Sharkey family, and being around the casino, pubs, and clubs they owned, Mack had a lot of women flirting and giving her fake smiles, just to get her attention. None were like the smile Flora just gave her.

Then Mack placed her palm to her heart and mouthed the words *thank you.* Finally she stuck out her tongue and pointed to the blue dye on it, to show she had enjoyed the fizz bombs already.

Flora started to laugh, and that was exactly what she wanted. Maybe she could try to talk to Flora tomorrow.

❖

"Kevin Drury's here to see you, boss."

Malcolm McDade—Malky—looked up from the files in front of him. "Send him in."

Since returning from London to take over the business after his dad died, Malky made his office in the back of one of the family's car mechanic businesses. It was only one of the many business operations that the McDade family used to launder money. Taxi firms, florists, hairdressers all gave the family somewhere to filter through their drug money.

Until recently Malky was based in London. He had a myriad of contacts that supplied the McDades with the drugs they sold on the streets of some territories in Glasgow and the surrounding areas. After his father's death he came back to Glasgow to take the helm of the family and make sure no one took advantage of the temporary shift in power.

Malky looked down at the pictures his informants had given him. Thomas, Nikki, and Mack Sharkey. "I'm coming for you."

The McDades and the Sharkeys were bitter rivals. They'd been good friends before vying for territory, and then ultimately Malky's grandad ordered a hit on one of the Sharkey children.

He heard the door open, and Kevin Drury walked in. Malky sat back in his seat and just stared at him. Malky was short, but stocky and intimidating to most, especially someone like the snivelling Kevin Drury.

Malky continued staring silently until Kevin said in a shaky voice, "You wanted to see me?"

"Believe me, Kevin. No one wants to see you, unless we have to."

Kevin was one of their dealers on the street, and an essential part of the plan that Malky had convinced his dad to give the go-ahead for. It didn't go exactly to plan, but it had struck a blow against the Sharkeys and reminded them that the McDades were still here.

"I'm sorry about your da, Malky," Kevin said.

As much as it saddened him to lose the man who brought him up, Malky had been waiting for this day for a long time, too long. He was quite unsentimental about it. His dad Gerry had been happy enough to sit with the small territory they had, and not push the boundaries into the more traditional Sharkey territories.

Malky resented the Sharkeys, especially Thomas and Nikki. Since they went legitimate in the eighties, they thought themselves better than those in the Glasgow criminal underworld they had apparently left.

"I don't need your sorries about my dad. I need you to do what I tell you and when I tell you, and that means selling our merchandise where and when I tell you, along with my other little junkie minions."

Kevin was starting to sweat. Malky loved this, the surge of power you got from people being terrified of you. He remembered being picked on at school because of his height. When he'd complained to his dad, he told him to look after himself and stop running to him like a crybaby.

The next day he went into school with a knife, waited for one of the boys in the bathroom, and stabbed him through the hand. No one bothered him again, and the stories that grew arms and legs around this incident made people terrified of Malky.

"I want you to move into the city centre."

Kevin gulped hard. "The Sharkeys—"

Malky jumped up and leaned over the desk. "I don't give a fuck what the Sharkeys say. My da has let them have it all their own way for years. Not any more. I want you selling on those streets and making me money."

"But Mack's out of prison."

"I know that, but if they touch you, they'll incriminate themselves. Has Thomas or Nikki come after you in the last year and a half?"

"No," Kevin said, "but there's no way Nikki will let me off after trying to get her daughter. She'll put me in hospital for a month."

"And I'll put you in the ground if you don't do as I say. You have a debt to the McDade family," Malky said.

"You said if I could get to her daughter, my debt would be paid."

"But you didn't, did you? You only got the girl's friend, and every day thereafter the interest in what you owe has grown."

"They'll kill me. I came after Nikki's daughter, and her friend died."

Malky flew around the desk and slammed Kevin up against the wall. "I'll kill you if you don't. At least you'll have a fighting chance with me, ya fuckwit."

Kevin was choking for breath. "Okay, okay."

"Take your junkie mates and get selling. I want that money flowing in. My da might have been happy with the small time, but I want the McDades back at the top of the tree. Understand me?"

"Yeah, yeah."

"Are you sure you understand? If you want this to keep flowing in your veins." Malky lifted up a bag of drugs, and when Kevin went to grab them, Malky snatched them away.

"Please, Malky. I need them."

He had Kevin exactly where he wanted him. "Davey," Malky shouted out the office door. A big burly guy with tattoos all the way up his neck came in. "Make sure Kevin gets to his new patch and tells all his wee dealer mates that they've to push into Sharkey territory."

"Aye, nae bother," he replied.

Davey grabbed Kevin by the collar, and Malky handed Kevin the drugs. "On you go then, like a good wee boy."

Kevin nodded and was half dragged, half walked out the door. Malky sat back at his desk. He lined up the three pictures of the main Sharkeys—Thomas, Nikki, and the so-called Mack the Knife.

"I'm coming for you."

Malky's dad said he had an unhealthy obsession with the Sharkeys, but it was resentment. They had everything, plus the pretention to go legit and become respected businesspeople. He hated the respect and the fear people had for them. If only his dad was as ruthless as Thomas Sharkey, the McDades would be feared and respected just the same, and that was Malky's goal, while taking the Sharkeys down.

He took a pen and crossed out the faces of Nikki and Mack. He'd like to get Thomas as well, but he was old and retired. Taking out those two would destroy the Sharkeys.

## CHAPTER FIVE

It had been a strange long weekend for Flora. Strange in the sense that she had felt nervous and excited to get back to work on Monday morning.

On her way to work she looked in the window of the barbershop, hoping to catch sight of Mack, but even though the shutters were up, no one was in the front of the shop, which was disappointing.

As the day went on, Flora had been tempted to walk next door and say hello, which was unheard of for her. Of course she didn't go through with it, but the excited urge was there, and that was different enough for her.

Flora hadn't met a woman like Mack before, one who was physically strong and tough and clearly moved through the world without fear. That must be an amazing feeling. Flora had often daydreamed about inhabiting someone with that sort of confidence and surety, even just for a second. For someone so anxiety-ridden and fearful, that imagining was tantalizing.

It was midmorning, and while Sandra called the suppliers, Flora was putting out some stock. She heard a knock on the glass of the shop door. When she looked up, Flora got a rush of excitement. It was Mack with Dexter.

"Hi, can I bring Dexter in the shop?"

"Yes, of course."

Flora stood up from her crouched position and ran her fingers through her hair. Her hair was a mess. But why was she so concerned by her appearance all of a sudden?

Dexter pulled Mack through the door and jumped up at Flora excitedly.

"Dex, down," Mack said.

"It's okay. Can I pick him up?"

"Aye, of course."

Flora lifted the little dog, and he kissed her all over the face, making her giggle.

"I'm sorry, but he seems to like you," Mack said.

"Don't be sorry. I like him." Flora kissed his ears and his snout. "I love dogs."

"Do you have one?"

Flora shook her head. "No. I'd always thought a dog would be good for me, though."

"Well, feel free to borrow Dexter any time." Flora smiled and stroked Dexter's head. "I wanted to thank you for the sweets, and the dog treats."

"You're welcome."

Surprisingly for Flora, she felt nervous talking to Mack but didn't feel that awkward fear that she did with everyone else, apart from Sandra. It was an *excited* nervous.

Mack scratched the back of her head. "Listen, I'm not going to talk about anything in the past, but I know it was a shock to see me again. My note, did you—"

"Yes, I read it, and thanks—it made me feel better."

"Great. I didn't want you to be worried about what I might say. You can talk to me whenever or never. I don't want to make you feel bad."

Could Mack get any more attractive? Because that's what this excitement was. Attraction. It hadn't hit her very often and not for a long time. Sometimes she didn't even think she was capable of it, but once or twice it had snuck up on her. What with the gay pub around the corner and the club across the road, she had seen a few women who pricked up her interest, but none like Mack.

"Thank you." Flora looked down at her big cardigan and wished she had worn something less frumpy. She tried to make her mush of a mind come up with something to say. She cleared her throat and said, "How is the new shop going?"

"Really well. Last week we just had a few appointments to find our feet, but this week it's full on. I'm really enjoying it."

"That's good." Flora's mouth went dry, and she struggled with what to say next. She turned her attention to Dexter and scratched his ears. "You're a gorgeous boy, aren't you?"

"He knows it too," Mack said. "He's a spoiled wee boy."

"I'm sure he deserves to be spoiled."

Mack reached out and scratched him under the chin, "Yeah, he does, especially being away from him for so long."

"You were away?"

Flora saw Mack look down at the floor nervously. "Just a family thing. So I better get this little man his walk before my next client."

Flora put Dexter down on the floor. She sensed Mack was being evasive, but of course said nothing.

"Before you go, can I give Dexter a treat?"

"Aye, he'd love that," Mack said.

Flora hurried behind the counter and got out the tin of dog treats she had bought at the supermarket. She knelt down next to Dexter. "Here you go, sweetheart."

"He loves that kind."

Flora looked up from her kneeling position and saw Mack giving her that smile again. The one that made her shiver and her stomach twist. They looked at each other silently for a few seconds. Then Mack closed her eyes, and when she opened them up said, "You know, if you ever want to take a walk with us, just say. We'd love the company."

If she was neurotypical like she'd always wanted to be, and not this awkward socially challenged woman, Flora would have said yes straight away, but instead panic was besetting her brain. "I…"

Before Flora could get her excuses out, Mack said, "No pressure. The offer's there."

Flora stood up. Mack made her tense, conflicted mind settle in an instant. It was a first. It really felt like Mack understood her issues, without even being told.

"Thanks."

"And I'll need to show you around my barber's sometime. You can get a look at what we've done on YouTube."

"You're on YouTube?" Flora said with surprise.

"Yeah, I've had the channel for a few years. I give tips on cutting hair, shaving, things like that, but now that I've got my own shop, I'm going to do it more seriously. It's a good advert for the shop."

"Sounds great. I'll look it up. What's the channel called?"

"Mack the Knife. It's a nickname of mine. A lot of barbershops are on YouTube now. To be honest, most viewers watch to relax and fall asleep at night."

"ASMR," Flora blurted out excitedly. Autonomous sensory meridian response gave a sedative, almost brain-massage feeling. Not everybody had heard of it.

"Yeah, I wasn't sure if you'd heard of it. In fact I hadn't until I got feedback on my videos. So I try to make my uploads more for the ASMR viewer."

"Not everyone feels it," Flora said.

"No, I don't," Mack said, "but I wish I did."

Flora smiled. Every night she went to bed, popped in her earphones, and watched a few videos to relax and fall sleep. She didn't like the silence of being alone, and it covered up the noise from the two students upstairs.

"Yes, I love ASMR. I'll look you up tonight."

"Let me know what you think. My email is on the channel information," Mack said.

Flora was nearly bursting with excitement. She'd never had such an easy-going conversation with someone before. She hardly knew a thing about Mack, and yet this was so easy.

"I will."

"I better get this little man his walk. See you later, Flora."

As Mack walked away, Flora blurted out, "Flo, call me Flo."

Mack turned her head back and gave her that devastating smile that melted Flora from the inside.

"See you later, Flo."

Why someone like Mack wanted to talk to her, she had no idea. She wasn't beautiful, well-dressed, or sophisticated, like the people she was sure Mack was used to. But Mack was kind—that had been clear to see since the first night they met.

Friends had never been something Flora kept. Her anxieties had always made it more comfortable to be a solitary animal, but maybe she could be friendly with Mack. They were neighbours, after all.

Yes, that's what she would do. Try to at least have a neighbourly friendship. It wasn't as if she would have the pressure of seeing her any other time. This was her challenge—be friendly with Mack.

"Was that Mack?" Sandra said behind her.

"Yes, she was just going a walk with her little dog, Dexter."

Sandra put the boxes she was carrying on the counter. "You know, I was wondering if she was any relation to the famous Sharkey family."

"Famous?" Flora said.

"Well, maybe infamous is a better word to use. They were a criminal gang that ran most of Glasgow but went straight in the eighties. They still have a big influence on the streets and own a lot of property across the country."

"All I know is that she is kind."

Sandra smiled. "You seem to be comfortable with her now. Where was it you had met before? Because you were panicked the first time she came into the shop."

Flora did not want to talk about this. "She just helped me out one time when I was having a panic attack."

It wasn't a lie. She had been having a panic attack—she just had a group of men around her at the time.

❖

That evening Mack was having dinner with Nikki and Isla at Nikki's apartment in the Merchant City neighbourhood of Glasgow, where nineteenth-century buildings that had been converted into luxury apartments.

Nikki's parents lived out in the green outskirts of Glasgow, but Nikki was a city woman, and since she left home, the city centre had been her home. The Sharkey empire was run from here and at the office building, just five minutes away.

Mack and Isla had finished their food and were patiently waiting on dessert. Nikki had been eating at a rate of one mouthful per five minutes.

"Mum," Isla whined. "Put your work away. We're waiting for ice cream."

Nikki looked over at their empty plates. "Sorry, little bug."

"You aren't meant to do work at the table."

Nikki scooped up some of the food and ate it quickly. "I'm done. Can you take the plates, and then we'll get ice cream?"

"Okay."

Once Isla was away, Nikki asked Mack, "How are things at the shop?

"It's been fantastic. I'm loving every day. I was lucky to get Liam on board. He's going to help me so much."

"I'm so glad you're enjoying it. You deserve it," Nikki said.

"Don't, Nik."

"Don't what?"

"Don't keep feeling guilty. There's nothing to feel guilty about." Mack looked towards the kitchen area of the open-plan apartment, to make sure Isy was busy and not able to hear her. "You know how Isy has been. Can you imagine how she would have reacted if you went to prison? It wouldn't bear thinking about. She needs her mum."

Nikki shot a look over to Isy and said, "I know, but I still feel guilty. I'll never be able to repay you."

"Shut up, Nik."

Nikki laughed. Mack was one of the few people who could say that to Nikki.

She then shouted over to Isla. "Can you just bring the ice cream, bug?"

Isla sighed and rolled her eyes. "You're talking?"

Mack's niece was used to some conversations being adults only. It's how she was brought up.

"She's definitely going to be a moody teenager," Mack said.

"Don't I know it. If only she was as confident outside of the family. So, have you made any progress with your neighbour next door?"

"Yeah, the letter made things easier, but I helped her when some kids were getting out of hand in the shop, and that broke the ice. I haven't mentioned that night we met. I don't think she can face it."

They heard a bark and turned around to see Isla feeding Dexter ice cream from a spoon. Mack laughed but Nikki sighed. "Isy, stop that."

"Dexter helped," Mack said. "I mean with Flora. She likes dogs, so he's helped with the conversation."

Isla brought the bowls over to the table and went back to pick up the ice cream. "You're determined to make her your friend."

"I think she needs a friend. All the other shopkeepers around us think she's a weirdo—in their words—and that makes me angry. They have no idea what she's been through. I don't know anything apart from that one night we met, but she's obviously a shy, sensitive soul."

They both looked over at Isla carrying the ice cream, and Nikki said, "Like someone else we know."

Isla put down the ice cream, and Mack said, "You forgot the most important thing."

Isla's face lit up in a smile, and then they both said at once, "Sauce and sprinkles!"

Mack got up to get them while Nikki dished out dessert. When she got back, Nikki said, "Tell me more about this woman Flora."

"Who's Flora?" Isla said.

"My next door neighbour at the barber's. She runs a traditional sweet shop."

"Really?" Isla's face lit up.

"Yeah, when you come to get your hair cut, I'll show you."

Isla and Mack put the sprinkles on their ice cream liberally while Nikki kept hers plain.

"Is she pretty?" Nikki asked.

"She is beautiful, but she doesn't know it. She hides under oversized cardigans and things like that. I don't think she wants anyone to notice her."

"But you did?" Nikki said.

"Yeah, I did."

Nikki took a spoonful of dessert and said, "That's a rare thing in our world. Women not knowing how beautiful they are."

"She's special, and I think I found my way back to her for a reason."

"It's not like you to talk like that. This Flora must be something special," Nikki said.

Mack smiled. "She is. I feel it."

❖

Flora was eating dinner at the kitchen table. The TV was playing in the background. She was late with dinner tonight. When she returned home, her neighbours upstairs were at the front windows of their flat shouting and making sexual gestures at her.

She was so upset that she locked herself in her bedroom when she got in. Eventually hunger made her brave enough to go to the kitchen and cook. They hadn't done anything else since, thank goodness.

It was a shame they'd ruined her excited, happy feeling. She could have skipped home this evening, after her conversation with Mack. Talking with her wasn't hard, as it usually was with people, and she didn't feel judged.

And Mack was so gorgeous. Everything about her made Flora's heart flutter. Her kindness, understanding, and sensitivity—Flora didn't think someone like that existed.

Maybe she could make a genuine friendship with her, and admire her from afar?

Flora took another forkful of her pasta dish and then remembered what Mack had said about her YouTube channel.

Flora lifted her iPad from the table and set it up on its stand. She opened YouTube and typed in *Mack the Knife*. Lots of videos came up with Mack in them. Flora's heart started to beat faster as she subscribed to the channel.

She chose the very latest video so that she might see the inside of the new barbershop. Before she pressed play, Flora rubbed her nose and tapped her fingers on her chest. Nervous excitement could drive her OCD just as well as more negative emotions.

When the video started, she watched Mack whisper, "This is for you ASMR fans."

She then started to wash her friend Liam's hair over the sink. She had microphones strapped to her arms that allowed you to hear all the soapsud sounds.

Flora became mesmerized as she watched Mack dig her strong fingers into Liam's scalp and give him a head massage while she washed his hair.

Her forearm muscles bulged as she did, and Flora imagined herself in Liam's position. She felt a tingle spread from the back of her head down her spine. The ASMR tingle was so good. She'd felt tingles before, but not like this. These made her shiver.

Mack then rinsed and dried off her hands with a towel and led Liam back to the barber's chair.

There, Mack gave him an open-razor shave to tidy up his slight beard, then gave him a face massage followed by a back and shoulder massage, right down to his hands, cracking every knuckle as she went.

Flora couldn't take her eyes off the video, though she knew her dinner was cold. She kept putting herself in that chair and imagining Mack massaging and touching her like that. All of her nerve endings were sparking and tingling everywhere.

"Well, that's settled," Flora said to an empty kitchen. "I'm definitely gay."

She'd always suspected as much as she didn't show any interest in men, but then she hadn't trusted her instincts as she hadn't spent much time with men or gay women.

Now she was sure—not that it mattered. Flora knew she wouldn't be able to even begin thinking about dating. She wasn't socially capable, and she knew the panic that she would feel at the prospect of even talking to someone new, far less letting them into her life.

The one person she seemed to be comfortable with—at least she was able to talk to them—was Mack, and Mack was so out of her league. But maybe she could be a friend. Even having a friend would be a step forward for her.

Flora was transfixed with the videos and went from one to the next to the next, until loud shouts and music from above jarred her calm, relaxed feeling. The boys upstairs obviously had friends over as there were many different voices.

Anxiety started to creep into her bones again, so she quickly tidied up, then retreated to her bedroom, turned on the TV to make her feel less alone, then put in her earphones and played Mack's videos again.

She drifted off with Mack's voice in her ears and her face in her dreams.

## CHAPTER SIX

Every day it became Mack's routine to pop into Flora's and buy some sweets or chocolate before taking Dexter on his afternoon walk. She didn't even need or want the sweets every day, but it was an excuse to talk to the enigmatic Flora.

She was excited to see and talk to Flora, as was Dexter, who got treats each day from her. Mack had never met someone who grabbed hold of her interest like that. She had been attracted to many women, slept with a lot of them, but this was different.

Flora, it seemed, had grabbed hold of her inside that first night they met, and never let go. She was so beautiful but tried to hide it, with her plain clothes and hair, but that just made her more interesting to Mack. She wanted to know what made Flora tick—she wanted to know *her*.

Mack had never had that deep interest to know a woman better. All of the women in her life before were short-term girlfriends. They didn't know her, and she didn't know them, except physically.

"Liam, I'm taking Dex out now," Mack said.

She clipped the lead on his harness, and he jumped about, full of excitement. Liam came out from the back and said, "Bring me back some gummy bears."

"I'm going on a walk with Dexter."

Liam grinned. "But you always pop in next door before you do. Don't think I haven't noticed."

She'd been caught. "I'm just getting to know the neighbours—besides, Flora needs friends, and me and Dex would like to be."

"You're a puppy underneath all that scary Sharkey outside, aren't you?"

"Shut up. People have been punched for less," Mack said.

But Liam just laughed. "See you later."

Mack shook her head, and then she and Dexter walked out the door. He started pulling towards Flora's shop. It was part of his routine now—plus he loved Flora, and she gave him treats.

Mack held the door open for a couple of elderly ladies leaving the sweet shop. When they finally got in, Dexter pulled hard, and Mack let go of his lead. Dexter ran at top speed over to Flora and jumped into her open arms.

"Where's my little boy pal?" Flora said as she scratched his ears.

Sandra smiled warmly. "That wee terror is back."

"He is," Mack said. "Hi to you both. Can I have a quarter of gummy bears for Liam, please?"

"Coming right up," Sandra said.

Mack walked up to Flora. "You definitely have a pal there, Flo. He loves you."

Flora blushed as she often did. It made her all the sweeter. "How are you, Mack?"

"I'm fine. Business getting better all the time."

"I'm really pleased for you." Flora put Dexter on the ground and got a couple of chew sticks.

"But I've always got to make time for my wee pal," Mack said. She was desperate to ask Flora to come for a walk with them, though she thought Flora would probably say no. She was so shy. Well, she could only say no. "Flo, would you like to come for a walk with us?"

She saw panic on Flora's face, but just as Flora was probably about to say no, Sandra arrived with the bag of gummy bears.

"That sounds like a lovely idea," Sandra said.

Flora shot her a look, and Mack could see a thousand thoughts flutter over her brain, trying to come up with a reason to disagree.

Mack wasn't offended. She understood—Flora found social interaction difficult.

"Will you be okay on your own?" Flora said.

"Of course I will. The rush is over," Sandra replied.

Mack added, "I don't go for long. Just to the end of the road and into George Square."

She watched Flora rub her nose and tap on her chest. Although Flora clearly tried to be discreet, Mack had noticed it a couple of times. It was a strange little habit.

"Okay, then," Flora said softly.

Yes! "Fantastic."

"I'll just get my jacket."

When Flora went out to the back of the shop, Sandra said, "Thanks for inviting her. She really loves it when you and Dexter come in. Which isn't like her. She's very reserved."

"I'm happy for her to come. Dexter and I love coming in to see Flo."

Flora appeared from the back of the shop and looked nervous and unsure.

"Are you ready?"

Flora nodded and walked towards the shop door. She was so nervous. But she couldn't say no without hurting Mack's feelings, after Sandra put her on the spot. It wasn't like Sandra. She understood all her issues, but she'd heard Flora gabbing about Mack and Dexter all week, so she wanted to encourage her probably.

She was glad that Sandra had pushed her to go. Flora was excited about this walk with her new friends. Ever since she discovered Mack's YouTube channel, she had been glued to it every night. It felt like she was getting to know Mack by watching them.

When she finally went to sleep, she imagined herself in that barber chair, getting a massage from Mack, those strong fingers digging into her tired muscles and making her feel relaxed and hot under the collar at the same time.

They were outside the shop and leaving Flora's comfort zone. Probably sensing Flora's nerves, Mack held out Dexter's lead and said, "Do you want to have him?"

"I'd love to," Flora said.

Flora felt immediately better. Little Dexter had a calming effect on her. He was an open, loving boy, and he broke the ice between them. They walked along in silence for a few steps, and Flora said nervously, "I like his red and white stripey jumper today."

Mack smiled. "Aye, he likes to be fashionable."

Then Dexter pulled to the curb across from The Deep and sat nicely, waiting to cross the street.

"No, we're not going to the club today, Dexter." Mack patted her leg and whistled to get him back walking again.

Flora wondered why he wanted to go across to the gay club.

Mack explained, "My family owns the club over there. I sometimes stop by and have a chat with the staff. They always make a fuss over him, so he likes going there."

Flora remembered what Sandra said about the formerly criminal Sharkey family she'd heard of. She thought of the night they met and the big men that Mack was with. They saved her, but who knew what had happened to them.

But when she looked up to Mack's kind, gentle face, she couldn't imagine Mack ever hurting her. After all, she had no need to try to be so friendly to her. After their second awkward meeting, Mack tried hard to make friends with her. She didn't need to do that.

In fact, far from being intimidating like you would expect a gang member to be, Mack had been protective, and since the incident with the schoolkids, Flora had felt more relaxed in the shop, as if Mack's protective bubble extended from the barber's into Sweet Surprise.

*Don't think about it*, Flora told herself. She should just enjoy these little moments with the woman she now was having the biggest crush on.

They got to the end of the street and waited at the side of the road to cross to George Square. Flora flinched when she felt Mack's hand touch the small of her back, but she soon relaxed. She gazed at Mack as she concentrated on finding a safe gap in the traffic, so they could cross.

Heat spread up from her back and down to the tips of her fingers.

Excitement and trepidation were her overwhelming emotions, and these were new feelings for Flora.

"Okay, let's go," Mack said as she ushered both Flora and Dexter across the road. When they got safely to the other side, Mack let her hand fall from Flora's back and brush past her hand. Flora had the urge to grasp it and hold on tightly.

Another first. Normally Flora didn't like anyone getting that near, except for her family. When her mum and grandad were alive, she was always seeking out hugs of reassurance and safety, but never from anyone else. But now there was some invisible force drawing her hand to Mack's. It was so strange.

They walked onto the large square which was dominated at one end by the City Chambers and the war memorial. It was landscaped with grass, which people loved to lie back on in the summer, and was surrounded by Georgian and Victorian town houses.

"Do you want to take a seat? Just for a few minutes? I know it's cold," Mack said.

Flora wondered if Mack was going to talk about that night, and her excitement turned into worry. "If you like. I don't mind the cold as long as I'm well wrapped up."

They sat on a bench facing the City Chambers. Directly in front of them was the war memorial guarded by two recumbent stone lions, a famous and well-loved feature of the square. Dexter sniffed around the bench, always busy with other dogs' scents.

The tension was palpable for Flora. She had to steer the conversation away from anything that would make her uncomfortable. The urge to perform her OCD rituals was so strong and they would be hard to do discreetly.

Just as Mack was about open her mouth to talk, Flora launched in to a babble of words to stop any uncomfortable questions.

"It's nice here, isn't it? Beautiful architecture and flower beds, a lovely place to sit in the middle of a busy city."

"Yeah—"

Mack tried to respond but Flora didn't let her. "Did you know the square was named after King George III? And the streets around the square, Queen Street after his wife Queen Charlotte, and Hanover Street, for the German Hanover kings?"

"No I didn't know—"

Again she cut Mack off. "The grand Georgian buildings all around the square were houses for the rich families who lived here. Can you imagine how that must have seemed to the poor folk, to see people with so much? William Young, the famous architect, designed the City Chambers and it was built in—"

Mack looked at her with a grin and a raised eyebrow. She closed her eyes in embarrassment and said, "I'm sorry. I'm babbling, aren't I? I do that when I'm nervous. I'm a history and facts buff, and it just pours out sometimes."

"I like listening to you, but why are you nervous? It's just me," Mack said.

How could she explain the millions of worries that ran through her mind at any one time?

"I don't usually do this sort of thing, going for a walk with someone."

"But you can talk to me—you have been, every day in the shop."

Flora looked down at her lap. She was going to have to be a bit more open, or Mack would think she was a complete freak. She tapped her knee with her finger in a rhythm of threes. Always in threes.

She knew from all the failed therapy she had tried over the years that this and her other OCD behaviour were called stims. Stimming was a way of trying to calm the fear or anxiety you had, but sometimes it made things worse because it could be embarrassing if noticed.

As if Dexter understood that she needed some comfort, he jumped up onto her lap. She started to stroke him, and her anxiety started to lessen.

"Yes, I know. I have social anxiety, and I struggle with any kind of social interaction, but I do feel more comfortable with you. I wouldn't have come if it had been anyone else."

"Thank you." Mack smiled. "You can trust me."

This was so strange. Why was Mack trying so hard with her, trying to be her friend? A plain woman, and a social phobic. She wanted to ask why but didn't have the courage. She didn't have the courage to hear that her crush actually felt sorry for her.

"Do you mind me asking how long you've had social anxiety? Was it a recent thing?"

Flora felt her throat constrict at that question. Mack probably thought it was connected to the night they met, but it wasn't. She'd never had to explain it before. Sandra knew just by the fact that Flora grew up around her, but having to explain it to someone else was a different thing.

Flora cleared her throat nervously. "I—since I was about ten."

Mack turned around and slipped her arm along the back of the bench behind her. "Really? You were that young?"

Mack was obviously waiting on her to elaborate, but Flora couldn't speak. She struggled to even talk to therapists about that time in her life. She didn't want to remember. She didn't have a voice to speak the words.

After Mack must have realized Flora wasn't going to say any more, she said, "My little cousin has social anxiety."

Flora wasn't expecting that. "Really?"

"Aye, well, I say little cousin. Isla's mum and I are cousins, but we're more like sisters."

"What age is she?"

"Eleven, but a really young eleven. My family hasn't had experience of any kind with mental health issues before, so we've had to learn as we go. I've been away for a while, and when I came back she had gotten worse, if anything."

There it was again. Mack had mentioned being away from Dexter for a while too. Flora wondered where she could have been.

"Does she have a therapist?" Flora said.

"Lots, she hasn't been able to talk to any of them so far."

"I understand. It's hard to find someone to trust and open up to."

"I'd love to talk to you about her, and maybe bring her into the shop sometime. I know she'd love Sweet Surprise," Mack said.

"Any time."

"Thanks." Mack looked at her watch and said, "I suppose I better get you back. It's been nice."

Flora smiled. It *had* been nice. Spending some social time with Mack had been nice. She felt excited and safe with Mack, and feeling safe meant everything to Flora.

"Yes, it's been nice."

"Why don't we do this every day? As long as Sandra can spare you from the shop at this time."

Flora's heart hammered, and she managed to croak, "Okay."

This was strange. In a short time her life was expanding to places she hadn't even dreamed about. Could she actually make and keep a friendship, with a friend that she also had the hugest crush on?

Flora gave Dexter a kiss and put him down on the ground.

"You've got a new best friend there," Mack said.

When they stood up, Mack pointed to the big stone lions at the side of the war memorial. "I've always loved those lions."

Flora smiled. "My grandpa used to tell me they're called George and Mildred."

Mack laughed. "Then that's what we'll call them."

"Yes."

Mack offered Flora the crook of her arm to hold.

Her brain and her hormones screamed *take it*, but that anxious girl inside her told her to run from this offered connection. She had to take a snap decision, and she fought against everything that her anxiety told her and grasped Mack's arm.

Flora had taken the first step. She fought her demons, her anxiety, and won. A small victory, but a start.

# Chapter Seven

The next two weeks were a revelation for Flora. She was loving her new friendship with Mack. Every afternoon they walked Dexter, and as long as it wasn't raining, Mack would buy them a cake and coffee to sit and enjoy in the square.

Flora learned a little bit every day about how to be a friend. She couldn't have done it with anyone else. Mack seemed to understand her and never pushed for conversation or anything that Flora didn't want to talk about.

She was excited for every day now. It was only half an hour out of her afternoon, but it made her brighter, and somehow knowing Mack was next door made her feel safer. Today was the last day of the working week, and Flora was going through her morning ritual of filling her sweet jars and lining them up just right.

It was going to be a long weekend on her own.

Wait. Flora stopped in her tracks. That was the first she had thought about loneliness for a long, long time. Generally, Flora liked her own company. She was an introvert whose idea of a great night was being on her own, with her favourite book, TV show, or film.

But since she got to know Mack, she was breaking all sorts of new ground, and she'd miss her until they saw each other again. This was her new worry and anxiety. Flora was getting attached to her new crush, and although Mack had said she wasn't seeing anyone at the moment, there would come a day when she would.

Flora went out to the stockroom to get a new tub of sherbet

flying saucers. She crouched down to get them off the bottom shelf and thought of seeing Mack come into the shop, arm in arm with some pretty girl.

It would hurt. She stood, and the picture of Mack and her girlfriend floated around her mind.

She shouldn't have gotten so attached. Maybe she should stop going for a walk with Dexter and Mack every day.

Flora heard the bell on the door chime. It must be Sandra. She walked back out front and saw Mack standing just inside the door.

"I can't stop. I've got a client arriving any minute. Can Dexter come and spend some time with you? He's been pawing the door trying to get to you."

"Of course." Flora put down the tub of sweets and knelt to allow Dexter to jump into her arms. He ran to her and leaped onto her chest. "Hi, Dex." Dexter licked her face and gave her little yelps. "Good boy, good boy."

"Thanks. I'll come and get him when Isy arrives, later. Remember—I'm bringing her in to see you later, after her haircut," Mack said.

"I remember. I'm looking forward to meeting her."

Mack gave her that dazzling, sexy smile that she had, and Flora's stomach flipped.

It was too late not to be attached, wasn't it.

❖

Mack put the hairdryer down and started to brush Isla's hair. "What do you think, Isy?"

Isla smile was wide. "It's really nice. The only thing that would make it nicer is if it was shorter."

Mack grabbed some hair product and laughed. "Let's take it step by step with your grandma, okay? She's let you get a lot chopped off this time."

Isla wanted her hair as short as Mack's. Mack knew how much Isla hero-worshipped her, and she didn't know why, but she did. She wasn't like Isla's mum, an articulate, beautiful businesswoman.

Nikki was happy to go with whatever Isla wanted, but her grandma, the matriarch, wasn't so keen, and everyone listened when she spoke.

"I think your grandma doesn't want to lose her little girl just yet. Give her time to get used to it."

Mack ruffled the hair product through Isla's newly shorn locks. The hair had gone from the middle of her back to, now, collar length.

"It's really nice, Mack. Thanks."

"You're welcome, wee barra."

Liam came over with the brush to clear up the hair. "Looking good, wee yin."

Isla gave him a shy smile. She'd spent the afternoon at the shop, since it was a school holiday, helping out with sweeping and tidying.

Not that she went to school regularly. She fought her mum and grandma about it every day, which was a source of worry for them all. But today there was no fighting as she was off school legitimately, and Mack loved spending time with Isla.

"Do you want to go and see the sweet shop now?"

"Yes, I can't wait. Grandma says it's a lovely shop," Isla said.

"Grab your coat. It's cold outside." Mack then turned to Liam and said, "We're headed next door, mate."

"No bother."

"Go and get Dex," Mack said.

Isla came back with Dexter in her arms. He was wearing his spotty jumper today because Mack knew that was Flora's favourite.

Mack was actually a bit nervous. She wanted Flora and Isla to get on, but she was bringing two people with extreme social anxiety together, which was tricky. But she had a plan.

"Okay, let's go."

Mack led them out of the shop to next door. She opened the door of Sweet Surprise and encouraged Isla to walk through with Dexter. There were no customers in the shop—Sandra was out front, tidying up for the day. The shop would closing soon, so Flora would have more time for them.

Sandra looked up and smiled. "Hello, Mack. Is this Isla?"

Mack hadn't noticed that Isla had moved virtually behind her back. She put her arm around Isla's shoulder and encouraged her to move forward and pulled her close.

"Aye this is ma wee barra, Isla. This is Sandra, Isla."

"Hi," Isla said in the softest of voices.

Mack bent down and unclipped Dexter's lead. "Go find Flo, Dex."

Dexter sped off into the back of the shop, and Mack heard giggles. That made Mack smile. Flora was the most relaxed when Dexter was around. In a few seconds Flora came out from the back with Dexter in her arms.

"He found me," Flora said.

"He always does," Mack said. "This is Isla. Isla, this is Flora."

"Hi, Isla. Mack's told me so much about you."

It worked, Mack thought. Flora was holding on to Dexter and stroking him, making her feel more relaxed, almost like a therapy dog. Mack had hoped this was the best way to make her feel relaxed.

"Hi, Flora." Isla gripped Mack's arm.

"You call me Flo. Dexter told me that you're his best friend."

Isla laughed softly, and Mack felt a lot of tension leave her body. *Well done, Flo. You're doing well.* Mack knew that Flora's social awkwardness did not end with adults, so she was really trying hard.

"Aye, he is—he loves Isy." Now to help with Isla's social awkwardness. "Isy, get your list out. We've got shopping to do."

"Oh yeah." Isla fished into her pocket and brought out her iPhone.

This was Mack's plan for today. From all that she'd learned from her encounters with Flora, and being around Isla, she realized that there should be something to break the ice, something to relax both Isla and Flora, so the two socially anxious people didn't stand struggling with what to say.

As Mack lay in bed last night, she thought about the thing that they both shared, that relaxed them—Dexter.

Having Dexter there would break down the tension, and then giving Isla a list of things to buy would give her something to say, a structure of a conversation to start off with.

"What shopping?" Flora asked.

Mack didn't reply for Isla and encouraged her to speak. "My mum, Auntie Mary, Grandpa all gave me a list of things they would like from the shop. I've got it on my phone."

Flora grinned. "Lovely."

Mack gripped Isla's shoulders and gave them a reassuring squeeze. "Don't forget Murdo and Jamsey."

"Oh yeah, Murdo and Jamsey work for Mum," Isla said.

Flora turned to Sandra and said, "I think we should close a little early. We've got a big order to fulfil."

"Will do." Sandra went over and snibbed the door and turned the Open sign to Closed.

"Let me show you around, and then we can see to your shopping list."

Flora held out her hand, and Isla looked up at Mack. She gave her a small nod. Mack watched with pride as Isla walked off with Flora. She'd done it. With careful planning, she'd brought these two socially awkward people together.

❖

Flora led Isla behind the counter. She had been nervous about meeting her. As an adult you were meant to be relaxed and in control when meeting with youngsters, but high school children like the ones that came into her shop every day still made her shiver and shut down in fright. That's why Sandra worked the till at lunchtime and after school.

The noise high school children made made Flora freeze and took her straight back to navigating the corridors of school, while feeling like she was on the edge of meltdown. And more often than not, she was.

But when she saw Isla hiding behind Mack, she knew this wouldn't be the case with Isla, especially with Dexter there. He both calmed her down and gave her a subject to talk about when there was a lull in the conversation.

"I like your hair. Did Mack do that for you?"

"Yeah, I want it shorter, but Mack says we have to let Grandma get used to it first."

"Probably true. Your cousin is clever, isn't she?"

"She's the best," Isla agreed enthusiastically.

Flora looked up at Mack and grinned, and she could see Mack blush. It was sweet.

"Okay, come behind the counter, and I'll show you everything. Mack, can you entertain yourself?"

"Don't worry about me. On you go. I'll keep Dex here with me."

Mack appeared really happy seeing them get on so well.

Flora watched Isla look around all the shelves in wonder.

"Why don't we start in the storeroom." Flora led her through to the back of the shop and down the corridor to the storeroom. She opened the door and said, "In you go."

The shelves of the storeroom were packed floor to ceiling with jars of sweets and boxes of chocolate bars.

Isla gasped. "Wow, it's like Willy Wonka."

"That's what I used to think when I was younger, and"—Flora bent down slightly and whispered—"to be honest, I still think that. I love coming here to work just as much as I did when I came to help my grandpa after school and weekends."

"This was your grandpa's shop?"

"Yes, he loved it too. He wanted to keep it as traditional as possible."

"Like the glass jars?" Isla asked.

"Exactly, let me show you my system."

Flora was so surprised and glad at how easy it was to talk to Isla. As soon as she saw her hiding behind Mack, she saw the same vulnerability in her eyes as she had suffered her whole life.

Flora lifted one of the plastic jars of sweets down from the shelf. "The sweets come in from the wholesaler in these plastic jars and sometimes tubs. Most other shops display in these too, but I fill up the glass ones from these as needed. There's something so much more exciting about seeing your favourite sweets displayed like they would have been in the Victorian days."

Isla nodded. "It's more magical."

"It is."

Isla walked around the shelves pointing as she went. "They're nice. Oh, Granny loves them." Then she stopped and turned around in a circle. "They're in order."

Flora wasn't sure what Isla meant. She wouldn't have noticed her system, would she? "What do you mean—"

"Colour order, kinds of sweets, it feels safe. I like things in order too," Isla said the last part quietly.

Did she have OCD tendencies like her? She didn't want to make her feel uncomfortable. The way Isla lowered her voice made her think this subject wasn't easy for her to talk about. So Flora tried to make it seem not a big deal.

"Yes, I love everything to be in logical order. This is my Corner of Chaos, as I call it." She pointed to mixed sweet jars. "And then over there is my Corner of Calm. All single colour sweets."

"Then the toffees and chocolate things in the middle?"

"That's right. It's nice and logical." Flora smiled warmly.

Isla responded to Flora's reaction by visibly relaxing and smiling along with her. "Logical." Flora made a promise to herself to talk to and understand Isla the way she would have hoped someone would have talked to her as a youngster.

Flora went over to the mixed sweets and joked, "If I could get away with separating these and selling them this way, I would, but unfortunately not all the customers are as logical as you and me."

Isla laughed.

"I like calling it the Corner of Chaos. That's what it looks like to me," Flora said, "But come with me. I've got some jars that are especially for me."

Flora led them out of the storeroom and over to the small back area of the shop, where they gift-wrapped presents and sorted out stock, and there were a sink, a kettle, and a microwave for breaks.

"You have a slush machine?" Isla said excitedly.

They stopped by the machine that was churning blue, red, and green coloured ice.

"Yes, the kids like it, but we keep it back here with the drinks fridge, so it doesn't look too modern for our Victorian vibe out in the front. Would you like one?"

"Yeah, please."

"Which colour?"

"Blue, please."

Flora poured out a large clear plastic cup full of the blue slush and handed it to the excited Isla. Isla took a drink from the straw and then shivered.

"Mmm. It's so good."

Flora got another cup and poured out the same blue one for her. "I think I'll join you. You know there's some kids that want the three colours in the one cup?"

Isla's eyes went wide. "That's so wrong. It should be illegal."

Flora laughed. "You are so right."

She led them over to the shelves in the kitchen area. "This is my own personal stash. I love fruit sherbets and Love Hearts, but the mixed-up colours drive me mad."

Isla grinned. "So you separate them out into tubs?"

"I do. Then I can eat them as they should be."

"You know, when I have things like this"—Isla seemed buoyed by meeting a kindred spirit—"like fruit gums or Love Hearts, I eat them in colour order. Everyone thinks it's strange—"

"But it's only logical," Flora finished for her. "Well, any time you want some sweets in a logical way, you can have them from my secret stash."

"Thanks," Isla said happily.

"We better get your orders ready."

When they walked out into the front shop, they found Mack helping Sandra with the sweeping up, but Dexter was making everything harder by pouncing and barking at the brush.

"I thought I'd put her to work," Sandra said.

When Mack looked up at them, she furrowed her eyebrows. "Hey, since when have you had a slush machine?"

"Flo keeps it back there, so it doesn't mess with the Victorian vibe," Isla said confidently.

Mack seemed surprised at Isla's confidence in front of them all. "If I had known about the slush machine, I'd have been having one every day."

Isla stuck out her now blue tongue at Mack, and Flora asked, "Would you like one?"

"Yeah, please?"

Flora turned to Isla. "Would you like to do the honours, Isla?"

"Use the machine, you mean?"

Flora nodded.

"Yes, please." Isla hurried to the back of the shop again.

Mack gazed at her with soft eyes, put her hand on her heart, and mouthed *Thank you.*

Flora's knees went weak at the gesture. In fact she was surprised that she kept upright. Mack was making her life lighter, her heart lighter. She only wished Mack would feel the same way.

❖

Mack sat in one of the barber chairs with her feet up on the mirror unit in front of her. She scrolled aimlessly through Twitter while she waited on Flora closing up next door.

After a while Murdo came to pick up Isla, and Mack let Flora get on with cashing up. Liam had gone already, and Mack was waiting because Flora had promised to come in and finally see her shop.

Mack was completely alone because Dexter hadn't wanted to leave Flora, so Mack left him there. Even her dog loved being with her.

She smiled as she remembered how well Isla had gotten on with Flora. Unlike with most adults, Flora was open with Isla. Mack could see so many issues that Isla shared with Flora and knew it was a good idea to introduce them.

Mack felt herself start to doze off and tried to stay alert. "I must be getting old." Friday night, half past five? A few years ago, on the nights she wasn't working with Nikki, Friday evenings didn't start until eleven, when she'd head into The Reef for a pre-club drink before heading to The Deep.

But a few years later, and she was trying her best to stay awake at closing time. She jumped with she heard a knock on the shop door. Mack saw Flora standing there with Dexter. She moved quickly over to the door and opened up.

"Come in."

Flora walked in and gazed around at the interior of the shop. "It really is beautiful, Mack."

"Thanks, come in and see everything. I designed the inside to be steampunk style."

Flora put Dexter down on the floor, and he ran to Mack, who ruffled his ears. "Did you have fun with Flo?"

Dexter barked.

Flora walked around the seats and looked at the decor. "It really is lovely. Both our shops have a kind of Victorian feeling."

"That's true. I hadn't thought about that."

"Why is it called Mack the Knife? Is it your favourite song?"

How to explain you were called that because you were a gangland enforcer that used an open razor as a weapon?

"Not my favourite, but my theme song maybe?" Mack joked. "No, my middle name is Mackie, my granny's maiden name. The family always called me that as I grew up, and they realized what a tomboy I was. The knife bit came as I got older and trained as a barber." She reached into her back pocket and pulled out her trusty, extremely sharp open razor.

"Oh, I get it," Flora said.

Mack had gotten away with it so far. What would Flora think when she knew the truth? Flora was a sheltered middle-class woman, whose life hadn't been touched by the grimy Glasgow underworld.

Her open razor became her weapon of choice through necessity. Carrying knives had been illegal and still was, largely because of the gang culture in most Scottish towns. But you could carry them for work purposes—a chef, a fisherman, or a barber like her.

So Mack the Knife and The Barber became her titles in the underworld.

Flora walked further into the shop and said, "Your videos on YouTube don't do it justice."

"You've watched them then?" Mack said.

Flora smiled shyly. "Yes, I've watched a few."

"I'm glad you like the channel. It's a lot of fun. Here"—Mack spun round the barber chair and said—"sit down." Mack sat opposite her and noticed Flora rubbing the tip of her nose and tapping next to her collarbone. She did this when she was nervous, Mack had noticed. "You're like a little mouse."

"What? Why?" Flora asked.

Mack rubbed the tip of her nose, and she immediately saw Flora's eyes go wide with embarrassment.

"I'm sorry. It's just a silly habit."

Great, now she'd made Flora uncomfortable. "Hey, it's sweet. Don't ever feel bad about anything you do."

Flora smiled. "So did Isy get home okay?"

"Yeah, her grandpa and Murdo came and picked her up. Thanks for being so nice to her. She loved seeing around the shop. I've not seen her so happy and excited in a long time."

"I'm glad she enjoyed it. She's a lovely girl," Flora said.

"She definitely did enjoy it. There's something magical about a traditional sweet shop, isn't there?" Mack said.

"Yes, sometimes even more so for adults. It takes you back to the innocent joy of being a young child. Everyone that comes in the shop has their own special sweet that takes them back to happier, carefree times."

"Yeah, I suppose you're right," Mack said. "Isy loved it, anyway."

"She's a beautiful girl."

"Yeah, she is. We are all so proud of her." Mack then leaned forward in her seat. "So did you get the tingles?"

"What? What do you mean?" Flora said defensively.

"ASMR? When you watched the YouTube videos?"

"Oh, that." Flora blushed adorably. "Um yes, I get AMSR

tingles. It was really relaxing to watch. I usually struggle to get to sleep, but watching your videos helped me to drift off to sleep."

"Do you always struggle to sleep?" Mack asked.

Flora gulped hard. "When you're on your own—I mean there's two students that live upstairs, and they're quite loud, late at night."

"Oh, okay."

There was something more going on there. Mack guessed Flora's anxiety didn't help with sleeping soundly.

"I'm glad the videos help, in a small way. You'll need to let me give you the full treatment sometime—hair, massage, the whole works."

"Hairdressers are the worst for someone like me," Flora said.

"Why?"

"Social anxiety. Hairdressers feel obliged to talk to you about anything and everything, and I can't cope with the conversation. I just freeze."

"So how do get your hair cut?" Mack asked.

"A friend of Sandra's is a mobile hairdresser. She comes to the house. Sandra warned her about my difficulties. The only problem is her clientele are old ladies, and I don't really get a style I'm happy with. It's just to tidy up my hair really." Flora was embarrassed admitting that, but with Mack she never feared ridicule.

"You should let me cut it for you sometime."

Flora could feel her skin and her body heat up. All these nights watching Mack in the videos, she imagined herself in the chair. She imagined Mack's strong fingers running through her hair, massaging her scalp and then her neck—it was too much.

"Maybe," Flora croaked.

An awkwardness hung in the air now, and Flora didn't know what to say.

Thankfully Mack filled the silence. "Have any plans this weekend?" Mack asked.

The dreaded question to someone with social anxiety. That loaded question had been asked all the way back to her school years, by well-meaning people just trying to make conversation. The answer in her head was always, *No, the only plans I have are to put on my pyjamas, watch my favourite TV shows, and be on my own, and be perfectly happy at that.*

Instead, she would come up with a socially acceptable lie, to make herself seem normal in the eyes of the world. It could be—I'm meeting some uni friends, I'm decorating the flat, I'm meeting up with family. The family that she didn't have any more. Anything, just to make her seem socially acceptable.

But sitting across from Mack, Flora found that she couldn't lie. "Nothing. No plans."

Mack clapped her hands together and smiled. "Well how about coming for a drink with me at The Reef around the corner? I'd love to show you the family pub."

"No," Flora responded a little too harshly. "I don't go out at night." Mack must think she sounded like a freak.

But instead of questioning her about it, Mack just smiled and said, "How about a walk with me and Dexter on Sunday? I'd love to meet up with you. So would Dexter."

Flora couldn't really say no that. Not without it seeming like a rebuff. "Okay, there's a beautiful park near me. High Gate, have you heard of it?"

"Yeah, there's ducks and swans and things, isn't there?"

"That's right. My grandpa used to take me when he was still alive," Flora said.

"Dexter will love that. Is three o'clock okay? Mum will kill me if I'm not at Sunday lunch."

"I'll look forward to it." Flora looked down to her watch. It was half past five. "I better get going. I don't like to be home any later than seven."

As Flora stood, Mack got up quickly and said, "Do you want me and Dexter to walk you back to your car?"

"Are sure you don't have anywhere better to be?"

Mack looked offended. "No, there's nowhere in the world I'd rather be. Let's go."

❖

As they rounded the third set of stairs in the car park, Mack thanked God that she was fit. Dexter's little legs couldn't cope with the stairs, so Flora carried him in her arms.

Flora didn't like using lifts and not entirely because of claustrophobia—mainly it was being stuck in a small space with other people, so Flora told her. It was one of the many new things she observed about Flora, every time she went walking with her.

One of the big things she had noticed on previous walks and today was the way she flinched and tensed every time she went by groups of people.

That she understood, since Flora was harassed and threatened by a group of men the first night they met, but she flinched and tensed up even more when a group of high school kids passed by. But she seemed to relax when Mack put her hand on her back.

"We're on the right level now. The car's just over in the corner."

"Great."

Flora looked to the side. "You didn't have to walk me all the way."

"I wanted to. I don't mind a walk."

She smiled at her, and Mack's heart constricted in a vice, a new sensation for Mack since she'd met Flora.

They arrived at the white car, and Flora gave Dexter lots of kisses before handing him back to Mack. "Well, thanks so much for walking me back."

"Nae bother, Flo. If you head off now, you should get home well before seven."

Flora cleared her throat. "I don't normally tell people that I like to be home by that time. It's a bit embarrassing."

"Don't be embarrassed. It's just a part of who you are. Oh, can I have your mobile number in case I need to get hold of you about Sunday?"

"Sure."

They exchanged numbers, and Mack opened the door for Flora. Flora sat in the driver's seat and asked, "What are you doing tonight?"

"I'm going to have a drink at The Reef, talk to some friends, then head home. It's been a long day for Dex."

Mack stood back and waited for Flora to pull out of the space, but she just looked at Mack and waved back, as if she was waiting on her to walk off first, so she did but glanced back and saw Flora tapping the steering wheel, like she did on her collarbone. She was sure Flora had OCD.

That feeling of protectiveness and caring washed over her. She wanted to make Flora feel safe, and going by their conversations each day on their walks, that was something Flora hadn't had for a long, long time.

Mack got the lift down to the bottom of the car park and hurried around the building to the exit the cars took. She stood there waiting, and eventually Flora's car came to the barrier at the exit.

At the last minute Flora spotted her and smiled and waved, before driving off. Hopefully she could show through her actions that Flora could feel safe.

"Come on, Dex, let's go."

Dexter trotted along as they walked to The Reef. It wouldn't be packed till later, but a lot of people came in after work, or university, or college. The pub was just around the corner from her barber's. Really handy to go in and see good friends.

She lifted Dexter and walked up the steps. In front of her was a door that led down to the loos, and the door to the right took you into the main bar. Mack took that door and heard the murmured chatter of people sitting in chairs and booths, above the background music.

It was a modern, stylish pub with dark hardwood floors and brown leather chairs and soft creams everywhere. Jay was sitting at the bar talking to her wife, Annie, who managed The Reef for the Sharkeys.

Jay beckoned her over, so she walked over and took a seat next to her.

"Hey, it's Mack the Knife," Jay said.

"Very funny. Annie, I don't know how you put up with her."

Annie rolled her eyed. "I don't know either. Hand over that little baby, so I can give him kisses." Mack smiled and lifted Dexter up and across the bar. Annie cuddled and kissed him. "I'll just take Dexter back to the kitchen and get him some food. Lilly will serve you with your drinks."

After Annie left with Dexter, Lilly, a young bartender, took their order and came back with two bottles of lager.

"Cheers," Jay said.

"Cheers, are you working tonight?"

"No, it's my night off, or I wouldn't be drinking. I'm just waiting on Annie. We're going to get something to eat on her break. The barber's doing okay?"

"Really good," Mack said.

Jay took a swig of lager and said mischievously, "I hear you've a nice woman next door."

"Yeah, she's lovely. As quiet as a little mouse, and Dexter is her shadow. He loves her."

"I must go in and get some sweets. Annie loves old-fashioned boiled sweets."

"She's very shy until she gets to know you, but she's warm and kind."

"Sounds really nice." Jay cleared her throat and turned to face Mack. "I know it's not strictly your department any more, but I heard a couple things on the street."

Mack was suddenly alert. "The safety of the Sharkey family will always be my business. What have you heard?"

Jay looked both ways and said in a low voice, "Word is Malky McDade's come up from London to take over from his dad, now his dad's planted."

"It's not surprising, I suppose."

"I think he plans to be more aggressive about his business and push his drugs into as many territories of Glasgow as he can," Jay said.

"He's always had a good supply filtering through his London drop-off points."

"Malky's already stepping into some other territories, north of the border," Jay said.

"He must have more bodies on the streets if he's that brazen.

Thanks for that, Jay, I'll tell Nikki, so we make sure he's not in our territory with any of that shite."

"I did also hear that Kevin Drury is working for him."

"That little shit? I wonder how long he's been working with the McDades."

"Here's Annie coming," Jay said.

She walked back from the kitchen with Dexter under her arm and a bowl of plain chicken. She came around to sit next to Jay and said, "Are you two gossiping?"

"Aye," Mack said, "how's ma wee boy?"

"Licking his lips at this chicken. Is it okay that I feed him?" Lilly said.

"I think he'd kill me if I said no."

Mack sat and chatted for a while longer. In her mind she was trying to make sense of the new information that Jay had given her. There was no way she was ever going to step outside of her former role as enforcer for the Sharkeys. If her family needed her, she was there, and nothing could stop that need to help protect those she loved, even after the jail time she had just served.

Her devotion to her family was unshakable. Kevin Drury was the reason she'd served time and the reason Isla was so traumatized. She had to find out what was going on. Mack took her phone out of her pocket and called Jamsey.

"Jamsey, I've heard Malky McDade is back in town, and Kevin Drury is working for him. Find out from our people what he is up to. Cheers."

How far back did Kevin's association with Malky McDade go? Could he have ordered the hit on Isla? She'd need to speak to Nikki.

After she hung up, she thought of Flora. Did she get home safely? Mack wanted more than anything to phone her, but she hadn't said goodbye to her that long ago. She might seem a bit overbearing.

Mack's finger hovered over Flora's number. What should she do?

# CHAPTER EIGHT

It was quite a bracing winter evening, Flora thought as she drove home. She'd had such a good day. She'd spent time with Mack and Dexter and met the lovely Isla. Such a sweet, quiet girl, not like Mack at all.

Nothing seemed to bother Mack, but Isla was sensitive, she could tell. With what Mack had told her, it wasn't surprising. Flora didn't feel anxiety talking to Isla—she recognized a kindred spirit. Someone with issues similar to hers. They just seemed to get each other.

Flora was nearly home and she couldn't wait to get in, make some food, and watch some Netflix. She pulled into her driveway and her heart sank. At the side of the house, her resident tormentors sat with friends around a firepit, drinking and smoking God knew what.

She absolutely hated having them downstairs, but this was even worse. The cool, crisp winter evening didn't stop them from being outside.

Flora switched off her engine, then gathered up her bag pretending not to look, but she could see them looking at her, saying things and laughing. Her worst fear was a group of men, drinking, just like the night she was very nearly assaulted.

*Just walk straight to the door, don't look back, get in and lock the door.* She gathered her courage and got out of the car. Flora let the hair fall down over her face so she could pretend they weren't there.

Flora walked as quickly as she could to the door. She wasn't looking, but she could hear everything.

"Is that the weirdo you were talking about?"

"Yep, frigid bitch. Come on and show us your tits!" one said.

"Sit on my knee, hen, I've got something big for you."

Flora's heart was hammering and her hand shaking as she lifted her keys to unlock the door. She got through the door and locked it, put on the chain, and rushed into the hall.

"I can't keep going on like this."

Maybe she had to move. Those boys were just going to get worse. But the thought of going through the selling and buying process was frightening. Could she do it on her own?

Flora put her keys down on the hall table and began to take off her coat. She jumped when her phone rang. Flora searched quickly through her handbag and finally found her phone. She was surprised to see Mack's name displayed on the screen.

"Hello?"

"Hi, it's Mack. I hope you don't mind me phoning. I just wanted to know if you got home safely."

Flora was still shaky but felt safer now that Mack was on the phone. "I'm okay, yes."

"Your voice sounds a bit shaky. Are you sure you're okay?"

"It's nothing. Just those university guys that live upstairs saying some things as I came in from the car."

"Do you want me to come over? I can be there quickly and have a word with those dicks," Mack said.

Flora was starting to panic again. "No, no, please don't—it'll make things worse."

Mack sighed. "I'm not happy about it. I hate bullies, but if that's what you want. Keep your doors locked and windows shut. I'm always at the end of the phone, so call me any time."

"Thanks Mack. I really appreciate that."

"Okay, well, stay safe then, little mouse."

Flora laughed when she had been terrified minutes ago. Life

was feeling safer, and she was more connected to the world with Mack's friendship. At work Mack's bubble of safety was extended into her shop, and now it was beginning to make her feel less alone at home.

❖

"This is amazing. Thanks, Mum and Auntie Chrissy," Mack said.

Sunday lunch was sacrosanct in the Sharkey family. Nikki, Isla, herself, and her mum all attended her aunt and uncle's house every Sunday lunchtime. After a busy week it was a chance for them to reconnect and talk about family and business and bond over roast beef. Her mum and her aunt cooked the whole meal together from scratch.

Although her mum was Uncle Thomas's sister, she and Chrissy were more like sisters than sisters-in-law. It had been like that since they'd first met, and the bond had only grown stronger over the years. Uncle Thomas loved it. When he was dealing with the business, he felt happier knowing his wife and his sister had each other.

"Thank you, my darlin'," her mum said.

"That's your third helping," Nikki said. "Where do you put it all? Plus nearly a whole tray of Yorkshire puddings."

"That's the best bit," Mack said with a smile.

Isla took the opportunity to slip some of her meat under the table for Dexter, who was lying at her feet.

"Isy," Aunt Chrissy said, "what have I said about feeding Dexter at the table?"

Mack winked at Isy after she was caught.

"Sorry, Granny, but I always share with him. Mack always does."

Nikki shook her head. "Do you see what a bad influence you are?"

Mack laughed. "I hope I always will be."

Mack and Nikki gathered up the dirty plates and dishes while their mothers dished out the dessert.

"What's for dessert, Mum?" Mack asked.

"Apple crumble and ice cream," her mother replied.

"Yes, my favourite. I hope you've made enough," Mack said.

Aunt Chrissy replied as they walked out of the kitchen, "Oh yes. Plenty."

Nikki smacked her on the arm. "You're a glutton—you know that?"

Mack laughed. "Guilty as charged."

Nikki became more serious. "You said you had something to talk to me about."

"Yeah, I was just waiting until we were on our own."

"Okay, quick, while we're alone," Nikki said.

"I was at The Reef on Friday, teatime. Jay was there, and she wanted to let me know what she'd heard."

Nikki held up her hand. "Wait, you're not supposed to be involved in this kind of thing."

Mack held out her forearm to show Nikki her tattoo of a shark tooth. "I'll always be involved, Nik. I might not be working with you every day, but you know I'm always going to be involved."

"Yes, I know. I just want you to be happy in your new life, but I suppose being the Sharkey enforcer never leaves you. What have you heard?"

"Malky McDade is back in Glasgow to take up his dad's position as head of the family."

Nikki sighed. "Christ. That's all we need. His dad was happy with his little patch, but Malky was pressing him to go further. No doubt this will cause problems up ahead. I don't want this family drawn back into turf wars. We're professional businesspeople now. But at same time. I'm not going to let them push their shit on our streets."

"There's more. Kevin Drury is selling for him. Which makes me wonder—how long has he been working for Malky?"

"You mean Malky could have ordered the attack on Isy and Charlotte?"

Mack nodded. "It's a possibility."

"Little prick. I want his head on a platter, but I'd be the first under suspicion," Nikki said.

"Do you want me to have a quiet word?"

"No, let's see what happens first. I'll get Jamsey to organize a watch for him. Keep your nose clean for now, okay? But if I find out the attack was Malky's doing, I'll make him wish he was dead."

Just at that moment Isla came into the kitchen. "Granny says hurry up so we can have dessert."

"All right, we're coming." Mack followed them both back into the dining room and took a seat. She rubbed her hands together. "Double portions for me and Isy," Mack said.

"Oh, we know," her mum said.

The crumble and ice cream got dished out, and everyone dug in.

"This is amazing, Mum and Auntie Chrissy," Mack said.

"It's wonderful as usual, ladies," Thomas said.

Mack knew her mum and Aunt Chrissy thrived on looking after their brood by feeding them and looking after them. That's why Sundays meant so much.

Mack put a tiny portion of her dessert on a side plate, then nudged Isla discreetly. She made sure everyone else was talking and distracted when she put the plate on the floor for Dexter. He lapped it up. He had a very sweet tooth. Mack winked at Isla, and she laughed silently.

"Don't think I didn't see that, Mack Sharkey," her mum said.

"It's only a little taste, Mum." He deserved it.

She just shook her head and sighed. "You are a troublemaker."

"And you're a bad influence on my daughter," Nikki said jokingly.

Both Mack and Isla sniggered.

After a few moments her mum said, "A little bird tells me you're taking a young lady out on a date this afternoon."

"It's not a date, Mum, Flora and I are friends. She owns the sweetie shop next to mine," Mack said.

"What's she like?" Chrissy asked.

"Very quiet and shy. I thought she needed a friend."

"I met her, Granny. When I was at Mack's barbershop. She's lovely," Isla said.

Nikki looked at her daughter. "I've heard about nothing else but her new friend, Flora."

"Yeah, Flora shut the shop early and showed me all the jars of sweets and let me pick what I wanted."

"She certainly sounds nice. I liked her grandad a lot. A good man," Thomas said. "Where are you taking her?"

"High Gate Park. It's near her house."

Nikki laughed. "My cousin, going to a park on a date. I've heard it all now. Are you going to feed the ducks?"

"Aye, look, I want to be a good friend to her. She's got no one else, and I don't want to just take her for a drink at The Reef. Flora is the most sensitive and shy woman I've ever met. I want her to feel comfortable."

"My, you really must like her," Chrissy said.

"I do, but it's not a date," Mack insisted.

"Well, if you continue being *friends*"—her mum made air quotes around the word *friends*—"then you must bring her for dinner sometime."

Mack could just imagine how overwhelming this loud family dinner would be for Flora. Mack had never brought anyone home to the family. She'd never trusted them enough. Flora she was sure she could trust, but Flora knew nothing about her. That was what was worrying Mack.

If they kept up their friendship, Flora would eventually find out she'd been in jail, and more about her family background. That could frighten her. She hoped their friendship could get past that, because Mack did feel something for Flora, something very protective. Flora needed someone to stand up for her, and she would like to be that person.

## CHAPTER NINE

Flora had lots of clothes all over her bed. She'd changed her outfit a million times already. She wanted to look nice and presentable for Mack, but her wardrobe consisted of jumpers and cardigans that were oversized and didn't attract attention.

The only thing was, she did want Mack's attention. "This is stupid. You aren't someone she would look at twice." *Just pick something.* She picked a nicer cashmere jumper that wasn't too big, jeans, and boots. She got dressed and went to her dressing table to put on her make-up.

*Why are you doing this?*

She was so nervous and had nearly texted Mack to cancel so many times. This was a big step for her. But she didn't cancel because she wanted to know Mack better, much better. She'd made her feel so much safer since her arrival. And it was so rare for Flora to feel comfortable with someone that she had to explore it.

She finished her make-up and ran a brush through her hair.

Flora sighed. "I bet she meets women at her club who aren't as boring looking as me." The doorbell rang. "Oh no. She's early."

Flora's stomach was turning with nerves, and she did her rituals all the way to the door to try to calm down. The urge to continue was almost overwhelming, but she forced herself to open the door.

When she did, all her fears and the urge for her OCD rituals calmed. Mack was standing there with a loaf of bread in one hand

and little Dexter in the other. He was wearing the cutest jumper with dogs on it.

"Hi, we brought bread for the ducks and swans," Mack said.

Flora chuckled. "Come in. I just have to get my jacket."

They stepped into the hallway and Dexter was wriggling and barking to get to see Flora.

"You better let him say hello. He's really taken to you."

Flora took him from Mack's arms and gave him kisses. "I love your little jumper, Dex."

"Cute, isn't it?" Mack said.

"You always have the nicest clothes for him. Where do you get them?"

"Mostly online. I've got to keep my handsome boy well-dressed."

Flora handed him back. "You hold the boy, and I'll get my coat on."

"You look really nice today, by the way," Mack said.

Flora slipped her coat on. "No, I don't."

Mack put Dexter and the loaf of bread on the floor and then helped Flora on with her coat. "You look nice if I say you do."

"Who made you the judge?" Flora said. "You don't just have to humour me. Sorry, I didn't mean to say that sharply."

"One, Dex made me the judge, and I would never humour you or patronize you. You are the nicest woman I've ever met, and I'm lucky that I have you as my friend."

"Thanks," Flora said. If only she could be more than a friend. Mack was exactly her type. She'd never known what exactly her type was until she met Mack, but now she knew. Mack was her one and only type.

"Have you had any more trouble with the idiots upstairs?"

"Just loud music. It's only when they see me coming in from the car, and loud noise at night. I put my earphones in and just fall asleep that way."

"I'll go and have a word with them," Mack said firmly.

"Please don't," Flora pleaded. "It'll just make things worse. I've got to live here after you go away."

Mack sighed. "Okay if you insist, but if they terrorize you any more, I'll talk to them."

❖

"This was fun," Flora said as she threw the last piece of bread into the pond.

It was nice, Mack thought. Being with Flora eased her strain and tension. It was such a relaxing way to spend a Sunday, and Dexter loved having Flora with her. When the bread was gone, Mack said, "Do you want to walk around the pond?"

Parents and children, joggers, people on bikes, and all kinds of dogs sauntered past them, even though it was a frosty day. Dexter was having great fun talking to all the other dogs too.

"Yes, that would be nice," Flora replied.

"You hold Dex."

Flora took his lead, and they walked off at a gentle pace. "I haven't done this since I was young—well, since my grandad died."

"Will you tell me about your family?" Mack asked.

"There's not much to tell. My dad left when I was a baby and then my mum died when I was about ten."

"I'm sorry about your mum. My dad isn't in the picture either. But luckily, I had a strong family. My mum, my aunt Chrissy, Uncle Thomas, Nikki, and Isla."

"Isla's a lovely girl," Flora said.

Mack smiled. "She is. We adore her, but she's really such a sensitive soul, so unlike her mum and me."

"What's Nikki like?"

"Super confident."

"Like you?" Flora smiled.

"In a different way. She's our leader, and a natural one at that, just like my uncle Thomas. She runs our business, The Sharkey Group. We have property, the Sharkey casino, gyms, the pubs and clubs, and some other companies we've acquired over the years."

"You'd need to be confident to manage all that. What does she look like?"

"Much more sophisticated than me. She went to university, and I went to train as a barber. She's the clever one."

"I'm sure that's not true," Flora said.

"We're just different. I'm butch, in case you hadn't noticed, and a little rough around the edges," Mack joked, "and she's a sophisticated femme."

"I'd noticed."

She stopped and looked at Flora with a grin. That comment had sounded flirty and so unlike Flora. "Do you want to take a seat?"

Flora nodded and they walked over to a bench. They sat and watched the water while Dexter ran around at their feet.

"So, Nikki?" Flora asked.

"Aye, she's a powerful woman. I've seen people quake in her presence from just a look."

"I think I would be a bit frightened to meet her."

Mack laughed. "No, she isn't frightening to her family and friends, which I'm sure she'd be if you met her. She's a big softie when it comes to Isla."

"I wanted to say, bring Isla in to see me at the shop any time she's visiting you. She really enjoyed being in the shop, I think."

"She did, but she liked you more than anything. She hasn't stopped talking about you." Mack smiled.

"I think we get each other. I see a lot of me in her."

"Yeah, I noticed that connection. I think it would be good for her to have a friend that isn't a Sharkey. Give her a different perspective."

"I'd be happy to have her any time at the shop. In fact, I'll be decorating the shop for Christmas before long—maybe you both could help?" Flora said in a soft tone.

"I know Isy would love it. She said it was like *Charlie and the Chocolate Factory*. Well, a smaller version. And I would too."

When she said that, Flora had the biggest smile on her face.

"I was the same when I was a girl," Flora said. "My grandad's shop was the most exciting place in the world to me. Warm, comforting, and safe, while he was there."

Mack took a chance and covered Flora's hand with hers. "You feel safe now that I'm next door, don't you?"

Flora looked at her silently. "I do, but I don't know why you're being so nice to me, helping me, being so supportive."

"I'm being a friend. That's what friends do. You're the most gentle, sensitive, kind woman I've ever met."

"I've never had a friend like that before. In fact I haven't really had a friend."

Mack squeezed her hand again. "Well, I'd like to be that person for you, but I…"

"What?"

"You don't know who I am, what I need to be sometimes. Not really, and I'm worried…" Mack faltered. How could she explain to the most shy, nervous woman she'd ever met about her life and that she'd been to prison?

"What are you worried about?"

"It doesn't matter," Mack said. She never had worried about what other people would think of her before. Mack wasn't ashamed of who she was and the part she played in the Sharkey family.

Her mind went to the razor in her pocket, how she had gotten the name Mack the Knife. She'd never hurt anyone who hadn't come looking for trouble, only those that took liberties. But would Flora see it like that? She was being a coward.

"No, tell me what you're thinking."

"Honestly, it's nothing." Changing the subject, Mack said, "What a beautiful day, isn't it?"

"It is. A clear winter's day. It'll be Christmas in no time."

They looked at the water and listened to the sounds of the ducks and swans splashing about. Flora had never felt so comfortable with someone outside her family before, and in fact even her grandad hadn't known everything about her conditions.

For some reason she wanted Mack to know, in the hopes that she could explain that she wasn't as strange as she might appear, tapping all the time. But could she muster the courage?

"Mack, I—" The stress of saying out loud what was wrong with her made her compulsions all the more urgent. She rubbed the tip of her nose discreetly and tapped, but every time she performed the routine, her mind said she got it wrong, and she had to start again.

Mack must have sensed her anxiety because she touched her hand gently. "What is it?"

Flora had a lump in throat stopping her from speaking. "It doesn't matter."

She supposed they both had things they struggled to talk about. Flora felt the warmth of Mack's hand on hers and looked down at them touching. This was as close as she had been to anyone, without flinching or feeling desperate to run away.

Mack must have noticed her staring and said, "Sorry, is this okay?"

Was it? Yes, she thought, it was. Everything about this was nice. Mack was so gentle with her. She smiled and nodded.

"Listen, there's an ice cream van over there. I know it's cold, but do you fancy one?" Mack said.

"Only if Dexter can have one too."

Mack stood and ruffled his ears. "My boy always gets an ice cream, don't worry."

Mack winked before walking away and made Flora's heart flutter. What was happening to her?

This was new territory for Flora.

❖

Mack and Flora spent a few hours at the park, then began to stroll back to Flora's house. It had been as nice an afternoon as Mack could remember. When she had lain in bed at night, while in jail, it wasn't nights at The Deep that she'd longed for. It was something like today, with Dexter and someone special.

Flora was special. She was beautiful, and she didn't even know it, which made her even more special. Dexter was tired, and Flora carried him home in her arms, and that made Mack feel things she never had before.

But maybe Flora could only be her friend. Would Flora ever want someone like her?

Mack made a joke and Flora laughed at her bad humour, as they walked into the driveway of her house. Mack stopped by the entrance to the driveway to let Dexter have a sniff around. She spotted something on the windscreen of Flora's car.

"What's that?"

Flora walked over and looked at the paper, then up at the windows of the house. Mack followed her gaze up and saw two young guys at the open window. They jeered, said some disgusting things, and then one of them with darker hair used a Super Soaker water gun to shoot at Flora's head, while the other filmed it with his phone.

Flora stood, clearly paralyzed with fear, and then ran to her door, opened it quickly, and ran in crying. Mack felt a cold fury rise up inside her. She caught the eye of one of the laughing students, and Mack was sure he could see the ice in her eyes as he stopped laughing immediately, pushed his friend back, and shut the window tightly.

Was this the intimidation Flora was going through? Mack hated bullies, detested them, but doing that to someone as gentle and kind as Flora was a different level of disgusting. She would be dealing with them, but first of all she had to check on Flora.

"Come on, Dex. We need to look after Flo."

She walked through the front door and found Flora sitting on the floor with her hands over her ears and her heart breaking. It was a shock to see Flora so upset. Her heart broke for her, and she hurried over to Flora and fell to her knees. She put her arms around Flora and pulled her head underneath her own chin.

"I'm here, Flo. You don't have to worry. I'll keep you safe."

Flora grasped on to her frantically, as if trying to hold on to the safety that Mack offered.

"Take deep breaths. No one can hurt you," Mack said.

This emotional meltdown resembled the ones that Mack had seen Isla have. She tried her best to calm her, while beside her Dexter whined and pawed at Flora. When Flora didn't respond to Dex, he pushed his snout underneath Flora's arm, forcing her to sit back.

"He doesn't like anyone to cry," Mack said.

Flora scooped him up in her arms and hugged him tightly. Dexter licked the tears from her face.

"You see?" Mack ran her fingers through Flora's wet hair. She was disgusted with the two men who'd wanted to humiliate Flora, pure and simple.

"Is this what you've had to live with?" Mack asked.

Flora wiped the tears from her eyes and tried to slow her breathing. Dexter was helping, Mack could see.

Flora took a few deep breaths. "I can't cope with this any more. It's mostly just crude words and gestures. This is the first time—" Tears came again and stopped Flora from finishing her sentence.

Mack cupped her cheeks and wiped away Flora's tears with her thumbs. "You won't have to cope with it. I'll deal with it."

"How will you?"

"By having a chat." Mack stood up, took off her jacket, and hung it on the coat stand.

"No, please don't. It'll just make things worse. It always has in the past. I called the rental management company and the council noise control department—it just got worse."

Mack saw Flora rub her nose and tap her chest frantically. She crouched and brushed the wet hair from Flora's eyes. "I promise you that you won't have to worry about them again. Do you trust me?"

Flora looked into her eyes and nodded.

"Good, because I'll never hurt you, and I'll keep you safe from anyone. Okay?"

Once again, Flora nodded.

"Now take Dexter in the kitchen, and shut the door. I won't be long."

❖

Once Mack got outside, she tapped the back pocket of her jeans to make sure her razor was there, not that she'd need it.

She pressed the security buzzer, and a man with a well-spoken Highlands accent answered. "Yes?"

"Delivery," Mack said.

The door unlocked, and Mack walked upstairs to the front door of the upper flat. She knocked, and a weedy man opened the door. There was a look of surprise on the man's face. He'd obviously seen her walking in behind Flora.

"Did that crazy cow send you up to complain?" This one sounded local but just as posh. "Are you her boyfriend?"

He obviously thought that would upset her. It didn't. "I'm more of a man than you'll ever be, ya prick." Mack grabbed him by the throat and pushed him into the flat. She slammed him up against the wall. "You like intimidating women, do you?"

He had a look of surprise on his face. It was probably the first time he'd been confronted by a woman in his life.

"What's going on, Mark?" his Highlander friend shouted from the other room.

Mark tried to struggle, but then his gaze fell to the tattooed shark tooth on her forearm, and the fight left him.

His friend came into the hall and shouted, "Who are you? Get off him."

"Leave her, Gavin. She's a Sharkey."

"Aye, you better leave me, *Gavin*," Mack said. She might be angry, furious, but she was calm and controlled on the outside, one of the reasons she had such a fearsome reputation.

"What the fuck is a Sharkey?" Gavin said angrily.

Mack smacked Mark on the cheek and said, "You stay here and don't move while I talk to your friend."

She turned around and said, "Your worst fucking nightmare."

"You think I'm frightened of you?"

Mack stepped closer and said, "You should be, Gavin."

"Leave now while you can."

Mack laughed at the threat.

Again Mark pleaded, "Don't, Gav, please."

"You both are pathetic bullies. You've made a woman's home life miserable, and what you did today was cruel. Does it make you feel like big men to bully a quiet, kind woman like my friend?" Mack said.

"Fuck off." Gavin pushed her.

"Whoa, you're a big, tough man. Show me how tough you are."

"Gav, no."

He moved to push Mack again, but she dodged, and in frustration he threw a punch. Mack ducked, then headbutted him in the face. Gavin crumpled to floor and held his hands over his nose and cried out in pain. "You're not from around these parts, Gavin, but that's what some call a Glasgow kiss, or me sticking the nut on someone."

"My nose, you broke my nose."

Mack would have preferred to have left them unharmed—she was just out of jail. But she knew they wouldn't involve the police. She walked back over to Mark, who was staying against the wall as instructed. He flinched when she got up close, but she simply patted him on the chest.

"Now are you ready to hear what you're going to do to make this right?" Mack could feel him tremor. He nodded quickly. "Good." Mack gave him a deadly stare. "You and your wee pal are to pack all your clothes and whatever other shite you have here, and you're going to leave tonight. Understand?"

"But we have a lease—"

"It'll be paid for you." Mack gripped his chin tightly. "Just go and pray I never see either of you again, all right?"

"Yes, yes. I promise."

"No, we fucking won't," Gavin said. He staggered to his feet and had his mobile phone in his hand. "I'm calling the police. You're finished."

"You're not calling the police," Mack said.

Gavin looked up from his phone with blood dripping down his face and his nose at a slightly odd angle. "Why the fuck would I not?"

"Because when they arrive, I'll tell them that I came upstairs to break up a fight between you and your pal here. He thought it was out of order that you were so cruel to your neighbour."

"Are you mental? They'll ask him what really happened."

"Let me explain something, Gavin. You're not local like Mark here. He knows the score. Who headbutted him, Mark?"

Mack didn't look back at Mark—she was so confident in his reply.

After about ten seconds Mark said, in a soft voice, "I did."

Mack smiled. "You see?"

"Why are you saying that, Mark? You're so frightened of some dyke you'd go against your friend? I want her in jail for touching me."

Mark ran his hands through his hair frantically and said, stress evident in his voice, "You don't understand. She's a Sharkey. I have to live here—my family has to live here. You can go home, but I can't."

"I can't believe this. Are they gangsters or something?"

"I'm insulted," Mack said. "We left that behind a long time ago."

It was true, they had left it behind, unless people took liberties. But the very name Sharkey dripped with decades of gang warfare, and the mention of it made most people of a certain age in the west of Scotland, if not the whole country, instantly on the defensive and fearful.

"Mark, you can't do this," Gavin shouted.

"He can, because he knows I'd punch the fuck out of him if he didn't."

"I'm sorry, Gav."

"You are pathetic, Mark." Gavin spat blood onto the floor.

Mack took out her phone. "I'll leave you two boys to chat and pack. I'll just be on the landing making a few phone calls." She tapped her watch and said, "Two hours, remember. Tick-tock."

As soon as she shut the front door, Mack called her cousin. "Hey, it's me. I need a favour."

"Anything, you know that," Nikki replied.

"I need to find out who owns a property in Dunvale Street and pay off a remaining lease."

"Do you have trouble?" Nikki sounded concerned.

"Two bully boys that live in the flat about Flora—they've decided to leave tonight, in two hours. I said I'd cover the rest of their lease."

"I see." It would have been clear to Nikki exactly why and how they'd came to that decision. "Is Flora okay, and do you need any backup?"

"She's upset but okay, I'll make sure of it, and no, I don't need anyone. They're packing as I speak."

"Were you careful, Mack? You're just out of prison."

"Nae worries. They were both easy to deal with."

"Okay, what number Dunvale Street was it?"

"Ninety-one B."

"I'll get my PA on it. It'll be dealt with."

"Thanks, Nik," Mack said.

"No thanks needed. I hope Flora is okay. I'll let you know when it's done. Just be careful. I want you above the radar with the police."

"Nik, Flora's had nobody to give her safety for most of her life. I want to give her that safety. She's been through too much."

"Well, Isy's been talking about her non-stop, so she must be nice."

Mack thought of all the days Flora must have put up with this bullying, and especially after her attack the night they'd met. Flora must be stronger than even she knew to keep going every day.

"She is, Nik. Thanks for your help."

Mack hung up the phone and headed back to her new friends.

❖

Flora went from sitting at the kitchen table with her hands over her ears, to pacing back and forth to the hall and back. She hated confrontation and avoided it like the plague, which usually left her being walked all over.

At the same time, she wanted to hear what was going on. It

helped having Dexter with her. He was like her favourite teddy bear when she was a little girl, except that he was able to follow her mood and gave kisses and comfort when Flora needed it.

Eventually Mack texted her that everything was fine and she would be back with her soon. Flora couldn't imagine what Mack was doing. At first she was worried they would be fighting, but if they had, Mack wouldn't have stayed up there for so long.

Dexter, who was standing next to her in the hall, all of a sudden was barking and going crazy at the front door. Finally the door opened, and Mack walked through. Dexter jumped and barked around her feet.

"Hi, Dex, were you a good boy?"

Flora scoured Mack's body for any sign of injury that would indicate a fight, but there was none.

"Mack? What happened?" Flora asked.

Mack walked a few steps and held out her hand. "I want to show you something."

She took Mack's hand and was led to the door. When Mack opened the door, Flora saw a taxi waiting and her two horrible neighbours packing bags into it.

"What's happening?"

"I had a little chat with Gavin and Mark, and they came to the conclusion that they should both leave."

Flora was confused. "Why would they do that?"

"Because you have a friend that won't tolerate bullies."

"Did you fight them?" Flora asked.

"No—well, hardly."

"What does that mean?"

Just at that Gavin turned around, and Flora saw the bloody injury on his face. "Did you do that?"

This was going to be difficult. "He threw a punch at me. I defended myself."

Her neighbours got into the taxi, and it slowly pulled away. "I want you to watch them leave and know that you never have to be fearful again."

"I don't understand. How could you make them leave?" Flora was confused.

"Let's talk in the kitchen. Come on, Dex."

Flora followed Mack into the kitchen, and they both sat down. Dexter lay at their feet under the table.

"How did you get them to leave?" Flora repeated.

"I'll always tell you the truth—I want you to know that. I hate bullies, and that's what those two boys were. I wanted to confront them and make them pick on a woman like *me*. I never intended there to be any violence. Normally the name is enough to persuade people around to my way of thinking."

"The name?" Flora asked.

"Sharkey. The Sharkey family were on the wrong side of the law for quite a few generations."

"Sandra thought she recognized the name. Do you mean gangsters?"

"We were involved in criminal activity, but the family went straight in the eighties, and now we're just business owners," Mack said.

"But people still remember who your family used to be."

"That's it. Don't get me wrong—we still operate on the edges of the law when people take liberties, like tonight, or try to sell drugs in the Sharkey territories of Glasgow. My family don't want that stuff on our streets."

Flora's mind was whirling. She should be frightened of someone like Mack, but she wasn't. She could not imagine Mack hurting her, ever, and she was normally frightened and thought the worst. But not of Mack.

"Tonight the name wasn't enough?" Flora asked.

"One of the boys wasn't from around here, and he thought he could bully me with violence. He was wrong."

Flora gazed down at the tattoo of the shark tooth on Mack's forearm. "What does that mean? I saw that boy at my shop change in a second when he saw it."

"This?" Mack pointed at the shark tooth.

Flora nodded.

"Everyone who is part of the Sharkey family, either by blood or proven loyalty, has this tattoo."

"And people get scared because of who the family is?" Flora asked.

"Only criminals or those who take liberties. As I said, my family and I hate bullies. I know it's a lot to take in. I'm your friend, and you will always be safe with me."

"Is there any more I don't know?"

"Some. If you look up the Kevin Drury case on the net, you'll find out some more. I'll go now and let you think about what I've told you. If you don't want to keep being friends, I'll understand, but at least you'll have your eyes open," Mack said.

"Will they come back tonight?"

"No, there'll be no neighbours upstairs for a while, I promise. You'll feel safe in your home at last, and at work. I better get my jacket. Come on, Dex."

Flora followed her to the hall and said, "That's three times you've come to my rescue."

Mack put on her jacket and attached Dexter's lead. She looked up at Flora and said, "Maybe you are rescuing me."

What did she mean by that? Flora wondered. How could someone who was afraid of her own shadow save a confident and in-control person like Mack?

"I better go—remember, I'm at the end of a phone. And lock your door, okay?"

Flora nodded. "Thanks for being with me. I had a lovely day up until they…" Flora hesitated.

"I know. Me too. Good night, little mouse." Mack smiled.

Flora realized she had been unconsciously performing her ritual, and Mack had noticed. But Mack never made her feel embarrassed about it, which was very freeing.

"Goodnight, Mack."

❖

Mary Sharkey walked into the family room of her large home, holding a big plate of sandwiches and a small plate of meat for Dexter. Mack was sprawled out on her mum's couch waiting for her food and watching TV.

After spending the day with Flora, she didn't want to go home to an empty flat, so she headed to her mum's, where she knew she could find comfort. Her mum loved her to bits and always spoiled her and made her feel better.

"Here you are, roast beef sandwiches and some for Dex. Your aunt Chrissy had lots of leftovers."

Mack sat up quickly and rubbed her hands together. "Yes, look what we've got, Dex."

Her mum believed in big portions, and that suited Mack just fine. Her mum set two cups of tea on the coffee table in front of them.

"So, what brings you to your ma's on a Sunday night?"

Mack furrowed her eyebrows. "You make it sound as if I never visit."

"No, I don't mean that, but Sunday night you usually go out for a drink to the pub or to the casino."

That had been her routine before she'd gone to prison. The weekend was a time for checking in with all their establishments, meeting Nikki, and talking over any issues that came up.

Mack loved her weekends. She usually dropped off Dexter with her mum or Isla and headed off into the bright lights and loud noises of the Glasgow evening, the buzz of the crowds of partygoers. She would meet her friends who worked behind the bars, the security guards, and everyone else who gave their loyalty to the Sharkeys—not to mention the women.

Being a Sharkey brought with it notoriety, and Mack's image of being the bad girl of the family added to that. To those outside their immediate family, people saw Mack the Knife, Mack the Sharkey enforcer who used a blade to keep peace.

That image brought her a lot of female attention, and Mack took the opportunity to enjoy it. The fact that these women didn't know who she really was inside was fine by her, since Mack had no intention of making anything permanent. Her mum had brought her dad into the family, and that had been a big mistake. Mack had no want or need to repeat the same mistakes.

Her life was simple—support Nikki in every way she could, and help protect her mum, Uncle Thomas, Aunt Chrissy, and especially Isla.

But all those long months in jail had given Mack a lot of thinking time. She didn't want to return to the jail, or her former life of living for the weekends. She hungered for something more. When her family came to see her in jail, Mack looked around the room and envied those with long-term partners and children who had come to see them.

But how she would achieve that different kind of life, Mack didn't know. Then, out of the blue, the woman she had rescued that very night her life was about to take a different turn happened to be her next door shop neighbour.

Her friendship with Flora had changed her in even a few weeks. She wanted to know her, wanted to make her safe, wanted to kiss her and make her feel wanted and cared for.

"Well?" her mum said.

"Well what?"

"What are you doing here on a Sunday night?"

Mack took a big bite of her sandwich. "I just fancied seeing my ma—is that okay?"

"I always am happy to have you. How was your day at the park?"

"Really good. Dex had a great time, Flo and I talked about everything, and then..." Mack hesitated as the image of a crying Flora stuck in her head.

Her mum nudged her. "Then what?"

"I've told you how Flo has social anxiety."

Her mum nodded. "Well, she's been dealing with some bullying behaviour from her upstairs neighbours, and she'd reported them to the council and police, but that just made them retaliate. Today we were walking back from the park, and they were waiting for her. They couldn't see me behind her because Dex had stopped to sniff around the hedges at the driveway."

"And what did they do to the poor lassie?"

"Left her a disgusting letter on her car, then soaked her with water guns, just to humiliate her. She was so upset, and I was fucking raging."

Her mum softly slapped her arm. "No bad swear words in front of your ma."

"Sorry, Ma, but knowing her history as I do, I knew how that kind of humiliating behaviour would make her feel."

"What history?"

Mack told her about the night she first met Flora, and her mum was astonished.

"God knows what would have happened to her if you hadn't got down there."

"I know, and since we've met, that night hasn't been spoken about, so it obviously had a huge effect on her," Mack said.

"What did you do?"

"Flo ran inside in hysterics. I left Dex with her and went to pay them a visit."

Her mum covered her mouth with her hands and said, "Oh no. What did you do? I'm not going to get a chap at the door from the police? You're only just out of jail."

Mack put her plate of food down and took her mum's hands and said, "Don't panic, Ma. I'm not an idiot. Words were enough for those cowards. I persuaded them that they should move out in two hours, and happily they agreed."

Her mum raised an eyebrow. "As easy as that?"

"Well, one did throw a punch, and I stuck the nut on him, but apart from that it was really amicable," Mack joked.

Her mum sighed and shook her head. "They could go to the police, Mack."

"Ma, I'm not stupid. I made sure that they understood what a bad option that would be. Trust me."

"And your wee lassie, Flo, was she happy?"

"Not really, she was in a panic. She hates confrontation and thought they might come back and make her pay. She hasn't heard about the persuasive power of the Sharkey name and how safe that makes her, so I had to tell her some of our history."

"Did she not like what she heard? Is that why you're wanting to be with your mam, on a Sunday night?"

"No, I just don't feel like going out or going home to the flat on my own." Mack waited a beat and said, "I told her I was in prison. Well, I told her to look up the Drury case."

"And she didn't like that?"

"No, she didn't say much of anything. I didn't give her the chance really. I told Flo to look up the case. So I suppose I'll see what she think of that tomorrow, if I see her."

"You didn't give her any background or why it happened?"

Mack shook her head. "No, I just left. I don't want to see her reaction if she thought badly of me."

Her mum smiled. "You like her, don't you."

Mac nodded. "Flo is so alone in the world and frightened of her own shadow. She needs someone to lean on, and somehow, because of our first meeting, I feel like I know her better than I do. Plus she's beautiful and doesn't even know it."

"She sounds lovely, but you took a chance dealing with those bullies yourself. You could have phoned Nikki or Uncle Thomas, and they would have sent people to deal with it. People who weren't just out of jail."

"It had to be me, Ma," Mack said.

Her mum grasped her hand. "I'm selfish. I don't want to lose you again. You were in my thoughts night and day when you were in jail. It was hard."

Tears came to her mum's eyes, and Mack pulled her into a hug. "I'm sorry, Ma, but I had to do it."

"Your uncle Thomas used to say that to Chrissy all the time too, but I don't want to lose any more time with you."

Mack kissed her mum on the cheek. "Can I stay tonight?"

Her mum squeezed her much tighter in the hug. "That would be nice."

She knew her mum loved to spoil her—feeding her, taking care of her—and Mack enjoyed it too.

❖

Flora checked the locks on the doors for the hundredth time it seemed. Her OCD was bad tonight, between the doors and checking and rechecking whether all the switches were off. In fact she had to go as far as taking pictures of the switches in the off position and pictures of the door locks snibbed, because she knew as soon as she got through to bed, the worries and urge to recheck everything and not trust her memory would be too strong. But with the pictures on her phone, she could prove to herself that everything was fine.

When Flora was particularly stressed, her OCD could get quite bad, and if other people knew she went around taking pictures of electric sockets, they would think she'd lost her mind. But simple little tricks like that could make her mind rest easier, so she did whatever she had to.

Since Mack had left, she had been too nervous to look up the news stories about her. Flora had never connected with anyone like she had with Mack, and she was frightened that whatever Mack had served time for would erase that.

She got herself comfortable in bed and perched her iPad on the cushion stand in front of her. She thought about what to type in and realized she didn't know Mack's real first name. So she started searching for the Sharkey family in Google, then clicked the link for news articles. A whole host of newspaper articles were returned in the search.

Flora picked the newest one.

> *First jail sentence in the Sharkey family in thirty years. Laura (Mack) Sharkey, niece of the infamous Thomas Sharkey, was sentenced to two years in jail today, for grievous bodily harm on a Mr. Kevin Drury, a known drug dealer. The Sharkey family were allegedly involved*

*in the criminal underbelly of Glasgow since the early 1900s but have since become respected members of the west of Scotland business community.*

*Ms. Sharkey lured Mr. Drury to an isolated place and took revenge for his selling drugs outside a Glasgow private school, which ended in the death of a young girl.*

"Oh my God. That must be the friend of Isla's that passed away."

It must have been a horrible, distressing incident, and knowing how much Mack adored her little cousin, she must have been pushed to her limit. Then she cast her mind back to today and the injury that one of her neighbours left with.

Mack said he had swung for her, but had he? Or had Mack simply lost her temper? It didn't square with the kind and gentle way in which Mack treated her. As she looked at the pages and pages of older information on the Sharkey family, Flora knew she should be overwhelmed and scared of Mack's reputation, but she couldn't be afraid of her.

Maybe she was just being naive, as she often was. Then her phone beeped with a text.

*How is everything tonight?*

*It's quiet. For the first time in a year.*

It wasn't till she typed and sent the text out that she really thought about how Mack had changed her life. The boys upstairs had bullied and harassed her, and without Mack's help they would still be up there laughing at her and making her home life a misery.

Was it selfish to think that way? Her grandpa always said to her that she needed to stand up to bullies, but of course Flora never had the confidence or ability to do that.

Mack was making Flora's world safer, bit by bit, over the weeks, and in fact had been like a guardian angel to her at the times when she needed her most.

A text interrupted her thoughts. *Are we still okay?*

*What do you mean?* Flora typed back.

*With what I told you about my prison sentence?*

Oh, that. Flora's stomach twisted. The newspaper articles hadn't made clear to her if the violence could have justified.

She typed out, *We need to talk about it.*

Flora just prayed it wasn't a story that would ruin their friendship. She got a message back asking if Mack could call her.

Flora's heart began to thud. She hated phone calls. It was part of her social anxiety, even with people she knew—her mind went blank, and she became tongue-tied. But if she said no, then Mack would assume that she thought badly of her, and their friendship might be over.

She jumped out of bed and started pacing back and forth, all the time gripping her phone with a vise-like grip. What should she do?

"If you want this friendship," Flora said out loud, "then you're going to have to push yourself."

Before she could change her mind, Flora typed out, *Yes.*

Flora's mouth dried up and her chest went tight waiting on the call, but to her surprise, when the phone came alive, it was a FaceTime call.

"Oh God, that's even worse. She's going to see me."

She had a split second to make the decision and on impulse she accepted the call.

Suddenly Mack appeared on screen and smiled warmly at her. "Hi."

"Hi, Mack," she croaked. She needed a drink. "Excuse me a minute." Flora reached for the water bottle on her table and took a cooling drink.

Mack was looking delightfully ruffled. Her hair was sexily floppy on top, and she had a casual sleeveless T-shirt on.

"You don't mind me phoning, do you?" Mack asked.

"No, no." Flora didn't mind—she was just so nervous. She caught sight of herself in the corner of the screen and was horrified. She quickly ran her fingers through her hair, trying to make it look less messy. "Sorry, I look a mess," Flora said.

"No, you don't. You look sweet."

Flora could feel heat in her cheeks. She'd never had compliments like she had from Mack.

Mack was gorgeous, and she loved to linger on her biceps in that T-shirt. Mack was strong, no doubt, compared to most women, but it was her strength and confidence from within that really attracted her. When they were in the park today, Mack strode around as if she owned the place. To someone who couldn't look people in the eye, that was sexy as hell.

And when she was in Mack's company, she felt more at ease than she ever had. Flora loved that. She hoped Mack's story was something she could live with.

Suddenly Dexter came into view and was licking the screen. Flora laughed at his antics and relaxed a lot.

"Dex, calm down," Mack said. "He heard your voice and shot into the room. I thought he was staying in his granny's room tonight."

"Granny?"

"Sorry, I'm staying with Mum tonight. I didn't really want to go back home on my own. Sometimes you just need your ma."

Flora couldn't help but smile at that. Mack sounded so far away from the criminal she had read about online.

"Hang on," Mack said. "I'm just going to lie back, so Dex can cuddle."

Flora followed suit and slipped under her covers. Now that she was over her initial terror of being seen, Flora become excited. Talking on FaceTime was much easier for her than a voice-only call.

Mack lay on her side and leaned her head on her arm while Dex cuddled in at her chest. "So, um…I suppose we have to talk."

"Yes, I looked at the newspaper stories like you told me, but I know that's not the full story," Flora said.

"Not even close. Have you got time for a story?"

"Of course, I want to know. I want to understand you."

Mack smiled back at her. "Okay. You asked for it. There's a family called the McDades. Back in 1900, two friends came over to Scotland from Ireland, as a lot of Irish did back then. Malcolm McDade and Patrick Sharkey."

"Your ancestor," Flora jumped in.

"Aye, the first Sharkey to live in Glasgow. So the best friends were dirt poor. They thought they were coming to a better life, but back then Catholics didn't get the best of jobs."

Flora knew this only too well. Sectarianism between Catholics and Protestants had blighted the west of Scotland for generations, and for the longest time Catholics were seen as second-class citizens. She herself had come from a Protestant background, although they were never churchgoers, and her grandpa hated that kind of discrimination.

"Yes, I know it was hard for Catholics back then."

"Aye, it was tough. With families to support, they both got involved with the criminal underworld of the city. They did well and made a name for themselves, until they came up against one of the biggest gangs in the city, the Munros."

"That name's familiar."

"Yeah, they were linked to a police officer's murder, in the seventies. Six months later, Davey Munro's son Stewart was taken for a walk in the hills."

"What does that mean?" Flora asked.

"If you die after a walk in the hills or a fishing trip, that's code for the police did ye in."

Flora was shocked. "What? The police would kill someone in retribution?"

Mack smiled softly. "You really are innocent, little mouse."

Flora's stomach flipped at Mack's use of her cute nickname for her, and it made her rub the tip of her nose and discreetly tap out her ritual.

"Aye, they did," Mack said, "especially back then. Anyway, long story short, years later, Malcolm McDade took money from the Munros to lure Patrick to a place where the Munros would execute him."

"I thought they were friends."

"They were—that's why the betrayal cut so deep. Malcolm thought Patrick was getting a bit too powerful in the city. It was jealousy."

"So from then on, your families have been enemies?" This kind of criminal underbelly of Glasgow was not something Flora had any knowledge of, and if nothing else, it was interesting. Two people could have such different experiences in Glasgow, depending on where they grew up. There were areas of extreme deprivation, where drugs, crime, and alcohol were a way of life, compared to Flora's existence in the leafy suburbs.

She often made herself think of that when she was feeling sorry for herself, missing her mum and grandpa. Flora might have lost so much, but she never worried about having money in the bank. The shop kept doing well, and her mum and grandpa left money when they passed on, although she would give it all up for five more minutes with them.

"So how does that relate to what happened when you went to jail?" Flora asked.

An embarrassing noise trumpeted across the call, and Mack's eyes went wide. "That was Dex, honest."

Flora started laughing. "I know. He's terrible for that."

Mack rubbed his little pink belly and kissed his snout. Again, Flora couldn't equate this soft-hearted person with the one that committed grievous bodily harm.

"Erm…where was I? Oh yeah, there's been bad blood ever since, but the Sharkeys grew to prominence, and the McDades remained more small-time. The Sharkeys have never been into drugs. We were always into bricks-and-mortar—pubs, clubs, property—while bending the law, and a generous view on taxes, but the McDades are heavily involved in drugs."

"I see," Flora said.

Mack put her hand on her heart. "I'm not saying we were saints. We guarded our territory jealously, and my role in the family was to enforce the law of our streets, but we never hurt any innocent member of the public. Selling drugs is taboo with us even more so than it used to be. My granny's little brother died of an overdose. It devastated her, and Uncle Thomas promised her that he would redouble his efforts to protect our streets."

There were fine lines in criminality, but Flo could never be friends with someone who was involved in the drug trade.

"Flo?"

"Yes?"

"I want to be your friend, and I want you to know I've never talked this openly to anyone outside my family before. I really hope this won't change your opinion of me, but I promised you I'd be truthful."

"Tell me why you went to jail, and we can talk it through." Flora prayed it was something she could live with.

"Over time, the McDades grew frustrated about not being able sell drugs in our territories, especially when we went straight in the eighties. Our business grew and grew. There had been skirmishes over the years, but it wasn't until the last McDade got older and was influenced by his son Malky McDade that things got bad. Malky got one of their dealers, Kevin Drury, to sell drugs outside Isy's private school. Some of the older sixth years bought some, and he kept returning every day. Eventually, he got Isy's best friend to take cocaine. She overdosed and died."

"Oh my God. Poor Isy, did she see—"

Mack nodded. "She was in hysterics. Nikki didn't know what to do with her. All she kept saying was *It was for me. It was meant to be me.*"

"Poor girl."

Mack nodded. "It broke our hearts. Nikki made inquiries, and it turned out there was a hit out on Isy, but no one knew who from. We now know it was probably Malky McDade."

"A hit? Like an execution? But she's just a little girl." Tears started to fall from Flora's eyes.

Mack nodded. "It goes against all the unwritten rules of the street. You don't involve children or families of your rivals."

"I can't imagine what Isy went through, losing her best friend."

"She's always been a quiet, sensitive girl, and she just couldn't cope. Nikki and I had to deal with Kevin Drury and find out who paid him. Nikki took the lead—she's never been frightened of getting her hands dirty, and this was for her daughter, and the family of her friend. Kevin said some disgusting things about the girls, but just as he was about to give us a name, we heard the police sirens coming. Someone had called them, hoping to get Nikki arrested, no doubt."

"What did you do?"

"I told Nikki to go. We had a car waiting at the other side of the building. She didn't want to, but I knew Isy couldn't have coped if her mum was convicted and taken away from her."

"She left?" Flora asked.

Mack nodded. "Eventually. I was there with him when the police busted in."

"You were arrested?"

"Aye, I had to do it for my family. Nikki is our leader, and Isy needs her. I was convicted and got a light sentence. We had a really good lawyer."

"Wow, you really do love your family, don't you?" Flora said.

Mack waited a beat and said, "I'd do anything for those that I love."

Flora's breath caught at that statement. "I believe you."

"We now suspect it was Malky McDade who ordered it, as I said. He was based down in London, running the drug side of the McDade business, but then when his dad died, he came up to run the firm. We couldn't touch Kevin after that. It would just lead the police back to us, but Nikki is playing the long game. One day they'll get justice."

"Why did you open the barber's when you got out?"

"Nikki and my uncle Thomas insisted I take a step back from the business when I got out and pursue my own dreams. I trained as a barber when I left school—that's where I met Liam. I made the plans while I was inside, and Nikki made sure I had everything I needed." Flora didn't quite know what to say next, and her silence seemed to worry Mack. "That's the truth, like I promised you. Now you just have to decide if you can live with who I am and be my friend. I have the barbershop now, but I'll always be a Sharkey."

Flora thought about her answer carefully. "You've been like my guardian angel ever since I first met you. I can't believe that you would want to hurt anyone who doesn't come at you first."

"I protect those I care about. Like with your upstairs neighbours."

Mack cared about her? Why? She didn't understand it. Flora desperately wanted to ask that question—*why?*—but she was frightened by the answer, frightened Mack felt sorry for her.

Instead, she said, "I want to be your friend."

Mack's face lit up. "Thank you. I was convinced that the truth of who I am would end our friendship."

It astonished Flora how much their friendship meant to Mack. She looked at the time and realized they'd been talking for two hours. "Look at the time. We got lost in conversation."

"It's easy to get lost in conversation with you." Flora felt herself blush again. "I better let you get some sleep. I hope you enjoy your first night of peace since those idiots are gone."

"It's very peaceful. Thank you."

"You're welcome. Goodnight, then, little mouse."

"See you in the morning."

# CHAPTER TEN

Kevin Drury had been watching this street for a few days now. He stood on the corner, pretending to wait for the bus. A few times a day he walked down the road, with his hood up, and sat in the coffee shop, watching the barber's. But he couldn't stay for long, in case he was spotted by Mack.

He was filled with memories and fury when saw her going about her business, enjoying life. Kevin remembered how Mack held him while Nikki gave him his punishment. She didn't deserve to come out of prison and start up a new, happy life.

Kevin wanted her to pay as much as Nikki, the woman who injured him. He fantasized about it every night when he looked at his scars in the mirror, but Kevin was scared. The Sharkeys could end him if they found out what he was doing, but then, so could Malky McDade and stop his supplies of drugs. He had to just hope Malky would come out on top.

Kevin had a baseball cap under his hood, and he pulled the brim down further as he spotted Mack coming out of the barber's with her dog and walking to the sweet shop next door. He'd noticed that a lot. Kevin didn't think she needed traditional sweets every day, and sometimes she went in a few times a day. In the afternoon she came out with a woman and walked along the street, headed to George Square.

That confused Kevin. The woman was pretty enough, but

not Mack's usual type of glamourous women that hung around nightclubs and the casino.

Kevin had to know more about her, but he couldn't go into the shop and risk Mack seeing him. He would need to enlist some help.

❖

Mack was happy to say that things hadn't changed for her and Flora since her confession. In fact, Mack felt they were closer than ever. In the afternoon Mack stopped by Sweet Surprise to take Flora out for their daily walk with Dexter.

As was her practice now, Mack carried Dexter out of the shop, placed him on the ground, and handed his lead to Flora. She knew how much Flora liked to walk him. She saw Flora's gaze flit over to The Deep nightclub. Bar staff were polishing the silver facade at the entrance to the club. At night there were blue lights that simulated waves moving through the sea. It really was nice.

"Have you ever been in a club before, Flo?"

"No, I never had a group of friends to go with, and then I developed the fear of going out at night. Loud noise and lights are a lot of stimulation and not good for me. But I have always been fascinated by *your* club."

"How come?" Mack asked. She wanted to find out if it was because Flora thought she was gay.

Flora shrugged, looking a bit embarrassed. "I suppose I just always wondered what it would be like to be normal and walk into a pub or club."

Mack put her hand on the small of Flora's back and rubbed it. "You are normal—pubbing and clubbing isn't for everyone. I've been growing out of it for years. A lot of people pretend to like that kind of nightlife because they think that's what they should be doing. You stay your authentic you, Flo."

"Still, it would be nice to see what it was like once, but the lights would be too much for me."

Mack had an idea. "Listen, once we've had our little walk with

Dex, why don't we go into the club for a drink instead of sitting in the square? It'll only be some staff on, not big numbers. We can get a table and chat."

"I don't know." Flora sounded worried.

"I'll be there every step of the way, and if you're uncomfortable, then we'll leave straight away. I promise."

Flora looked at her nervously. "Um…what about Dex?"

"It's his second home. The staff love to give him treats, and he runs around the dance floor."

"Okay, then."

"Fantastic." Mack was excited to show her a bit of her world.

They walked around the square and headed back towards their street. As Mack passed the bus stop, something caught her eye, but when she turned back, no one looked out of place. She brushed it off and put her attention back to Flora.

"It's one of the nicest streets in Glasgow, I always think," Flora said.

"It is—that's why the Sharkeys bought property here."

Flora looked up at her. "Oh, your family owns it? I thought maybe the club, pub, and your shop were leased."

Mack shook her head. "We own every building on this street except one surprising shop."

She grinned when the penny dropped in Flora's mind. "My shop?"

"Aye, I asked Nikki about it. She said your granda didnae want to sell, and since it was my granny's favourite sweet shop, we backed off."

"That sounds like my grandad. He was so proud of his shop."

Mack stopped and took Flora's hand. "The next time you feel nervous or anxious, in the shop or walking to and from work, look around and think, *I'm protected by the Sharkeys*. If you're ever worried or need me, and I'm not at the shop or something, you can run across to the club or to the pub, and the security staff will help you. Okay?"

Flora gulped. "But they don't know me."

"They will once I introduce you. Let's go inside."

Flora stopped at the door of the club. "I—I'm not good at meeting people. I never know what to say."

Sometimes the easy way she and Flora talked made Mack forget the social anxiety she had. As the thought passed through her mind, it gave Mack an ache in her heart. Flora trusted her, was at ease with her, and that was such a huge thing.

"There's not that many staff in at this time, and you have me." Mack took Flora's hand. "If you don't know what to say, then I'll be your voice."

Flora looked down at their clasped hands and rubbed her thumb over the back of Mack's hand.

"That's one of the nicest things anyone has ever said to me." Flora met Mack's eyes. "I don't think anyone has ever understood my difficulties the way you do."

"Thanks, I'm just trying to do my best to make you feel safe," Mack said.

They looked into in each other's eyes, and Mack caressed Flora's cheek with the back of her hand. It was so intimate, even though they were on a busy Glasgow street. Someone bumped Mack, and she jumped out of their little moment.

"Will we go in?"

"Okay."

Mack held the door open, and Flora stepped into the entrance hallway. It gave the feel of a deep ocean with the dark background and fluorescent blue lights. Coming from the afternoon light into this darkness was strange, but the blue lights were beautiful.

Dexter barked, and Mack took off his lead. He ran off down the hall and turned the corner. "Don't worry—he knows where he's going."

"How big is this place?" Flora asked.

"There's three floors."

They walked out into a huge open room with a large bar along one wall, and booths, tables, and chairs. It wasn't like clubs she'd seen on TV because the normal room lights were on, so no dark room with flashing lights that worried her.

Some staff worked behind the bar, busying themselves with glasses and restocking drinks, while some cleaned tables and got ready for the customers who'd arrive later.

"This floor is more a meeting area for clubbers or for those who want to chat," Mack said. "The music's always played, but low. Upstairs there's the cheesy music floor with all the old favourites, and the top floor is for serious dance music. There's something for everyone."

The thought of this place packed with people was scary for Flora, but like this she could handle it. She heard a bark and saw Dexter getting petted and hugged by a tall, solid woman at the bar.

The woman turned and shouted across the room, "Awrite, Mack?"

Mack whispered to Flora, "See, I told you he knew his way around here. Let's go and say hello to Jay."

Mack walked a few steps, but tension and anxiety had made Flora still and immovable. Instead of making her feel strange or odd, Mack just gave her a soft smile and extended her hand. Before she knew it, Flora grasped Mack's hand, and it felt like confidence travelled from Mack's body to hers and got her to move.

They walked over to the bar, and Mack said, "Jay, how's it going?"

"Good. I was just working on the staff rotas, and I found this wee sausage."

Dexter barked when he saw them and struggled to get over to them.

"C'mere, Dex," Mack said, and she handed Dexter over to Flora, knowing he would be a comfort to her during this introduction.

"It's just a quick visit, Jay. I wanted to show my friend Flora around. She owns the sweet shop opposite."

"Sweet Surprise?" Jay said enthusiastically. "My wife Annie loves that shop. Nice to meet you, Flora."

Jay held out her hand to Flora. Mack felt Flora move closer so she was hip to hip with her, and it reminded Mack of when Isla did similar.

Flora took Jay's hand and in a soft voice said, "Nice to meet you, Jay."

"I can tell you that Sweet Surprise, along with the florist at the end of the street, has saved me a lot, after an argument with the missus."

Flora smiled but Mack could tell, by the way she was stroking Dexter, that she was struggling to answer, so Mack stepped in.

"Your profits are safe then, Flo, because the amount of times this one is in the doghouse with Annie is...a lot."

Jay laughed. "Aye, that's true. Do you want a couple of drinks?"

Mack looked at Flora. "What do you think? We've time for one and a chat?"

"Okay," Flora managed to say while Dex covered her cheek in kisses. He must have felt her tension.

"Why don't you go and take Dexter to one of those booths over there, and I'll get the drinks. What would you like?"

"A ginger beer and lime, please."

That just added to Flora's sweetness. Ginger beer evoked images of upper-class children in the countryside, depicted in those private school sleuthing books Mack had avoided like the plague when she was young.

"I'll just be a minute, okay?"

Flora nodded and walked away with Dexter towards the booths.

"Nice woman," Jay said. "Quiet, though. It wasn't me, was it? I know I can look a bit intimidating but—"

"No, no. Not you, Jay. Flora is really quiet. She has anxiety issues, and I'm trying to be a good friend to her."

"Good, what can I get you?"

"Just a Coke, thanks."

Jay turned to the barmaid and asked for the drinks order. While they waited, Mack said, "Jay, if you're ever out and about, can you keep an eye on Flora's shop? She doesn't have anyone else in the world, and I've told her she has the protection of the Sharkeys now."

"Absolutely, and if she ever needs any help, just tell her to come here. I'll sort it if you aren't about."

"Cheers, mate."

Mack was slowly but surely ringing a network of safety around Flora and hoping that she would feel the care and safety she so desperately needed.

❖

Flora sat in the booth while Mack brought the drinks. Even though the club wasn't open, and it was far from the full clubbing experience, this was exciting and new.

She had noticed Jay had a shark tooth tattooed on her forearm. She must be a very trusted employee of the family.

"Here you go." Mack put down her ginger beer and lime and her own Coke.

Flora put Dexter down and he went running off towards Jay.

"Thanks." Flora took a sip. "Mmm, delicious. I haven't had one of these for ages."

Mack smiled. "I've never known anyone have a ginger beer and lime before."

"It was my mum's favourite drink. If she was somewhere everyone was drinking alcohol, she had this. She always said it was a bit more special. Either that or a tomato juice and pepper. Lovely."

Mack screwed up her face. "Um…I don't think I'd like that."

"It's delicious. What about you? Do you like to drink?"

"The odd bottle of lager here and there, a whisky with my cousin sometimes. I've only been drunk once in my life. I mean proper drunk. When we were seventeen, Nikki and I got a bottle of vodka, went to a party, and got steaming drunk. When we left, we got jumped and took a right beating. We were too steaming to fight back."

"Were you okay?" Flora couldn't imagine anyone getting the better of Mack.

"Aye, we had a couple of broken ribs and bumps, but mainly bruised egos. We were Sharkeys and were a bit arrogant, I suppose. We didn't expect anyone to get the better of us. When we got home, Mum and Aunt Chrissy fussed around us, but Uncle Thomas was furious. He gave us a big talking to about getting drunk and being out of control. We had to always be in control of our minds. We never got drunk again."

"I suppose, being Sharkeys, you had targets on your back a lot," Faith asked.

"Aye, we did. A lot of people over the years have wanted to find out if two women could live up to the Sharkey family name. Nikki is the first woman to lead the family and business."

"And did you prove yourself? Flora asked.

Mack grinned. "What do you think?"

Flora's heart fluttered, and her brain couldn't make sentences to reply. Instead she looked down and rubbed her nose and tapped on the table. She looked up and saw Mack watching her. Flora realized she hadn't been as discreet as she usually was, and for some unknown reason she blurted out, "I have OCD. I know I'm weird and strange, but this is just who I am. I can't change." She then squeezed her eyes shut in embarrassment. "I'm sorry, I didn't mean to—"

"Hey." Mack reached across the table and grasped her hand. "You are not weird or strange, and if you are, then we all are. There's not one person in the world that doesn't have some kind of quirk. It's what makes us different."

"But I don't want to be different. It's taken over my life. OCD is my life." Flora covered her face with her hands. "I've never said that out loud before."

Mack wished she could wrap her arms around Flora and protect her from the world. "You can say anything to me. Can you tell me about it? I'd like to learn."

Flora let her hands fall from her face. "I don't know if I can explain."

Mack tried to coax her into talking. "The thing I think of when you say OCD is washing hands over and over."

This seemed to break Flora's embarrassment. "Yes, a lot of people think that, but it's less about the act and more about the compulsion to take part in a ritual that soothes your fear. It's meant to calm you, but it ends up taking over."

"It's because you feel anxious or nervous, but doing your ritual—"

"Sometimes they're called stims, a stimulation to calm yourself, but then it becomes the fear, and you think, if I don't do it, something bad might happen. Then it's embarrassing, and you try to hide it," Flora explained.

All Mack could feel was sorrow that Flora had been on her own and fearful for so long. "You know, you don't have to hide in front of me."

Flora took a sip of her drink. "It'll be hard to shake off the shame of it."

"Did you mind me calling you little mouse?" Mack asked.

But Flora smiled. "No, it's nice, because you saw it and instead of making me feel foolish, you turned it into a sweet thing."

Mack cleared her throat and spun her glass of Coke around on the table. "You know, one of Isla's counsellors said she thought Isla had OCD, amongst other things, but Isy refused to go back to see her. Maybe you could talk to her about it sometime."

"Of course I will. I did get that idea when we talked at the shop. I see a lot of problems we share. I'd be happy to help. It's hard to find a therapist who you click with. If you don't, it's a waste of time really. I've seen two. When I was a teenager, I was put on medication, and I didn't go back. I couldn't talk to them, couldn't admit to things that I find easy with you."

That did make Mack happy, like the difference in Flora when she was talking to Jay and to how she was talking to her.

"That's because we're good friends."

Flora looked at her silently. "I don't have friends—what I mean is I've never had friends, I don't know how to, but you—"

Mack's heart was thudding as Flora looked deep into her eyes. Something in this woman's soul called to her. Mack had never been in danger of losing her heart before, but this was different.

"But I?"

"You've been my guardian angel since the first moment I met you. That's what makes you different. I feel safe."

*I want to kiss you* was all Mack could think about. "I'm no angel, Flo."

"You are to me," Flora said seriously.

*I want to kiss you,* Mack thought again.

A yelping bark interrupted them. Dexter was standing at Flora's feet. The intimate moment was lost.

"Hiya, Dexter." Flora picked him up and he got the kisses that Mack wished she could get.

"Did you have fun with Jay?" Mack asked him.

"He's adorable," Flora said. "I'd love a little dog like Dexter."

"You can borrow him any time or…"

"What?" Flora asked.

"We could come over together, Dex and me, I mean." Mack wasn't usually tongue-tied with women. She was super confident, but Flora was so, so different.

"That would be nice. Where do you live?"

"A flat down by the River Clyde," Mack said.

"They're nice."

Mack shrugged. "It's okay—not really a home, but it's fine for now."

"What we were talking about before, about Isla? I'll be happy to talk to her any time. I'm not a shining example of getting over mental health issues, but I understand them, at least," Flora said.

"That would be great. Do you ever think about trying again to get help with your conditions?"

Flora snuffled into Dexter's neck and gave him a kiss. "All the time. I feel like it's getting worse as I get older, but I don't know where to start. I mean, even to lift the phone and make the appointment is too much for me, and I don't know who to choose."

"Maybe I could help you—only if you were ready and you wanted help. I don't mean to…ugh."

"What?" Flora asked.

"I just don't want you to feel like you have to say yes to my help."

Flora just smiled at her. "Why wouldn't I want my guardian angel to help me? Oh, and I *could* say no to you."

There was a flirtatiousness in that statement, and that surprised Mack. "Oh?"

"Yes, because you make me feel safe to be me. I'm not frightened of you ever."

"I would be hurt if you ever felt frightened of me. So, how was your first experience of a club?"

"Good," Flora smiled. "But I'm sure it's quite different at night. I always wished I was the type of person who could just walk into this club."

Mack rested her head on her hand and gazed lovingly at Flora. "How come?"

Again Flora covered her apparent embarrassment by turning her attention to Dexter. "Just because…because I think I might be gay."

*Yes.* Mack knew it. "Oh, okay. Me too, in case you haven't guessed."

Flora chuckled. "Yes, I guessed. I sometimes daydreamed about coming to somewhere like this and meeting The One."

"The one?"

"The one who would understand me. I could never see their face, but…I feel so silly telling you this."

"No embarrassment. I'm your guardian angel, remember? What happened?"

"Well, I'd get a drink, and this person, this gay woman, would walk up to me and—"

Mack held her hand up. "Wait. Would she be butch, femme, or androgenous?"

"No, butch—I like butch women, I think."

Perfect, Mack thought. "Okay, carry on."

"She would take my hand, and I wouldn't have to worry about talking because she would just understand me. Then she'd take me to the dance floor and dance with me."

Mack was invested in Flora's dream and wanted to make it come true. "Is it just the lights that would bother you? Not the music?"

"Yes, just the lights."

"I'll be back in a minute." Mack was going to make it true.

❖

Flora had no idea why Mack had hurried off. She looked at her watch and saw that she didn't have long left in her break. When she talked to Mack, she always seemed to get lost in conversation and forget about time.

Dexter was enjoying Flora stroking his ears. It was funny. Conversation was terrifying to her with everyone else—even sometimes with Sandra, she had to search for what to say next—but with Mack, words weren't hard to find.

The time they'd spent together today had been perfect. Outside of the club when Mack caressed her cheek, Flora thought she might melt. She didn't have words to articulate to herself, even, what was going between them, but it was different from friendship.

Flora felt that, but maybe Mack felt very different. Maybe it was friendship for her.

Just then some music came on. It was Ed Sheeran's "Thinking Out Loud"—she'd know that intro anywhere. Mack came striding across the dance floor, took off her jacket, and threw it into the booth.

Flora didn't know what was happening, but Mack seemed to. Mack took Dexter from her and put him on the floor.

"Go play, Dex."

Mack held out her hand to Flora and said, "Dance with me?"

Flora was lost for words. She opened her mouth, but nothing would come out.

"You don't need to say anything or search for what to say. Just dance with me. You need the full nightclub experience."

It was like her dream, and she didn't need words with Mack. Flora gathered all her courage and stood up, took her jacket off, and was led to the dance floor.

"I don't know how to dance," Flora said.

"Lucky I'm going to lead then, isn't it?"

Mack put one arm around her waist and took Flora's hand with the other. It was the kind of slow dance you'd see in an old movie.

"Who taught you to dance like this?" Flora asked.

"Granny Sharkey. A tough old woman, but she loved to dance. I've only ever danced this way with her and now you. The bar staff are going to think I've gone mad."

Flora looked over Mack's shoulder and saw Jay and the bar staff watching them with smiles on their faces.

"Why did you want to dance this way with me?"

Mack slowed and looked deeply into her eyes. "Because Granny always said if you ever meet a proper lady, dance with her like this. You're the lady that deserves this dance."

Flora was dancing on air, it felt like. This was much better than any dream she'd ever had. Mack spun her around, making Flora giggle.

"Your friend Jay is watching, you know."

"I don't care."

Flora allowed her hand to wander lower on the small of Mack's back. She wished she had the courage to slip her fingers under the hem of her T-shirt and feel Mack's skin but, instead, grabbed the bunched up material of the shirt and held on tight.

She gasped when Mack put one hand on her hip, then used the other to put Flora's arm around her neck. Flora followed Mack's lead and laced her other arm around her neck.

This could not be happening. She was slow-dancing with Mack. Flora could feel her soft skin with her fingers and the short, spiky shaved hairs at the nape of her neck. Quite naturally her hips got closer to Mack as she gently held on to her hips.

Their heads got closer, inch by inch, until Flora placed her head on Mack's chest. They swayed slowly in that position for who knew how long, Flora having completely lost all sense of time. She was in her guardian angel's arms, and there was no safer place in the world.

Then everything changed. A fast-paced dance number came on, and Flora's shyness returned. "That was lovely, thanks. You're my first ever…dance."

"I'm glad. I suppose we better get back. I've got an appointment in ten minutes," Mack said.

Things were slightly awkward as they went back onto the street and into the daytime outside. To break the silence, Flora said, "I was thinking about Isy, Mack. I thought maybe if she ever feels like a little part-time job, I'd be happy to have her work at Sweet Surprise."

Mack smiled. "That would be amazing. I know she'd love that. I'll ask her mum about it. Isy's not getting to school very much at the moment, because of her anxiety. Maybe a real job of her own would give her some confidence."

"I think so."

They arrived at Sweet Surprise, and the awkwardness returned. "Thank you for a lovely walk and dance, Mack." She then kissed Dex on the cheek, just as she would have liked to kiss Mack goodbye.

"You're welcome. See you later."

## CHAPTER ELEVEN

Mack paced around her cousin Nikki's office, waiting for her to finish a meeting in the boardroom. The Sharkey business office was in a Georgian building, a large former bank. It gave all of those called Sharkey such pride that they'd arrived as penniless immigrants from Ireland and grew to occupy a former bank as their headquarters.

Her thoughts were interrupted by Nikki coming through the interconnecting door from the boardroom to her offices.

"Idiots," Nikki said with frustration as she dropped her iPad on her desk.

"Who are the idiots?" Mack asked.

"Local councillors." Nikki sighed and sat at her desk. "I want to bring jobs to the area, and they're quibbling about a planning regulation."

"Where for?" Mack asked.

"The former shipbuilding office building on the Clyde. It's a Category C listed building, but it's been empty for fifty years, mostly just used by junkies and as a drinking den for teenagers."

"Is that where you wanted to put the hotel development?" Mack asked.

"Exactly. It's a perfect spot near the town centre, but those idiots would rather keep it as it is. A historical building that's falling down that people use for drinking and drug taking."

"Maybe a few back-handers to the council members?" Mack suggested.

"It's probably what they're expecting, but they don't deserve a penny." Nikki sat back in her chair. "I'll leave it for a while, then maybe…who knows what could happen down there?"

Mack played along. "You're right. The homeless building fires to keep warm? The teenagers messing about with matches…"

It was a tried-and-tested method employed by both underworld figures and even more reputable firms. If you couldn't get a plot of land because of planning restrictions, you'd wait for an accidental fire to engulf the building, then swoop in with a lowball offer for the land.

Mack had made it happen before.

"That's right, but you"—Nikki pointed her pen at Mack—"you are having nothing to do with it. My ma has warned me. You are to be kept out of the firing line."

"Hmm…we'll see. Anyway, I wanted to ask you about something. Flora's going to put up the shop's Christmas decorations, and I'm taking her to the wholesaler on Sunday to pick out some new things. I thought Isy would enjoy it."

"If you trust Flora, then that's fine. I trust you."

"I think it'll help Isy. The last time she came to visit, she was so excited and interested in everything about Flora's shop."

Nikki sat back in her chair. "Yes, she seems to like her a lot."

"Flora said Isy could also have a part-time job there, if she wanted."

"That's nice of her. I don't know if Isy could cope with that just yet—I can't get her to school most days. I'll need to make some decisions on that soon. So, what's the story with you and Flora?"

"What do you mean?" Mack said.

"Well, I don't normally see you take that much care of someone outside the family. Is she just a friend or—"

"She's a friend that I really care about, and I don't know if she can feel that way about me, but she's got in here." Mack pointed to her heart.

There was no one else in the world Mack would be so honest with.

"Well, that's something. I thought we both were never going to lose our hearts."

"I never thought so, but it just creeps up on you," Mack said.

Nikki got up and sat on the corner of the desk next to Mack. "It wouldn't creep up on me. I've got a heart of stone, except for my family. But if it would make you happy, then go for it."

"We're going to spend the day together on Sunday. Ma and Aunt Chrissy say it's okay to miss Sunday lunch."

"Wait." Nikki sat forward and frowned. "I never get to miss Sunday lunch because of a woman."

"That's because you're generally just trying to sleep with them."

"And you're not interested in that with Ms. Sweet Shop?"

"No...yes...no—shut up, it's different."

"I'm only kidding," Nikki said. "You have a good day. You deserve it."

❖

Flora must have tried on every new outfit she had bought, before settling on a pair of jeans and a blouse. She was so late.

Flora hurried to the barber's and saw Mack and Isla sitting on the couch. Isla was throwing nuts for Mack to catch with her mouth. They were adorable together, and watching Mack like this, it was hard to imagine her being the Sharkey enforcer that everyone seemed to fear.

Flora opened the door and said, "I'm so sorry, I'm late."

"Don't worry about. We've lots of time," Mack said.

Mack and Isy followed her next door, and Flora quickly unlocked the shutter and let them in.

"I pulled all the decorations out of the storeroom last night. They really need updating, but I never did because Sandra and I were never good with going up ladders and things."

"Well, I'm here now. So is Isy. We'll help, won't we?"

"Yeah, let's go shopping," Isy said. "I'm so excited."

❖

Mack and Flora waved goodbye to Isy as she was driven away by Uncle Thomas's driver.

"Thanks for today, Flo. Isy really enjoyed that."

"Please, thanks for your help. The decorations look the best yet."

Mack smiled and rubbed her hand on the small of Flora's back. "Don't be daft. We're here to help. Why don't you close up, and I'll go and get everything ready for you at the barber's."

Flora looked unsure. "You don't have to cut my hair today. You've done so much already."

Mack could tell it was Flora's anxiety speaking. "Go and get locked up. It's only me, remember?"

Flora nodded. "Okay."

Mack hurried back to her shop. She got out lots of towels, brushes, and scissors that had been tidied away on Friday afternoon. Mack was really looking forward to this, not only because she could get close to the woman who was stealing her heart, but she didn't get the chance to style women's hair, apart from Isy's, very often.

She looked around and checked that everything was there that she would need. Then she remembered. "Music, need music." She took her phone from her pocket and selected a spa playlist to play over the shop speakers. Mack let out a sigh when the music came on.

She was actually nervous. She'd never really experienced that with anyone before. Mack generally was very confident with women that took her interest, but Flora was different.

She tapped her fingers on the headrest of the seat, then spun the chair around fast, practising for when Flora walked through the door. That move was one of her small trademarks when she recorded videos for YouTube.

Then Flora walked up to her door and came in.

*Stay calm, stay cool.* "Everything's ready you." Mack spun the chair around, but she must hast taken a step closer than usual, and the chair smacked her right in the midriff.

"Are you all right?" Flora came rushing to her.

"Ugh, aye. I just knocked the wind out of myself. That was supposed to look cool."

Flora begun to laugh. "I know you do that in all your videos."

"I'm glad my pain makes you laugh." Mack pouted.

"No, I checked to see if you were okay first."

"That's true." Mack straightened up. "I'll try not to do anything cool again. Let me take your jacket, and you take a seat."

Flora sat down and gripped the hand rests. She knew what was coming, she'd watched all the videos and imagined herself in this seat so many times, but now reality was setting in. Mack was going to touch her, and she wanted it so much it scared her.

"Okay, we're all ready," Mack said. "So, you know how I do it, but this time I'll start with the massage, and then I'll wash and cut your hair, okay?"

Flora looked up at the camera mounting and said, "You're not filming this one, are you? I don't think I'd feel comfortable on YouTube."

"Would I do that to you? But just to make you feel more relaxed..." Mack pulled the camera off the mounting and put it in a drawer with the brushes.

"You didn't have to do that," Flora said. "I trust you."

"I know, but I think you'll relax more if it's out of the way."

"Okay."

Mack got out cotton wool and cleanser and said, "Could I take off your make-up?"

"Oh, sorry. I never thought about that."

"That's all right. I'll do it, then your massage, hair wash, and cut. Sound good?"

"Sounds really good."

Just the simple act of Mack taking off her make-up was enough to let her enjoy Mack's touch already. She was so gentle, so tender in the way she touched her, that Flora couldn't imagine that the same hands were used for gangland violence.

Once that was finished, Mack binned the cotton wool and picked up a bottle of cream. She dabbed little dots of it on her chin, her cheeks, her nose, and her forehead. Mack then stood behind the chair and looked at her in the mirror. "Remember—you can stop any time, okay? Just say."

Flora smiled. "I know. I will."

Mack placed her hands on Flora's face and began to rub gentle circles on her cheeks. As Flora relaxed into Mack's touch, Mack became bolder, using bigger strokes and encompassing the whole of her face, from her neck to her forehead. She got shivers when Mack was touching her neck and collarbone.

Mack must have realized because the massage stayed on her neck and became gentle strokes and the lightest of touches, a caress almost of her collarbone. Flora's heart hammered, and her breathing became short. She kept her eyes closed, trying stay in control. The more she was trying to show Mack that she wasn't being affected, the shorter her breath became.

Flora was so turned on, and Mack had only started. How was she going to cope when Mack massaged her back and arms? It would be impossible.

The touch on her face stopped, and Flora felt Mack's hands on her shoulders. Her eyes were still closed, and she felt Mack's breath close to her ear.

"Was that okay?"

The sensation of breath on her ear made her shiver. If Mack had kissed her just now in this moment, Flora wouldn't have been frightened of the intimacy. She would have shown no resistance.

"Yes, it was nice," Flora squeaked. *Nice* was a huge, huge understatement.

Mack continued to whisper in her ear. "We'll wash your hair now over at the sinks, and I'll give you the best head massage you've ever had."

Flora's eyes popped open, and she saw Mack grinning. *She knows what she's doing to me.* It would be the only head massage she'd ever had. No one had ever gotten this close to her. Flora would have run from this intimacy if it was anyone else but Mack.

Mack held out her hand. "Follow me—this is going to feel so good."

Flora was glad Mack offered her hand because she wasn't certain her legs were going to support her as she stood up. They had turned to jelly. She took Mack's hand to steady her and held on tightly. As she did, someone tried to walk in the shop. It was a slightly dishevelled looking woman.

"Hang on. I'll get rid of her. You'd think she'd notice the closed sign." Mack unlocked the door. "We're closed."

"Aww, sorry. Nae problem. Have you got a pound for a cuppa tea?"

Mack stuffed her hand in her pocket and brought out her wallet. "Here. Buy something to eat." Mack gave her a ten-pound note.

"Thanks, mate."

When the door shut, Mack watched the woman walk away. "I hope she doesn't spend it on drugs. If I see someone who's homeless, I usually take them and buy the meal."

Flora gazed at Mack and lost another piece of her heart.

"Now, back to you, wee mouse."

❖

Flora pulled into the driveway, with Mack not long behind her. As she stopped the car, instinct made her look up at the upstairs window. This was always a moment that gave her anxiety. She never knew if she would manage to get out without receiving a torrent of abuse or sexual innuendos, but then she remembered and let out a sigh of relief. *They're gone.* She looked into the driver's mirror and smiled when she saw Mack looking back from her own car. Life was different now.

She ran her hand through her nice new hairstyle. Everything

was different. She felt lighter, she felt cared for, not to mention the new feelings that Mack's massage and haircut brought out in her. Flora was aching to be close to Mack and didn't want to let go.

She got out of the car, just as Mack and Dexter were getting out of Mack's.

"I can't get over how much nicer my new haircut is."

"You look even more beautiful," Mack said.

"Shut up," Flora said with embarrassment in her voice. She wouldn't have had the nerve to say that to anyone, even in jest, but with Mack she felt safe.

"Hey, I won't hear any of your nonsense." Mack walked up next to her. "You are beautiful, and that's it. Now, are you going to feed me?"

Since Mack wasn't going to charge her, Flora insisted on making her dinner, which suited Flora because she just wanted to spend more time with Mack.

"Of course I am. Your favourite, lasagne."

"Yes," Mack said with a first pump.

Flora had asked Mack what her favourite food was, and it happened to be lasagne, followed closely by macaroni cheese, so she had prepared a lasagne and left it in her fridge. All she had to do was pop it in the oven.

"Come on, then." Flora walked up to the front door, Dexter following at her heels. Once inside they dispensed with their jackets and moved through to the kitchen.

"Take a seat, and I'll get dinner going."

"Can I put some music on?" Mack asked.

"Yes, there's a radio there on the work surface, or you could put on the music channel."

Mack grabbed the remote and quickly put on one of the music channels. Then she returned to sit at the kitchen table.

"This is a nice cosy room," Mack said.

"I like it. I think when the house was changed into two flats, the kitchen and dining room were combined. By the way, it was so good coming home and remembering I didn't have to worry about the boys upstairs."

Mack got up and walked over to lean on the kitchen counter. "You don't ever have to be worried about anything."

Flora gazed at Mack and thought how sexy she looked, leaning against the kitchen counter with her arms folded. She looked so strong, not just physically but mentally, and to someone like Flora, with all her issues, mental strength and confidence were such an attractive feature.

"Why don't I have to worry?"

"Because I'm your friend, and you've had to deal with things on your own for far too long."

Flora could feel the heat of the preheating oven on her legs, matching the rising heat in the rest of her body. She had to ask the question she had wondered about for so long.

"Mack, why do you want to be such a good friend to me? You have family, Liam, and lots of other friends, male and female, I'm sure."

Mack pushed away from the counter and approached Flora slowly. She took her hand and held it lightly. "Because since the first moment we met, and it was only for a few minutes, I've never been able to forget you. When I was lying in jail with the lights off, your face, your beautiful but scared face, used to be here in my head. I won't talk about that night until you're ready, but I need to explain. I tried to find out if you had made a police report, and nobody could find anything. Then through sheer luck I turn up next door, and you are everything I thought you'd be—kind, sweet—but I don't want you to be alone any more. I want you to have people to lean on."

Flora could hardly take in a breath. Mack had thought about her that whole time they were apart?

Mack took a step closer and caressed Flora's cheek again. "When you are friends with a Sharkey, then you have a family of friends to look out for you."

Was it wrong to feel safe if that safety came from a person, a whole family of people, that others saw as criminal? Because she didn't. For the first time in her life, Flora didn't feel alone.

Her grandpa was a great man and loved her, but he didn't

understand her mental issues, and certainly didn't have the same commanding persona that gave out a bubble of safety.

Flora leaned into Mack's hand before pulling away quickly, confused by feelings she was experiencing. Now that she'd experienced the intense feeling of Mack's touch while she was cutting her hair and giving her a massage, she was on one hand greedy for more, but on the other scared of how it felt.

"I better get the food in the oven," Flora said as she hurried to the fridge.

"Can I help with anything?" Mack said.

Flora lifted the lasagne out of the fridge. "Um…you could put the glasses and cutlery out on the table."

"No problem." Mack stopped speaking and stared at the uncooked lasagne. "Wait, you made it from scratch?"

"Of course. Why?"

"When you asked me my favourite food, I didn't expect you to go to a lot of trouble."

Flora placed the dish on top of the cooker. "I like to cook—besides, look at all you've done for me. It'll be the first time someone apart from my own family has tasted my cooking."

"I can't wait." Mack smiled. "Where are the glasses kept?"

Flora pointed across the kitchen. "That one over there."

Mack walked over and opened what she thought was the right one. Looking inside the cupboard really brought home to Mack how much Flora's mental health condition was a part of her life. There were rows and rows of carefully placed tins—like baked beans, soup, vegetables—all in perfect rows, similar to the sweets at the shop. She noticed how they were always ranked by size and type of product and alphabetically.

Flora said, "Not that cupboard, the other one."

"Okay."

Mack went into the other and found the glasses. They were also sorted into similar order. She picked two glasses and took them over to the table, then got the cutlery.

They chatted while the lasagne cooked. It was such a nice experience, being with Flora in her home, and just enjoying listening to her speak. Flora was so knowledgeable about everything, it seemed, and she might hide when she met a new person, but with Mack Flora was comfortable enough to open up and let everything spill out.

At one point Flora stopped and said, "I'm boring you, aren't I? The Kings and Queens of Scotland is a bit of a dry subject to most people."

"No way. I'm enjoying it. You know more than my teacher at school."

"No, I don't." Flora felt her cheeks turn red. "You can tell the truth—I'll still feed you."

Mack laughed. "Don't be daft. Honestly, I love listening to you."

"I just get interested in subjects, sometimes random subjects, from history to the evolution of marine arthropods, and dive deep into every fact I can find. I doubt any women you meet at the club talk to you about that."

"Hmm…no, but that's what makes you different, Flo. You are the most unique, wonderful human I've met."

"I'm weird, let's face it," Flora said.

"We're all weird, Flo, and I like your kind of weird."

The timer on the oven went off, and a blushing Flora jumped up quickly. She was just adorable. Mack would love her mum and family to meet her. Mum had been asking, but she knew she'd have to tread carefully and not frighten Flora.

Flora was lifting some dishes from the oven.

Mack asked, "Would you like a hand lifting anything?"

"No, no, stay there. I have a surprise."

Mack was intrigued. "Oh, really?"

Flora shuffled over with the heavy casserole dish of lasagne and put it in the middle of the table. Mack smacked and rubbed her hands together.

"This is going to be so good."

"There's more." Flora went back over to the oven and brought back a slightly smaller dish.

"What is it?"

Flora put it down next to the lasagne. "Macaroni cheese."

"Mac and cheese as well?" Mack said with delight.

"Well, you said they were both your favourite foods, so I thought I'd make them both."

Mack got up out of her seat and rushed around to Flora. She opened her arms and asked, before she got in Flora's space, "Can I hug you?"

"Of course you can."

Mack wrapped her arms around Flora and hugged. "You are some woman. All my favourite foods."

Flora giggled. "You're easily pleased. It's not à la carte."

"It's what I like." Mack inhaled Flora's perfume and felt like she was melting inside. She gently pushed her head into the crook of Flora's neck. *Don't push her too much*, Mack thought. She broke away and said, "Simple food is enough to keep me happy. My family will tell you, I'm a glutton, a bottomless pit, all that."

"Well, taste it, and tell me what you think."

"I will. The only thing I need from you, little mouse, is tomato sauce."

Flora scrunched up her eyes. "Ketchup? What, for the lasagne?"

"Nah, for the mac and cheese. It's not complete without tomato sauce."

Flora rolled her eyes but got up and went to get the sauce.

"Oh, and have you got white bread?"

Flora looked back. "White bread? No, I only use brown."

Mack shrugged. "Oh well, doesn't matter." She couldn't wait for Flora and dove into the lasagne. "Yum. That's so good."

"Really? You like it?" Flora said as she walked back with the sauce.

"It's amazing." She took the sauce from Flora, squirted it on top of the mac and cheese, and began to eat. "Oh my God. This is bloody heaven on this plate." Mack looked up and saw the look of happiness on Flora's face. "You have to try this."

"I will." Flora took a normal-sized portion of lasagne and added a side salad, which she had brought over earlier.

"Do you want some salad?" Flora asked.

"No, thanks, I'm not really a salad kind of person."

"Why did you ask for white bread? I suppose I should have gotten us garlic bread to go with it, but I didn't think," Flora said.

"This is great. No, the white bread is to make a mac and cheese, tomato sauce sandwich."

Flora looked at her in disbelief. "A macaroni sandwich?"

"Yeah, I'd probably put some lasagne on it too."

"Let me get this straight." Flora held up her hand. "You were going to have double carbs, possibly triple carbs, on white bread?"

Mack smiled and winked at her. "I love carbs. They keep me strong."

❖

Flora enjoyed her meal. It wasn't very often she would have gone to the trouble of making lasagne just for herself. The last time would have been when her grandad was around. When you lived alone, meals became more simple.

But as much as she liked it, she couldn't have enjoyed it more than Mack. She just about ate the pattern off the plate. But it made Flora feel so happy that she could do this for Mack.

Mack finally put her cutlery down and patted her stomach. "Man, I'm so stuffed."

"I think Dexter is too." Mack had given him a little slice of lasagne as well as the dog food she had brought.

"I like to see ma boy happy."

Flora looked at the casserole dish and shook her head in disbelief at the amount missing from the dishes, after Mack took seconds, thirds, and fourths.

"Where do you put it all?" Flora asked.

"My ma says I've got a stomach like a dustbin liner."

They hadn't talked too much about Mack's mum, and she knew nothing about Mack's dad. "What's your mum like? If you don't mind me asking."

Mack shook her head and awakened the iPhone beside her.

"Here." She handed her phone to Flora. "That's my mum, Mary, on the left, and my aunt Chrissy on the right."

Flora saw two very nice looking late-middle-aged women in a large kitchen, cooking with chef's hats on.

"That's them making Christmas dinner. Christmas is a big deal in our house."

"She looks nice. They both do," Flora said.

"Yeah, they are. I hope I'll be able to have you meet them sometime."

Flora would feel terrified meeting Mack's family. Only because Mack had described them as a loud, hustling and bustling type of family. It would be a lot for her social anxiety to cope with.

"What about your dad? If you don't mind me asking."

Mack smile faltered.

"If you don't want to talk about it, that's okay," Flora said.

"No, I don't mind telling you anything. It's just a sad memory. When my ma started going out with my da, he liked being with one of the Sharkeys, thought of himself as a bit of a gangster. He wasn't—he was just a sad bully."

"What happened?"

"My uncle didnae approve of him, but my ma says that just made her want to be defiant and see him all the more. They ran away and got married right after I was born."

Flora saw the look that had been there the night Mack had rescued her from the men that surrounded her.

"He took Mum and me to live in England, supposedly for a job, but I think it was to cut Mum off from her family. My first memories are of him punching and kicking her. Even at three and four, I was trying to get between them and protect her."

Flora's heart broke for Mack. "I'm so sorry. Why did he have the nerve? I mean, would he not have been scared of your family?"

"She never told them. He said he would start on me if she ever told my uncle. She was trapped."

It was no wonder Mack was so sensitive about violence against women and bullying.

Mack had a faraway look in her eyes as she recounted, "One

time he beat her up so badly, and I was so frightened. Ma was just lying on the floor. Dad had left after, and I went to the phone and pressed the button that Mum had told would get through to ma uncle. I just said, *Dad hurt Mum.*"

Flora wiped a tear from her eye. It was a heartbreaking story. "Did they help?"

"Later that day, Uncle Thomas and Aunt Chrissy arrived, and I was so relieved, because I was frightened. I'd always loved my aunt and uncle. Aunt Chrissy took me and my ma home in a car with a couple of ma uncle's men."

Flora could probably guess what happened next but was frightened to ask.

"Ma uncle and some more of his guys waited for my dad to show up home. From that day on we lived right next to my aunt and uncle, and I learned how a real married couple should treat each other. If my uncle had ever lifted his hand to my aunt, not that he ever would, she'd have killed him."

"Did you ever hear from your dad again?"

"No, I never did," Mack said quickly. "That's why I hate—detest—bullies."

"I can understand that. I'm really sorry you had to see that." Flora tried not to dwell on what probably befell Mack's dad.

"It's okay, I got brought up by a great man. My uncle Thomas is the man I look up to as a father." Mack rubbed her face with her hands. It looked like she was trying to cover emotions that had gotten the better of her. "I've never told that to anyone outside my family before."

"Thanks for trusting me," Flora said.

"Course I do. What about your mum? Do you mind talking about her?" Mack asked.

"No, she passed away when I was one, so I can't remember her. I have this image in my head, but I think that's just because my aunt and grandad told me so many stories about her, you know?"

Mack nodded. "Yeah, I do."

"My auntie Catherine and Grandad brought me up, but then Aunt Catherine died when I was seven. Breast cancer," Flora said.

"I'm sorry," Mack said.

Flora was overcome with the need to perform her rituals. She was still embarrassed doing them in front of Mack. "Sorry."

"Hey, I told you—you never have to feel awkward about anything like that in front of me. In fact, I'll do them with you if you want."

Flora felt panic rise in her stomach and chest. "Please don't. I'd just have to repeat it again."

Mack held her hands up. "Nae bother. I just wanted to show you that you didn't have to feel bad about it. I want to learn about your OCD and anxiety, so I can be a support to you."

Again, why was Mack Sharkey so concerned about her? They were good friends, but could Mack feel more?

*About you? Don't be so stupid.*

"Back then, when my aunt died, was when I first remember all this OCD starting, and my anxiety problems. My grandad was a great man, and he took care of me as best he could, but he'd now lost both his daughters."

"I get it."

"It's been in my life such a long time—well, I say a long time *in* my life, but it *is* my life now, and I'm tired of it." Flora had felt weary for years, but meeting Mack just amplified how much her condition hindered her life.

"That's why we're here tonight. We're going to look online and find someone that can help. Why don't we get cleared up and make a start?"

Flora nodded. It was going to be scary facing this, but maybe, just maybe with Mack's support she could do it.

## CHAPTER TWELVE

It was early evening, and Kevin walked quickly as he punched text messages into his phone. He was frantic with stress. Every one of his dealers that he'd set up to sell in the city centre had no money for him. As Malky had been reminding him all day, he was waiting on his money from the last lot of drugs he'd given Kevin to distribute.

But every one of the street dealers had nothing. They were too frightened to sell, afraid of the wrath of the Sharkeys.

If they didn't sell, Malky was going to call in his debt, and that would be the end of him. Kevin had one left to try. Just as he rounded the corner of Glasgow Central train station, he stopped abruptly and stood back against the wall.

The bridge that brought the trains into the station building created a dark underpass that was filled with questionable shops, the homeless trying to be safe and remain unseen, and sex workers plying their trade.

A perfect place to sell drugs. But what had stopped Kevin in his tracks was the sight of his dealer chatting to two Sharkey guys he knew, Jamsey and Murdo.

"Fuck," Kevin said under his breath.

A few well-dressed business people looked at him as they passed but soon looked away when he glared at them. All these people caught in the rat race, going to their comfortable offices, then home to their lovely houses, had no idea what went on right under their noses.

Or maybe they did and just pretended not to see what was right in front of them. These commuters hurrying home or young students heading out for a night out saw the bright lights, the cosmopolitan café and bar culture, the museums, the fine restaurants, but there was a different Glasgow if you cared to scratch beneath the surface, and that was his world.

Kevin's world was dark, frightening, dirty, and full of invisible people, people that would be born and die in grinding poverty just like he was and would be till the day it was his turn to die, and nobody would miss him.

Life was a constant struggle to survive, and that was what got him in trouble with the Sharkeys the first time around, and now put him in this position of being in debt to someone like Malky McDade.

He took a peek around the corner and saw the Sharkey guys get into their car and drive off. Kevin moved around the corner and walked as quickly as he could to get to one of McDade's dealers, a homeless boy called Shug.

When Shug saw him, he tried to run, but Kevin grabbed him and pushed him back into the alcove where Shug had been sitting.

"Going somewhere?" Kevin said.

"Kev, it's you. I was just coming to try to find you."

"Aye, so you were. Where's ma money, Shug?"

Shug was barely twenty but looked like he'd lived a whole lifetime, and while taking drugs he probably had.

"I haven't got it."

Kevin put his hand around Shug's neck. "Why haven't you got my money? I gave you that stuff this morning. Did you stick it up your nose or in your veins?"

"No, no, I couldn't sell it, Kev. The polis were everywhere this morning, and then Jamsey and Murdo found me."

"I know, they've been doing the rounds today."

"They said they better not see me selling in the Sharkey territory again. They'll take me for a swim in the Clyde. You know what that means?"

Kevin squeezed his neck with his hand, the anger and panic overflowing inside of him. "I need that money for Malky. If you don't sell for him, he'll end you and me!"

Shug was struggling for breath. "I'm sorry."

"Give me the stuff, then."

"They took it, Kev. I had no choice."

Kevin's stomach dropped. This was the third dealer that had given their drugs to Jamsey and Murdo. The rest had dumped it and run, or run and used, as the rumour went around that the Sharkeys were on the prowl.

"I'm dead."

He heard a car stop behind him. Kevin looked around and saw a blacked-out people carrier there. The door slid open, and he saw Malky sitting there.

"Get in, Kevin."

From the front seat one of Malky's heavies got out just to make sure he got the message. Kevin let Shug go, and in an instant he shot off running. Nobody made a move for him. They only wanted Kevin.

With no choice, Kevin got in and sat across from Malky.

Malky smiled and said, "Let's go for a little ride."

❖

Mack and Flora were sitting on the love seat in Flora's kitchen. The TV was still on the music channel, and they were having a cup of tea while they studied Flora's iPad.

Mack was enjoying being this close to Flora and being a support to her. They'd searched two or three therapists' websites already—a couple Flora had seen before, and a few Mack remembered Isla had been to and hated.

Mack scrolled up the new page they'd clicked through to. "This looks good so far—Glasgow Mental Health Team."

"Hmm," was all Flora said.

Mack went to another page on that site and saw something

helpful. "Look—they're recommended by Stonewall, and they sponsor Glasgow Pride. They must be good." Mack smiled.

"Yes, they do look good."

"Should we keep looking at other places and make a note of their number?"

Flora first rubbed her temples with her hands, then placed her hands over her ears. "I can't do it."

Mack remembered Flora had done this the first time they met. It must happen when she became overwhelmed with stress and anxiety. She dropped the iPad to the side and turned to face Flora on the couch. "Hey, hey, it's okay. We're just looking. There's no pressure to pick somewhere tonight." She could see the tears rolling down Flora's face. She pulled Flora into her arms. "It's okay. I'm here."

Flora dropped her hands from her ears. "I can't do it, Mack."

"You can't talk to someone? I told you that I'd make the call for you."

"I know, but it's the whole thing—going myself, traveling there, talking, and…it's all too confusing and too much."

Mack thought for a second. "Okay, what if I took you? You wouldn't have to worry about getting there, and I'll wait outside for you."

Flora's emotions calmed and she wiped away her tears. "But you can't leave the barber's on a weekday. I know Sandra's sister would cover for me in the shop. She helps at Easter and Christmas sometimes. But you have appointments."

"Let me worry about that," Mack said, her mind already whirling on what she could do.

"No, I can't expect you to turn your day upside down just because I'm frightened to go myself. Anyway, it's not just that. I'll be a nervous wreck, waiting on the appointment day to come around. It'll be too much."

Mack had an idea. "How about this. If you could choose to do anything in the city, for fun, what would it be?"

Flora took a tissue from the box on the coffee table and blew her nose. "What do you mean?"

"Just like I said, what's your favourite thing to do? Maybe that you did with your granda?"

Flora knew immediately. "The Glasgow Kelvingrove Art Gallery. I love museums, and that's my favourite. It has art, fossils, suits of armour, early human artefacts, everything."

Flora's face lit up when she talked about it. Mack had hit the right idea. "Okay, after you've had your appointment, we'll go to your museum, have lunch, and have a long walk around. If you could focus on that fun part of the day, would that help?"

Flora laughed through the tears before wiping them away. "I haven't been since Grandad died because I wouldn't go myself. I'd love to. It'll still be so stressful, but if I've got that to look forward to, then it'll help me cope. I can't believe you would do all this for me, put yourself to so much trouble."

Mack grinned. "I'm your guardian angel, remember? I've got to keep my halo shining bright."

She pretended to polish her invisible halo above her head, making Flora laugh. "You're so funny."

"So have we got a deal? Do we make the appointment?"

"But do you like museums? Have you been to Kelvingrove Art Gallery before?"

"I can't remember—we went to one at school, but I don't remember which," Mack said.

"It's not exactly your cup of tea, is it?"

Mack took one of Flora's hands and kissed the back. "Anything is fun with you, Flo."

❖

Kevin was trying hard not to show how much he was trembling. He'd expected Malky to go for him as soon as the door of the blacked-out car shut.

All he'd said was, "Let's go for a drive, Kevin."

Going for a drive with Malky was a very dangerous thing to do, and Kevin was terrified. As they drove, he realized they were heading to one of the disused pier and warehouse areas on the

Clyde. A reminder of the Scottish ship building industry that once built seagoing vessels for countries all over the world, now all but a few companies had relocated further up the river.

Malky gazed at him silently. He was much more terrifying than his father. His dad had at least a small glimmer of empathy inside him, but Malky looked dead inside.

"So, Kevin. Have you got today's money?"

Kevin was certain Malky knew the answer to his question already.

"No, Malky. I…the dealers were frightened off," Kevin said.

One of Malky's guys, Daniel, who was sitting beside Malky, took out a handgun and started checking that it was loaded and in good working order. He was going to die today if he didn't find a way to play this right.

"They were frightened off by Jamsey and Murdo. They're Nikki's men."

"Nikki Sharkey. Do you know what they call her?" Malky said.

Kevin knew exactly. "The Queen of the Glasgow Streets."

"That's right." Malky leaned forward in his seat. "You almost sound as if you agree with the name."

"No, no, I don't. You know I hate the Sharkeys," Kevin said.

That was true. He did hate them. Nikki had beat him badly, along with Mack's help, but he was also terrified of them. His position was a precarious one. Be killed by the Sharkeys? Or by the McDades?

That was no choice, but all he could do was try to stay alive as long as possible.

"You know the Sharkeys and the McDades go way back?"

"No."

"Aye, the Sharkeys were like brothers to the McDades, but then they betrayed us. It was bad enough that they took territory that was rightly ours in Glasgow, and then thought they'd gain respect by going straight, but now they have a woman leading them. Do you think a woman can beat me?"

Kevin's inner voice said *yes* immediately. He knew first-hand how scary she was, and that was without lifting a finger.

"No, Malky."

"So you find new dealers who are more desperate, and get those drugs sold. Let me see what you got left from the gear I gave you this morning."

Kevin gulped and pushed his trembling hands in his pockets. He brought it out and set it on the car seat.

Malky looked at it and then back to Kevin. "Where is the rest?"

Kevin closed his eyes and tried to calm his fast-beating heart. "I…so some of the dealers disappeared with it after they were warned off by the Sharkeys."

Malky simply said, "Get out of the car."

This was it. He was dead. Kevin was given a push out by Daniel. He got out, and his legs felt like jelly, and his hands were shaking so much that he had to squeeze them into tight fists to try to not let it show.

Daniel pushed him in the back and told him, "Follow Mr. McDade."

Malky was standing by the edge of the river wall. Kevin stood beside him, knowing his life was probably over. Malky took out a cigarette and offered one to him.

Since these were probably his final moments, he might as well. Kevin took one, and Malky lit it before lighting his own. Malky inhaled the smoke and exhaled slowly.

"The River Clyde is beautiful to look at, isn't it? Everything in Glasgow's history is tied to the Clyde, the river that snakes through the town. The ship building, the ships coming and going filled with tobacco and sugar, part of the town's dark history that made some people rich on the backs of others, but…"

Kevin didn't turn around, but he felt Daniel move inches from his back and felt the muzzle of what he assumed was a gun. His fear made him ache for a hit of heroin. He'd much rather die that way than this.

"It's a treacherous place. People are lost to the river all the time. There's vicious currents and whirlpools that pull you into the deep." Malky turned and smiled at Daniel behind him. "Would be a good place for the Sharkeys to meet their end, since Nikki has that queer nightclub." Then he nudged Kevin. "Did you know that Nikki and Mack the fucking Knife are dykes?"

Kevin managed a croaky, "Yes."

"The so-called Queen of the Glasgow Streets is a fucking dyke. That needs to be stopped, and I'm going to get every one of them. I would have been far further forward if you hadn't fucked up getting Nikki's wean."

"I tried to get Isla, but—"

"Shut up. I was good enough to give you another chance to work off the debt with me, but now you've lost my merchandise. I think your debt has gone up five grand. That makes your debt fifteen thousand. I take cash, no credit."

Kevin's panic overtook him. He brought his hands to his face and said, "Mr. McDade, I can't pay that much, but please give me a chance. I can be useful. Please, please."

Malky looked at him with disdain. "Stop being a snivelling wee dick, Kevin." He took a last drag of his cigarette and flicked it into the water, as if suggesting where Kevin was going next. "You know how many bodies were recovered from the Clyde last year, Kevin?"

Kevin was so scared, his mouth and throat were dry.

"Thirty bodies, Kev. Thirty bodies, that sounds a lot, but that was only people that were reported for falling in, drunks, accidents with kids getting too close to the edge, but then there are the ones no one knows went in. But you know as well as me, Kev, this river has always been a dumping ground for bodies. If they drained this river, it would be littered with the remains of people long gone."

Malky nodded to Daniel, who said, "Take a step closer."

The muzzle of the gun pushed into his back. Kevin's breathing was panicked. Was this it? His toes were now over the edge. "Please, Mr. McDade. Give me one more chance."

"It depends on what you can do for me."

Kevin thought frantically. "I'll get you new dealers. I'll make them sell…" And then he remembered one piece of new information he had, but could he interest Malky in it? He'd sent that bitch to barge into Mack's shop, and she'd seen how close Mack was to her new friend. They were almost kissing. "Mack," Kevin shouted.

"What about Mack the dyke? What about her?"

"There's a woman in the shop next door to her barber's that she's grown close to. I've been watching Mack."

"She's shagging a bit close to home. Not like her. Once she gets tired of her bird, she'll not be able to get rid of her."

"This is different. The woman isn't her usual type," Kevin said.

Malky turned to face him. "How?"

"She's in her sweet shop multiple times a day, and they go walking that stupid wee dog of hers after lunch every day. The other shop staff on the street say that she's weird, a bit backward, or something's wrong with her."

"Interesting," Malky said. "What in fuck's name would Mack be interested in someone like that for?"

"An easy fuck?" Daniel said.

"I don't know," Kevin said, "but she's really protective of her."

Malky flicked his head, and Daniel pulled him back from the edge. Kevin felt like he was going to vomit, and he had no idea how his jelly legs were keeping him upright.

Malky grabbed him by his jacket and said, "You've got one chance. Get my drugs on those streets, and get me Mack through this sweetie woman, and I'll cancel your debt to me. If not…"

Kevin felt a gun at the back of his head. "It might take some time to get a plan worked out. I need to work out their movements."

"I can be patient when there is a prize at the end of it. I want Mack, her uncle Thomas, and the fucking so-called Queen of the Streets. There's going to be a King of the Streets. You've got a month, Kev. No more."

"Thank you, Mr. McDade, thank you."

"Pick up the new gear from me in the morning. Let's go, Daniel. You can make your own way back, Kev."

Kevin was happy to. He didn't want to be in Malky's company any more than he had to.

He watched Malky and his men get back into the car, and before shutting the door, Malky shouted, "One month, Kev."

As soon as the car drove away, Kevin's resolve left him, and he fell to his knees and vomited.

❖

Flora was in the back of the sweet shop waiting for Mack to come and get her. She was going for her first appointment with her therapist today and had been so nervous and exhausted because she hadn't slept properly. She had absolute fear and dread about today, and even watching Mack's ASMR videos hadn't calmed her enough for sleep.

She'd spent the last hour separating some fruit sherbets by colour, then putting the separate colours in bags to take with her for the museum. At least gaining some control of the chaos of the fruit sherbets helped a tiny bit.

Flora jumped when the bell on the shop door rang. Her heart pounded. The time had come, and it felt like torture.

Sandra stuck her head around the partition and said, "Mack is here."

Flora nodded and said, "I'll be right out."

Sandra took the hint and left. Flora immediately fell into her OCD ritual to try to bring some calm, but it wasn't helping. She felt sick and didn't think she could get her legs to move. But yet she kept going, caught in the cycle of her OCD until she felt a hand on her shoulder.

Flora jumped and turned to find a smiling Mack. "I thought you might be struggling, so Sandra said it would be all right to come back and see you."

Flora looked Mack up and down. "You look nice."

She really did. Flora loved Mack's jeans, shirt, and T-shirt look, but today she was wearing a grey suit with an open-necked white shirt.

"Thanks, I thought I'd better dress a bit nicer for the doctor and your fancy museum."

"It's not some formal museum—you didn't have to do that. I like you how you are."

"But you like this too?" Mack said, holding her jacket out.

"Oh yes." Flora brushed her hand over Mack's lapel. "You brush up very nicely."

Mack smiled and held out her hand. "You look beautiful too. Is that dress new?"

"Yes, are you sure it looks okay? I'm not used to wearing this kind of thing."

Flora had been expanding her wardrobe since she met Mack. It was silly, but her friendship was giving her the confidence to stand out just a little more.

"It's perfect. Let's go, wee mouse. You'll feel better once this first appointment is done."

Flora said nothing and still couldn't move.

"Take my hand. I'll be with you every step of the way. Trust me. I'm your guardian angel, remember?"

Flora grasped her hand. She did trust Mack, and that was the only thing that was keeping her going.

"Come on. I've got a taxi waiting outside."

Flora allowed herself to be led out into the shop, then outside. She barely heard Sandra say goodbye. Sandra's cousin was helping out in the shop today to let Flora make her appointment, and Mack's mum was looking after Dexter.

Mack held open the door of the black cab, and she climbed in. Mack followed suit and said to the driver, "Bath Street, mate."

"Aye, right away."

Mack had gotten Flora into the taxi—that was the first step for today. Ever since Mack had phoned for the appointment, Flora had been so tense and worried, and as she looked at her now, staring ahead and so quiet, she knew it wasn't getting any easier for Flora.

"It'll be okay, Flo. I'm here."

Flora didn't look around. She just grasped Mack's hand tighter, as if trying to share some of Mack's strength, and that's what she wanted Flora to feel. Mack had more than enough confidence and strength for both of them.

When she'd visited her mum and Aunt Chrissy yesterday, Chrissy had asked, "Why are you going to such lengths to help this woman, Mack?"

Mack had answered as honestly as she could. "Because she's kind, brave, has had to deal with so much shit in her life alone, and she has no idea how beautiful she is."

Her mum and Chrissy had looked at each other with surprise, before her mum said, "We'd like to meet this special woman."

Mack would love to introduce Flo to her family, but that would be too much for Flora at the moment. The Sharkeys were a loud, different kind of family. Maybe soon, and maybe if she could start small.

It wasn't far to the clinic they were visiting. It was a small practice in one of the nicer parts of Glasgow's town centre. They turned into Bath Street, and the driver pulled into a space in front of a Victorian building.

"That us, Flo."

Flo looked at her with terror in her eyes.

"It's okay." Mack took out her wallet and said, "How much, mate?"

"On the house, Ms. Sharkey."

Mack knew it was around a five-pound fare, so she held up a ten-pound note. "Nah, no freebies, thanks, though. Keep the change."

The driver took the money reluctantly. "Thanks."

Mack got out and held out her hand to Flora. She had squeezed herself into the furthest point of the taxi seat and was almost trying to melt into the door.

"Come on, just give it one chance?"

After a few seconds, Flora started to move and got out of the taxi, holding tightly to Mack's hand. When Mack tried to lead her up the stairs, Flora stopped.

"Give me a minute. I feel like I can't breathe."

"Okay, okay." Mack took both of her hands and said, "Breathe deeply. In and out."

Flora closed her eyes and followed Mack's instructions. "I don't have to come back if I don't like her?"

"You can do whatever you want. You're in charge."

Flora nodded. "Let's get it over with, then."

They walked up the stairs and Mack pressed the door buzzer.

"*Yes?*"

"Ms. Buchanan to see Dr. Carrson."

"*Come in.*"

Mack led them up a short set of stairs, through a door, and into a traditional-looking waiting area. Polished wood and wooden panels made up the decor, interspersed with some paintings.

The reception desk was over in the right hand corner of the room, while three doors at least led off from this main reception.

"Ms. Buchanan?" the receptionist said.

"Yes, this is Flora Buchanan," Mack answered.

"I'm Mrs. Woods. Dr. Carrson won't be long. In the meantime"—Mrs. Woods brought over a clipboard and pen—"could I get you to fill out the new patient form?"

Flora took it and nodded. They sat down, and Mack said, "You're doing great."

Flora looked terrified, but Mack was pleased to have got this far. She really hoped this first doctor would suit her, because she didn't want her to give up after just one try. It wouldn't matter to Mack if Flora never got help, as long as she was happy, because she loved all the differences that made Flora special. But she knew it was causing Flora distress that she couldn't live a so-called normal life.

Mrs. Woods's phone buzzed. She answered it and then said, "Ms. Buchanan? Dr. Carrson will see you now."

Flora looked at her with terror in her eyes.

Mack took the clipboard from her and smiled. "I'll be right here waiting for you."

Flora got up without saying a word and walked into the doctor's consulting room.

She was a lot braver than she knew.

Mack's stomach twisted with nerves on Flora's behalf. She wished she could be in there giving her strength.

She thought back to what her mum and aunt had said to her. No woman had ever made her feel these emotions. Flora was her first thought when she woke up in the morning, and her last thought at night. She was falling head over heels for her.

❖

Flora was shaking inside. She hated every part of this—meeting someone new, talking, talking about herself, frightened she'd make a fool of herself. As Flora shut the door, Dr. Carrson was on her feet and coming over to meet her.

"Flora, it's lovely to meet you. Come in and sit down."

"Hi," Flora said softly. Her urge to practice her ritual was strong. She had no choice but to do it, but she tried to make it as unnoticeable as possible.

Once they both were seated, Dr. Carrson picked up her pen and continued to smile openly. "Thank you for coming to us, Flora. I see from your questionnaire that you've seen a few therapists through your life but haven't really connected."

"Yes," Flora croaked.

"Well, hopefully I can help. If you feel uncomfortable at any time, just say, and if you don't feel that connection with me, then we can try you with another doctor in our centre. I won't be offended, honestly."

That declaration actually made Flora feel better. It took the pressure off and made her like the doctor's honesty.

Dr. Carrson looked down at her notes. "I see you also put down that you have issues with OCD and social anxiety."

Flora nodded. She couldn't speak, couldn't organize the thoughts in her head. Her whole brain was screaming *panic*.

She suspected the doctor noticed that, because she put down her pen and pushed the notebook to the side.

"Let's forget all that. Tell me about yourself, Flora."

Flora opened her mouth, but nothing would come out.

So Dr. Carrson said, "Is that the worst question to ask you?"

Again Flora nodded.

"You don't know what to say. You need a structure to the conversation?"

"Yes."

Dr. Carrson sat forward. "Is that your partner outside?"

"What? No, just a friend." Flora was so surprised that the doctor would think that.

"Do you have lots of friends?"

"No, none."

Dr. Carrson nodded. "If you were to describe how your symptoms make you feel, how would you describe it?"

The description jumped right into her head. "Tired, it makes me tired living this way."

"I understand that feeling, Flora. I have bipolar disorder, which I manage with medication. It's the reason I became a psychiatrist. So I understand the weariness of trying to cope with all your difficulties alone."

Flora was so surprised at what Dr. Carrson had said. It put them on a more even footing.

"Thank you for telling me," Flora said.

"I can help you. It won't be easy. No quick fixes, but I can help. Are you willing to give it a try?"

"Yes." This was more openness than she'd had with any of her previous therapists. "Yes, I want your help."

"Good. Let's begin."

❖

Flora walked out of the consulting room, embarrassed to have a red puffy face and still wiping away tears.

Mack jumped up and said, "Are you okay?"

Flora nodded and headed to the desk to pay. "Dr. Carrson said to make a new appointment for next week." Before today she'd said she would think about another appointment, but Flora felt this doctor got her, so she went ahead.

When they got out of the door, Mack said, "How did it go?"

"Can we talk about it when we get to the museum?"

"Aye, nae bother. I'll get a taxi."

Mack flagged one down and they got in. Flora's head was pounding, as it always did when she cried, so she went into her handbag and got a few painkillers and a bottle of water. She had prepared knowing this would be likely.

Reading her mood, Mack simply held her hand on the taxi ride over to the museum. She needed just to calm and collect her thoughts. When they arrived, again the driver tried to give them a free ride, which was weird. She would need to ask Mack about that.

They got out and Mack said, "Kelvingrove Art Gallery. I've always driven past here and never been in. I don't think this was the place school took us to."

The beautiful Victorian red sandstone building was surrounded with pleasant grass, trees, and benches.

"Can we have a seat over there before we go in?"

"Aye, let's go."

They sat down, and Mack looked at her, waiting for her to talk. Flora knew what she had to say, but getting started was a difficult thing. She opened her mouth, but something else came out. "The art gallery was built in 1888. It's a lovely building, isn't it?"

Mack smiled. "It is."

"It's Baroque architecture."

"What's that?"

"A style of art, architecture, music, dancing, that kind of thing that flourished in the seventeenth century."

"Wow," Mack said, "you know everything."

Flora laughed. "No, I don't. I'm just interested in learning facts that most people would find boring."

"Well, I want you on my pub quiz team, I know that."

Flora's head dropped knowing she had to talk about what happened at the therapist.

"Is everything all right, Flo?" Mack asked. "Did you like Dr. Carrson?"

Flora nodded. "She was lovely. So sympathetic and understanding. I'll go back."

Mack grasped her hand tightly. "I'm so proud of you. Today was a big step for you."

"I couldn't have done it without you. Your support is something that I've always—" Flora wanted to say *craved*. But instead she said, "I've always wanted."

Mack moved closer and put her arm around her shoulders. "That makes me happy." Mack motioned to her arm on Flora's shoulders. "Is this okay?"

Flora gave her a shy smile. "Yes, it's nice." She cleared her throat. "This is so hard."

"What is?" Mack said. "You don't have to tell me anything, you know."

"I told Dr. Carrson about you. She recognized your name."

"Did she tell you to run?" Mack was only half joking.

"No, she recognized your name because she volunteers once a month at a homeless group run by your family."

The penny dropped. "Oh yeah, my mum and Auntie Chrissy run a homeless charity project. Aunt Chrissy started it when she married my uncle. To give something back and look after the people on the streets. There's a group that goes out every night to give out food and stuff, and then once a month they set up big tents in George Square, to distribute food and more. There's medical help, like your new doctor, legal, things like that."

"That's a wonderful thing to do. So the Sharkeys aren't all scary?"

"Nah, we're angels," Mack joked by polishing her invisible halo. "Nikki and I usually volunteer once a month. You should come too, sometime."

"I'd like that," Flora said.

"So, what did your doctor say?"

Flora closed her eyes for a second and remembered the

claustrophobia of being surrounded by all those men. "I told her about the night we met. Dr. Carrson said that I need to talk to you about it, so the memory can't torture me as much."

"You know you don't have to."

Flora turned her head and looked at Mack. "I think I need to. That night I was going to an OCD group therapy session. It was my worst nightmare, talking in a group, and it started at eight at night. Sandra talked me into it. She thought it was worth a go."

"You must have felt you really needed the help if you did that," Mack said.

"Yes, but it was the wrong thing for me, and I needed support like you have been."

"When you were in your OCD group, Nikki, me, and her security people were having a meeting about what happened to Isy and her friend. Nikki wanted Kevin Drury's blood. Isy was at home, inconsolable after her best friend had died."

"It must have been awful for Isy."

"It's so weird how our lives came together that night. I think it was fate."

"You believe in fate?" Flora asked.

"I don't know for sure, but in my gut I feel it's true. Nikki and I were having a pretty intense conversation, and if I hadn't glanced up at the security monitors—"

"Thank God you did. I was counting down the time in the meeting to get away. It was excruciating being there, and when the others hung back for tea and coffee, I ran out, knowing I'd never be back. Then I ran to where the car was parked. I heard rowdy men coming towards the car, and I just couldn't find my keys in my bag. Then they were there, making lewd jokes, pawing me. I couldn't take it. I put my hands over my ears and screamed. I had a meltdown, they panicked, I think, and they dragged me around the corner. Then you were there, and I held on to you, knowing that I would be safe."

"Why did you run? I wanted to help you, take you to the police."

"I'm sorry, but I just wanted to go home to safety. I couldn't have gone through a police complaint and facing them in court. I know it's wrong, but I'm just not capable." Flora lowered her head on Mack's shoulder.

"Nothing is wrong. People handle events like that in different ways, but from now on I promise you that you'll always be safe."

"How do you know that?"

Mack looked into Flora's eyes and said softly, "Because I will keep you safe. I promise you."

Flora touched Mack's cheek and caressed it with her fingers. "You are the kindest, most understanding person I've ever met."

Mack replied with, "Shut up."

Flora giggled, and it interrupted their intimate moment. "You don't take compliments well."

"No, I don't. How do you feel talking about it? That night, I mean."

"Better. It's still scary, but I feel stronger having shared it with you," Flora said.

"Do you want to go in now?" Mack asked.

"Yes." Flora was really proud of herself for acknowledging what happened to her and facing the fear in the face. They got up and walked hand in hand towards the museum. Flora loved that.

"Mack? Why did the taxi drivers not want you to pay the fare?"

"Oh, that. It's a respect kind of thing, because I'm a Sharkey, but I'll always pay. The Sharkeys aren't some two-bit gangsters. Now, come and tell me all the facts you know about the stuff in here."

"You'll be sorry you said that," Flora replied.

## CHAPTER THIRTEEN

On the way back to Flora's they picked up a couple of pizzas for dinner. The enormity of the day had really hit Flora hard. She was exhausted.

Mack carried the pizzas into the kitchen and said, "Go and have a seat on the couch, and I'll bring these over."

"Thanks, I'm sorry I'm so tired and not better company."

"Don't be daft. You've been through the emotional wringer today."

Mack got a couple of bottles of water out of the fridge and carried them and the pizzas over to the coffee table in front of the couch.

"Here's your pizza—"

Flora had slumped over in the seat and fallen asleep. She must have been so tired. Mack took the pizzas back to the kitchen. She looked around and found a blanket to put over Flora and tucked her in.

She wondered if she should leave and let Flora have her space, but after such an emotional day, she couldn't. If Flora wanted her to go when she woke up, then at least Mack would know she was okay.

So Mack took off her jacket and sat on the end of the couch. Mack took her phone out and called Nikki's home number.

Isla answered, and she heard Dexter bark in the background. "Hi, wee barra, you got Dex from Granny? How's ma boy?"

"Hi, Mack, he's fine. We ate chicken and had some ice cream. His little belly is full."

"See? That's why you are the best doggie sitter. Do you think you could keep him till tomorrow?"

"Yes! I'd love that."

"You'd love what?" Mack heard Nikki say in the background.

"Put your mum on, Isy."

"What have you got my Isy to agree with?"

"Looking after my boy till tomorrow," Mack said.

She could almost see Nikki shaking her head. "You're making this puppy argument really hard."

"Shut up, he's a wee darlin'. I'll pick him up tomorrow if that's okay," Mack said.

"Okay, okay, you've made my little girl happy anyway. How did your day go?"

Mack gazed at Flora's sleeping form and felt another bit of her heart lost. "It went well. She really liked the therapist. Dr. Carrson volunteers at Mum and Aunt Chrissy's homeless charity."

"Hmm. I wonder if she would suit us."

Mack knew she was meaning Isla. "Maybe. I'll give you the details."

"Isy and Mum said you had a suit on when you dropped off Dexter."

"And what?"

Nikki laughed. "She really must mean a lot to you if Mack the Knife wore a suit."

Instead of making light of it, Mack said, "Aye, she does."

At that moment Flora began to waken, and her eyes fluttered open. When she saw Mack gazing at her, Flora smiled.

"I'd like to meet her," Nikki said. "Can you bring her to poker night? Isy keeps asking about the offer to help out in the shop. I'd like to meet her in person first."

Mack couldn't blame Nikki for being so protective. She'd nearly lost Isla. "I don't know. I can ask."

"Okay, I know she has her issues, but it's important. Listen, I wasn't going to tell you this, but there was a lot of merchandise on the streets today, mostly around the train and bus station."

That concerned Mack. "Why wouldn't you tell me? It's important." Mack was trying to keep her voice calm now that Flora was awake.

"Because I want to keep you away from anything that could cause difficulties."

"I need to know, Nik. I'm always going to be involved. It's in my blood. Who was it?"

Nikki sighed. "Kevin Drury was seen, using his little helpers. Jamsey and Murdo sorted most of it out, but if Drury is back on the streets, I'm sure he's being backed by McDade."

"And he knows we can't touch him."

"We can't touch him yet. His time will come. I'm a very patient woman. If there hadn't been a tip-off that day, we wouldn't have a problem." Nikki was trying to carefully choose her words so Isy wouldn't catch on to what they were talking about.

"Aye, he will."

"Like I said, I don't want you getting your hands dirty. Leave it to me," Nikki said.

"We'll see." When Mack left prison, she'd had every intention to take a step back from the business, but when people like Kevin Drury were on the street, she knew she would always be the Sharkey enforcer.

"Have a good night, okay? Bye, Mack."

"Bye." Mack turned off her phone and said, "Hey, sleepyhead."

"You stayed?" Flora said with excitement. "I'm sorry for falling asleep on you."

"I wouldn't just walk out when you fell asleep. You had a really hard day, and besides, I'm your guardian angel, remember?"

Flora moved a few inches closer to Mack and said, "Yes, you are, aren't you."

She took Mack's hand. Usually, Flora wasn't so bold. Mack moved a loose piece of hair behind Flora's ear. "Nobody's ever accused me of being an angel—a criminal gangland enforcer, maybe. Do I need to go on?"

"Well, you're the kindest person that I've ever met. I hope—" Flora shook her head. "It doesn't matter."

"No, tell me what?"

"You don't just feel sorry for me, do you?"

"Flo, that is the last thing I feel for you. What I do feel is that I admire you for being so brave and coping with everything you've had to deal with, alone, for most of your life. I feel bad that you have had to be alone, but never sorry for you. You're beautiful, brave, and strong."

"I don't feel strong and I'm definitely not beautiful." Flora let her head fall.

Mack put her fingers under Flora's chin and held it up. "I'm sorry that nobody has ever told you that, but it's true, and if you don't believe your guardian angel, who can you trust?"

Mack got a sweet smile in return and had a desperate need to kiss Flora but was unsure how it would be received, so she asked, "Can I kiss you?"

"Yes," Flora whispered.

Mack's heart was pounding as she inched forward, and she groaned when she met Flora's lips. They were so soft and yielding that Mack thought she could melt into them. She let the tip of her tongue run along Flora's lips, and she got Flora to moan in return and felt her hands grasp lightly around her neck.

The next second Flora pulled back, her breathing heavy. "You need to know something. Something that might make you feel differently about me."

Mack ran her fingers through Flora's hair. "Nothing could."

"It could. There was something else Dr. Carrson said today that might make you feel differently."

"I don't think so, but if you think it's important, then tell me."

"It's something that I've always suspected, and Dr. Carrson still has to give me the official test next week, but from what I told her, she thinks it's a pretty safe bet that I'm on the autistic spectrum. High functioning autism some call it."

Mack was only somewhat aware of the autistic spectrum. Up until recently, she thought only some children were deeply affected by autism. That was until Isla had been assessed for various disorders as she went through phycological evaluation, after her friend died.

Isla turned out not to be on the spectrum, but Nikki and her aunt explained that someone could have some of the symptoms and not be so severely affected by it.

"What exactly does that mean? I want to understand."

"Dr. Carrson went through some of the difficulties. Emotional sensitivity, fixation on particular subjects, social difficulties, devotion to routines, dislike of change, repetitive habits—apparently OCD symptoms go hand in hand with it."

"That definitely sounds like you. Why do you think that changes anything?" Mack asked. She honestly didn't know what that would change about her feelings for Flora.

"Because a lot of people wouldn't want to take that on."

Mack scrunched up her eyes. "Why would I be taking it on? You had the same symptoms yesterday, and the day before, and the first moment I met you. The only difference is you have a title for it now."

"A title for my craziness?" Flora shook her head.

"No, you are just you." Mack cupped her cheek. "The same woman I've felt connected to from the first moment I set eyes on you."

Flora pulled away from her caress. "No, you can't be involved with me. I'm not going to change the fact that I have autism or OCD by seeing Dr. Carrson. She can help me learn techniques to cope with the symptoms. You could go out to The Deep and meet a roomful of beautiful, nicely dressed women, who wouldn't give you half the trouble I would and will."

"You don't need to dress a certain way, behave in a certain way. To me you are perfect as you are, and I've been falling for you ever since that first night we met," Mack said passionately.

Flora went quiet but took Mack's hand. "You know, I've never had a friend. I couldn't understand the dynamic. The truth is I've never missed friendship. I've been lonely, but I didn't know what for. I've tried at points in my life, but all I could think about was when would the torture of conversation end, so I could go home, shut my front door, and leave the world outside. I felt safe there. But you…"

"What about me?" Mack took her other hand.

"You are just different, and I don't know why. I want to be in your company, I don't panic thinking of what to say next, and we can sit in silence without it being awkward. You anticipate what's going to make me uncomfortable or give me difficulties, and you're so sensitive. No one, and I mean no one, has ever made me feel like that. That's what makes you special."

Mack understood the significance of what Flora was saying. It meant so much to her to be that one.

"I've never been called sensitive before," Mack said jokingly. "But seriously, thanks for letting me in, because I'm falling for you."

"But what if I can't—"

"Can't what?"

"Be everything that another woman could be for you."

Mack understood but wanted to allay her fears. "I want a chance to be with you, to help you, to be your guardian angel, whatever you need me to be." Tears filled Flora's eyes. Mack used her thumb to wipe away the first stray tear that fell from Flora's eye. "Why are you crying?"

"Because I didn't realize just how much I wanted you to say those things. From the first moment I was held in your arms that first night we met, we connected, and there was something different going on."

"Listen, we both have feelings, so let's just explore and see what happens, eh?"

"But what if I can't cope with everything—"

"We'll see what happens. In the meantime, we're going to have fun together—you, me, and Dex."

"Poor Dex. He'll be missing you. Are you going to pick him up?"

"Nah, Isy's going to keep him till tomorrow. He always gets spoiled by Isy. I was on the phone with Nikki when you were waking up."

Flora gasped. "What about the pizza?"

❖

Flora heated up the pizzas in the oven and got some plates out. She looked back at Mack sitting on the couch, and her heart and other areas fluttered. Things had changed. Her heart had fluttered, pitter-pattered, and hammered in Mack's company plenty of times before, but now it was different.

There was a new buzz, an electricity in the air, and it was so exciting. How Mack had feelings for her, she didn't know, but Flora trusted Mack like no one else, so if she said she felt it, then she did.

It was funny—excitement made her have the urge to perform her OCD ritual. Flora didn't know why. Maybe she was afraid of the unknown ahead of her, and the ritual gave her some sense of control.

So she performed it, rubbing her nose and tapping three times on her chest, and then she went through it again. Flora was frustrated the urge was here in this happy moment too.

Flora put the pizza slices on the plates and carried them over to Mack. "Here we go. I can't believe you didn't just eat while I was sleeping. It won't be as good reheated."

Mack took a plate. "I'm not going to eat without you."

"That means a lot," Flora joked, "because I know how much you love to eat."

"Aye, you're right. That's a big compliment to you." She patted the couch. "Come sit with me, wee mouse. I'm starving. I could eat a scabby horse."

Flora laughed. "That's enough to put me off my pizza."

"Sorry, come on."

She sat and put her plate on her lap. She grabbed the TV remote and switched to her favourite channel. At this time, *The Simpsons* and *Futurama* ran back to back. "You don't mind watching this while we eat, do you?"

"What? No, I've usually got them on if I'm home at this time."

In the spirit of openness, Flora said, "This is one of my things."

Mack narrowed her eyes. "Your things?"

"You know, one of my oddnesses, rituals. I always watch the same things at different points in the day. It makes me feel safe to have a routine."

"You're not odd. What's the problem with watching what makes you happy? Come on, eat your pizza and watch Homer."

Flora smiled. Mack was so understanding. It was like she was made for her.

Mack hummed with delight as she munched into her pizza. Mack's pizza was groaning with toppings, every meat and hot topping they had.

"It's good?" Flora asked.

"Oh, aye."

Flora went about moving the slices of tomato from their original positions to line up to make a perfect circle on the pizza. She looked to the side and saw Mack smiling at her.

"One of your things?"

For once in her life, Flora didn't feel embarrassed. It was just funny. "Yes, one of my things. Your pizza freaks me out. Everything is just everywhere on it."

"Don't worry, I'll eat it quickly. Do you not like any other toppings but tomato?"

"Yes," Flora said. "I love all the vegetables that go on pizza, but I can't exactly ask them to place them in a certain way, so I just get tomato. It's easier, but I prefer to make my own at home. That way I can put the vegetables on in the correct order."

Mack smiled. "I didn't know there was a correct order?"

"Oh yes, in my goofy head, anyway. It's mostly by colour, type, and size."

"That's good to know. Maybe you could make me a meat one and come up with an order?"

"I'd love to."

Mack plopped her slice into the dip she had and ate with gusto. Flora liked to watch her just enjoy eating so much. She nibbled her slice like the little mouse Mack called her.

"This is nice," Flora said. "To me it's nice, anyway. Probably to you staying in with pizzas and watching TV is boring."

Mack shook her head. "You seem to think I'm some sort of party animal. I'm not. Maybe when I was young, but after the first experience of drinking, I kept sober, and going to the pub was just about meeting friends or dealing with business."

"You really don't mind?"

"Flo, I've just spent a year and a half in prison. I used to dream of quiet nights in with Dex and someone I loved, but I came out and the reality hit that my flat was big and empty. If I didn't have Dex, I would be going mad. This is what I want."

"Have you not had lots of girlfriends before?" Flora was sure she'd had lots of them and was worried about the answer.

"Not like you think. Friends that were girls? Yeah, but apart from that, only people I met—"

"For sex?"

"Well, aye, but that's not what I wanted deep down, but you know about my family. We're not always above board in some areas, and I couldn't trust that Sharkey knowledge with any woman I met. Look what happened when my dad was let into the family."

"But you told *me*," Flora said.

Mack put down her slice of pizza and wiped her hands and mouth. "I trusted you—why would I not? The history we share builds a bond. I feel it in here." Mack put her hand on her heart. "In here I knew you when I saw you, somehow. I know that sounds stupid, but all the time I was in jail I kept thinking about you, wondering who you were, if you were okay. You left a bit of yourself in my heart."

If Mack was trying to seduce her, which Flora knew she wasn't, she would have succeeded, but thankfully Mack knew Flora wasn't ready or prepared for that kind of thing. So she used all her courage and moved in to kiss Mack and wrapped her arms around her neck.

❖

Mack was so pleased that Flora was able to have the confidence to take this step. She'd experienced a lot of kisses in her life, but none quite like Flora's. Mack knew how much this kind of social courage took. It was a gentle, intimate kiss, but no matter how much her body was crying out for more, she didn't push Flora.

Everything was going to have to be at Flora's pace, especially after her probable autism diagnosis. But if she was worried about pushing Flora too far, she needn't have bothered. Flora pushed Mack back and began giggling.

"You taste of spicy pepperoni."

"That's not one of you your *things*, is it?"

"No, don't be silly," Flora said.

"I hoped that would be your answer. I mean, if it was between kissing you and pepperoni pizza, it would be a tight call, but in the end I'd choose you," Mack joked.

"Oh, that's really reassuring. I win, just above pepperoni by a whisker. That's good to know."

Mack took her hand and kissed it. It had taken a long time, but the girl that had haunted her was actually here and had kissed her. "I hope that the pepperoni hasn't put me at the bottom of your kissing list."

Flora looked a little sheepish. "I don't have a list. You were the first."

In a way, Mack wasn't surprised given her childhood and her difficulties at school and then into adulthood, but it was still a sobering thought. She was the first, and she had to live up to Flora's expectations.

"Don't be shy about it. I get to be your first. You sure the pepperoni hasn't put you off?"

Flora's smile came back. "Not a bit. I love kissing you."

Mack remembered what Nikki had asked her earlier on. She held up her arm and encouraged Flora to snuggle into her side.

"This is really nice," Flora said.

"You'll have to tell me at any time if our closeness is too much for you. I don't want to do anything that makes you uncomfortable."

"Thank you, I will, but that's the weird thing. My brain and heart just accept you. That's how I know you're special."

Mack held her tighter. "Thanks for letting me in. Erm…I wanted to ask you something."

"What is it?"

"First thing is, you don't have to do it, especially after what you told me tonight about being on the autistic spectrum. I'll totally understand if you can't do it," Mack said.

"Tell me what it is, and I'll tell you if I can do that."

"Well, I'd really love you to meet my family, but I know that's too much for you just now. So I wondered if maybe you could meet Nikki and a few of my friends at our poker night."

Tension and fear were already etched on Flora's face.

"Don't panic, and let me explain. Isy really wants to take you up on your offer of helping at the shop, but Nik would like to meet you first. She's so protective after everything that's happened."

"I can understand that," Flora said, while her insides were gripped with fear.

"Rather than make it a big formal thing, Nik suggested making it at our monthly poker night."

"Where do you hold it?"

"Either at one of the houses or a private room at the casino, but this time we can have it anywhere that makes you more comfortable," Mack said.

Flora had started to go through her rituals, so Mack got how big an ask this was for her.

"Hey, don't be stressed. We're just talking about it—there's no pressure."

"Who would be there?"

"Nikki, you and me, Annie and Jay, who you've already met—they're married," Mack said.

"I don't know if I could cope, Mack. I'd really like to meet them if it wasn't for my stupid brain."

Mack said, "Your fears aren't stupid. They're completely understandable. How about you think about it for a while?"

Flora nodded. "I will."

"The only other thing you'll find hard is that it's after seven o'clock."

Flora jumped quickly and started to pace. "I don't think I can do that, Mack. It's too much."

"Don't panic, it's just an idea."

"But it's important for Nikki and Isla," Flora said.

"I did think about either hosting the party at my flat or yours."

Flora shook her head. "I'm definitely not ready for others to come inside my house, maybe yours, but I don't know. I'll think about it."

"That's all I ask."

❖

Later that night Flora lay in bed after Mack went home. She started to read a book. It was so nice to have no noise coming from upstairs. But after five minutes she closed the book app. She had too much going on in her head.

Her visit to Dr. Carrson, being with Mack and explaining her difficulties, and also kissing her—it was all too much, and when she started to think about the poker night Mack suggested, her heart rate sped up, and tears of frustration tumbled from her eyes.

"I can't do this. I can't be what Mack wants."

She pulled a tissue from the box by her bed and dried her eyes. *Calm down.*

Flora was trying to remember some of the techniques Dr. Carrson suggested when she had meltdowns like this. She grabbed her iPhone and played a YouTube video of a thunderstorm at sea. She loved these sounds, and while it was playing, she did some breathing exercises.

Her heart started to calm, and her mind slowed down a little. Despite these fears, she did feel that the doctor was going to help her cope.

In the middle of her breathing exercise, her phone rang, giving her a fright.

Flora looked at the phone and saw it was Mack calling. She sat up and answered.

"Hi, wee mouse, I hope you don't mind me video calling you?"

"No, I'm always happy to see your face."

That made Mack smile wide. "That's nice to know. Hey, have you been crying?"

"Just a bit. The day's emotions got too much for me. I'll be fine."

"Okay, if you're sure," Mack said. "I thought I'd phone and let you see my flat. The whole guided tour, you know? Then you could picture in your head what poker night might be like. What do you think?"

"That would be a good idea."

Mack smiled. "I'm full of good ideas. Where will I start? Hmm…I'll show the flat as if you're just arriving, okay?"

"Yes," Flora said.

"Okay, I'm just going to the front door and out to the lift. You okay with lifts? It's not one of your *things*, is it?"

Flora chuckled at Mack's shorthand for her spectrum difficulties. "They're not my favourite thing, but I get through it."

"Good, I mean, I'd be there with you. I'd pick you up. So, anyway, you come out of the lift, and my flat is just around the corner." Mack switched the camera so Flora could see what it was like from her view. "You see the white door? That's mine and Dex's den."

Flora laughed at Mack's description and felt more relaxed already. Then she spotted a security camera above the door. She knew doorbell cameras were popular now, but this was a proper security camera that you'd see in a shopping centre or something.

"Mack? Why do you have a camera there?"

Mack flipped the camera view back to her face. "It's just the nature of the business the family is in sometimes, if you know what I mean. People might come to the door looking to do more that deliver a pizza."

She always felt a strange mixture of emotions when she was reminded of the darker side of the Sharkeys' business. Her initial reaction was worry about what she was becoming involved in, but then she told herself that Mack would never do anything illegal without being pushed, like after Kevin Drury tried to hurt Isy.

"So we go down the hall..."

Flora followed Mack's camera intently.

"Then we come out into the open-plan part of the flat. We have a couch and TV up in the other corner of the room, kitchen over here..."

Mack took her camera over to the back wall, and Flora saw a very stylish kitchen. "Your kitchen looks like it's in a showroom," Flora said.

"That's probably because I hardly use it. Look." Mack walked over to the oven and pulled down the door.

"Extremely clean," Flora said, "like it has never been used."

"It hasn't—well, apart from one time I had the flu and Mum came to look after me."

Flora laughed. "What do you use, then?"

"The toaster, the fridge, the kettle, and the dishwasher. That's all I need. Do you know how many things you can make with toast?"

Flora laughed and Mack continued, "It's the gateway to so many meals. Toast with marmite for breakfast, toasted sandwiches for lunch, beans on toast for dinner, french toast—the possibilities are endless."

Flora laughed and laughed. "I've heard of gateway drugs, but never gateway foods to meals."

Mack flipped the camera back to her and gave Flora a smug look. "I'm right, though, aren't I?"

"You're so silly, that's what I know. Show me the rest."

Mack flipped the camera back. "Okay, in the middle of the floor here we have a kitchen/dining table. If I have poker night at the flat, we always put this table aside and put the card table here."

"I've never known anyone who's owned a card table before," Flora said.

"Well, stick with me—I'm going to blow your mind." Again she flipped the camera back to her. "Wait till you see this." Mack walked backward with the phone to the far end of the flat, and a snooker table came into view. "Isn't this great?" Mack was all smiles.

"Is that a full-size table?" Flora asked.

"Aye, I enjoy beating Jay and Nikki on it."

"What a beautiful big flat you've got. I'm surprised you ever want to leave it," Flora said.

Mack's humour appeared to falter. "Nah, it's big and empty. I don't like being on my own. That's why I've always spent so much time out at the pub and the casino."

They were so different, Flora thought. Being alone was her idea of a good night, well, except for being with Mack. Mack was different.

There was a lull in the conversation, so Flora asked, "Do you have a nice view of the River Clyde?"

"Yeah, come and see."

Mack walked over to the bank of full-size windows that spread from behind the couch and TV area to the other end of the room, where the snooker table was.

"What a view," Flora said. "You're lucky."

Mack cleared her throat. "Just in case you ever want to stay over, I'll show you the guest rooms."

"Oh, okay." Flora felt the awkwardness, awkward because that was probably what they both wanted.

There was a corridor just off where the snooker table was at the far end. Mack opened a door and said, "This is the main bathroom."

It was a really nice modern bathroom with a beautiful, large shower.

"It's lovely, Mack."

"There's also an en suite in my bedroom and one of the guest rooms. I won't show you my room just now because it's messy, but I'll take you to the guest rooms."

They were both stylish and neat. "It doesn't look like you have too many overnight guests."

"None," Mack said flatly. "You'd be my first."

Flora made her decision after that answer and wanted to say it quickly before she chickened out. "I'll come to poker night."

Mack's face lit up. "You will?"

"Yes. It'll be difficult for me, but it's important that I meet some of your family, because I…It's hard to say."

"I know. I always know."

She did, didn't she. Mack was becoming everything to her.

"Here you are." Mack slipped her arms around Flora's middle and held her close. She could feel Flora go still then relax into her. Mack rested her face on Flora's shoulder and held her in an embrace. Flora held Mack's hands around her middle. It felt intimate, just like Flora had mentioned in the car. "What do you think of the flat?"

"It's so nice, so modern. It helped that I already had a picture of where I was going to. Thanks for showing me on the video call. This view is beautiful. You're very lucky."

"It's okay. The flat is pretty empty, but not tonight."

Flora turned Mack's wrist slightly and tapped her Apple Watch, to check the time presumably. Mack saw it was five minutes to seven, the time that Flora always wanted to be home by. It was one of her *things.* "Are you all right? It's okay if you're worried about the time."

"I am. It's like a preprogramed fear inside me, but I'm determined to fight it. I'm with you, in your home. I know I'm safe."

Mack kissed her cheek. "You're always safe with me, but it's okay if you feel scared or worried. If you do, talk to me, or go to your room if you need some space for a while, and if you freeze, I'll help be your voice."

"Thank you for saying that. I don't know how or why you're always able to read what I'm feeling."

"It's because I was meant for you." Mack squeezed her with as much love as she could convey. "So, what was that thing about intimacy you were talking about?"

Flora took a breath to speak, and then the door buzzer rang and Dexter ran to the door, barking.

Flora froze up. "Is it Nikki?"

Mack turned her around and cupped her cheeks. "Probably. Look, it'll be fine. I'm with you, and she's not that scary, honestly." Flora started her ritual, but Mack knew it was probably best for her not to mention it and make her feel like it was wrong. "Why don't you go and check I got the right food, and I'll bring Nikki in."

"Okay," Flora said in a small voice.

Mack cupped her face and gave her a kiss. "You'll do great."

Flora nodded and walked off to the kitchen. Mack ran to the intercom and buzzed Nikki into the building. She went out the front door and waited for Nikki at the lift.

After about a minute the lift doors opened, and Nikki walked out. "Hi, what's wrong?"

"Nothing, why?"

"Because you never meet me here, and you look like a cat on a hot tin roof. Why are you so tense?"

"It's Flora's first time in the flat and the first time meeting family, apart from Isy."

"I'm not going to eat her, Mack."

Mack rubbed her forehead. She was feeling tense. "I know. It's just that she has her difficulties meeting people, and you can be intimidating."

"I promised you I'd be on my best behaviour. I didn't even bring a date with me, so there wouldn't be too many people for her," Nikki said.

Nikki always brought her woman of the month, but never more than twice.

"She's very nervous, so just be careful, okay?" Mack said.

"I promise I'll be good. Now, can we get in and have a drink?"

"Sorry, I just want her to feel safe." Mack led them to the door. "Imagine you're talking to an adult Isy."

"Oh, for fuck's sake, Mack."

"Okay."

Mack opened the door and walked in.

❖

Flora had been tapping and tapping, waiting on Mack and Nikki coming in. She heard the door open.

This was it.

She hadn't been too far off when she'd imagined what Nikki looked like. She was powerful looking in a grey trouser suit and a gorgeous ivory silk blouse. Nikki was bloody beautiful.

"Flora, this my cousin, Nikki. Nikki, this is Flora."

"Nice to meet you, Flora," Nikki said. "Isla's talked so much about you. Thanks for making her smile again."

"She's a wonderful girl."

Mack rescued the slight lull in the conversation. "Follow me, and I'll get some drinks." Mack poured a large glass of bubbly for Nikki and an orange juice.

Nikki said, "I hear Isla wants to come work for you in her spare time."

"Yes, I would like that—if it was okay by you, of course," Flora said.

"Hmm." Nikki took a sip of her bubbly. "I've had to make some decisions about Isla. I contacted a tutoring agency. The school and I think there's little point in forcing her to go to school every day. So we're going to try private tutoring for a three month trial period and see how things go. I'm happy for her to help out at the shop, if she keeps up with her lessons."

"That's fantastic, Nik," Mack said. "She'll be so much happier. Especially with the job at Sweet Surprise. That will give her more confidence."

There was a buzz at the door, and Mack clapped her hands. "It's Jay and Annie."

❖

Flora was getting changed into her nightie, and she felt the absence of Mack acutely. They had been exchanging touches, kisses, and hugs all evening, and she didn't want to be without her. It felt wonderful to be close to Mack, and it helped with her nervousness. Dexter helped enormously too, just by being there, when there was a lull in the conversation.

Although it was wonderful to meet Annie, Nikki was the one she was most worried about meeting, but she was lovely. Nikki told her all about Isy and her likes and dislikes, and stories about the mischievous things she and Mack got up to. Nikki was intense and could be a bit scary, but she was extremely nice to her. If Mack hadn't been there, it would have been different. She still struggled with the conversation and got tongue-tied, but Mack was always there to fill in for her. Mack had been a tower of strength.

Flora looked at the bed and got slightly panicked and nervous. She was out of her own house at half past twelve. She needed Mack.

She left her bedroom and saw Mack and Dexter walking back from the kitchen with two bottles in hand. Mack looked gorgeous in her boxers and sleeveless T-shirt. The muscles in Mack's arms, shoulders, and neck made Flora crave intimacy. Her body so wanted her to be normal. If she was, she'd jump on Mack and never come up for air.

"Hiya, I was just going to bring you a bottle of water."

"Thanks." Flo took the bottle.

"Is everything all right?" Mack asked.

"Yes. I mean, no, it's strange being in someone's else's house at night."

"I'm just next door," Mack said. "You don't have to worry, but I do know how difficult tonight has been for you. But you did so well. I was so proud of you."

"Thank you. Nikki wasn't as intimidating as I expected."

"Nikki might be ruthless, but to our family she is strong and loving, and she would do anything for us," Mack said.

"I'm not your family. I'm not anyone's family," Flora said sadly.

Mack took her hand. "Come in and sit. I want us to talk."

Flora followed Mack into her room. Mack patted the bed. "Sit down."

She sat and said, "I want to talk to you too."

"You go first, then," Mack said.

"No, you." Flora was nervous to say what Dr. Carrson had suggested.

Mack lifted Flora's hand and kissed. "Having you here, with my friends, my cousin, it's made me so happy. Happier than I can ever

Buchanan. She wrapped her legs around Mack's hips, pulling them closer together.

That brought Mack close to the peak of her orgasm. Her thrusting got faster, as well as her moans.

"Come, baby," Flora said. "Come with me."

The thrusts against her clit were bringing her close to losing control too. When she heard Mack shout out her orgasm and felt her body go rigid, she followed her into that place of pure pleasure that now only Mack could take her.

Mack collapsed on top of her, and even in the midst of her own recovery, she took a moment to gasp, "Hold on to me, darlin'. You're safe with me."

After a minute her slightly confused brain became aware of Mack kissing her. "You are so beautiful." Mack then looked into her eyes and said, "I'm falling in love with you, Flo."

"Me too."

Mack stroked her cheek. "I think I have been since that night we met."

"It was fate," Flora said, and then she lifted Mack's wrist and kissed the shark tooth tattoo on her forearm. Their afterglow was interrupted by a small dog at the side of the bed yapping.

"Dexter loves us too," they said together.

## CHAPTER FIFTEEN

The next few weeks brought great change into Flora's life. Her new medication was starting to have an effect. It didn't take her OCD symptoms away, but it was making her slightly calmer. It softened the urge, so that just sometimes she would forget to practice her usual rituals.

She and Dr. Carrson were finding the right balance of medication, talking out her issues, and coming up with strategies to cope with social situations that she struggled with. So much so that Flora had agreed to pop in and meet the rest of Mack's family for a drink when they were finished decorating Sweet Surprise for Christmas.

But the biggest change was her blossoming relationship with Mack. Flora couldn't quite believe her luck to have found Mack, or Mack to have found her. She had tried her hardest to push her away in the beginning, but Mack had persevered, and here they were, decorating the shop with Isla, Jay, and Annie.

Mack and Jay were currently up on ladders, trying to hang a large and heavy Christmas garland, bedecked with pine cones and lights, above the shop sign.

"A bit to the left, Jay," Annie said.

"You said right a second ago," Jay complained.

"This thing is fuck"—Mack corrected herself—"bloody heavy, you know."

Flora laughed with Annie as they watched their partners struggle with the heavy decorations.

She liked Annie. Flora didn't know what Mack had told her friends, but they were all very accommodating to her issues. If the conversation lulled at any point, they always stepped in and drove it on if Mack wasn't around.

Flora noticed that Isla hadn't returned from the bathroom yet. She shouted up to Mack, "I'm just going to check on Isy."

Mack nodded, and she went into the back of the shop. She saw Isy standing alone by the sink, wiping her eyes.

"Are you okay?"

"Everything was just a bit loud and…"

"Gets overwhelming sometimes?" Flora asked.

Isla nodded.

"I know. Sometimes you just need a time out to quiet your mind." Flora put her arm around her. "How about we have a secret slush time out?" Isla smiled and wiped her eyes. Flora took her hand and led her to the machine. "Blue, red, or green?"

"Red, please."

"Oh, a bold choice. I'll go with that too."

Flora poured out the drinks and handed one to Isla.

Isla took a sip through the straw and said, "I miss Dex."

"I know, but with the doors open and closed today, putting up the decorations, he might have run out onto the road." She watched Isla play with her straw. She didn't look happy. "Have you enjoyed putting up the decorations?"

"Oh yeah, I've loved it. The toy Christmas train in the window is my favourite."

"It's so cute and traditional, isn't it? My grandpa bought that years ago. It's our tradition."

Isla went quiet again, and then out of the blue she said, "I get flashbacks a lot of the time."

"About your friend?" Flora asked.

Isla nodded. "And that man and woman who attacked us. It was meant to be me. They called out my name, and Charlotte said it was her. She was always joking that everyone made a fuss because I was a Sharkey. It was just a joke, and they grabbed her, and then she was dying right in front of me. It should have been me."

Flora pulled her into a hug. "It's okay. Nothing you are feeling is wrong. Are you talking to Dr. Carrson about this?"

Isla stepped back and wiped her tears on her sleeve. "Yeah. She's nice. I really like her. She said the more I talk about it, the easier it'll be."

"I'm glad you like her. She's really helping me. Listen, why don't I use my influence to get Dexter a sleepover with you?"

Isla's smile returned. "I'd like that."

"Good. I'm so glad your mum said you could work with me here. We'll have a lot of fun together."

"Yeah, I can't wait. Mum said as long as I keep up with my studies with my tutor, I can work here in my spare time."

Things had changed for Isla too in these last few weeks. Not only had she started to see Dr. Carrson, but her mum had reached an agreement with her school for Isla to receive private tutoring at home. That way she could concentrate on her studies and not worry about being so afraid at school.

Mack walked out to see where they were. "Is everything okay?"

She looked worried, but Flora winked at her and said, "We're just having a slush time out."

"Oh? Well, okay. We're finally ready for the big light turn on. Come on." Mack grabbed Flora's slush and said, "I'll take that."

"Cheeky."

Flora and Isla followed Mack out to the front of the shop.

"Quick, Isy," Annie said.

Annie put her arm around Isla, and Mack put her arm around Flora's middle. Jay was inside waiting to switch on.

Mack held the slush and straw up to her lips and winked. "Would you like a suck of my straw, wee mouse?"

"You're terrible."

"What? I only asked an innocent question."

"Of course you did, but since you asked, maybe later." Flora grinned.

# Chapter Sixteen

Isy, can you help me with these bags?"

Isla came jogging out through the back door of the shop. She had been helping out at the shop for a few weekends and was enjoying it. It was lovely to be getting close to someone who her girlfriend adored.

"If you get that smaller bag, Isy, I'll get these two big ones," Flora said.

When Flora stepped out into the backyard of the shop, she saw a white van sitting there. "That's strange. We don't have any deliveries—"

Just as she said that a hand was put over her mouth. She screamed into the hand, but there was no one to hear her muffled cries apart from Isla, as Sandra was on her break.

Flora was lifted off her feet and carried over to the van. She saw the same happening to Isla, except it was a woman seizing her. She thought she recognized the female assailant's face but couldn't place it.

Flora's panic was mounting, and when she was thrown in the back of the van, she was nearing meltdown. She closed her eyes tightly and put her hands over her ears. The fear, the terror were too much, and her feelings were overwhelming.

But then she heard the van doors slam and Isla's cries and screams. Flora's instinct was immediate. Isla was the most important person here. It was her responsibility to keep her safe while Mack and Nikki weren't here.

*You can do this. You can do it.*

Flora pulled Isla to her and held her tight in her arms. "It's okay, Isy. I'm here. We'll get out of this. Your mum and Mack will find us."

"It's her, it's her, and him," Isla said through convulsive tears.

"Who are they?"

"The woman and man that killed my friend."

"You're sure about that?" Flora asked.

"Yes, she asked who was Isla Sharkey, and my friend said she was. The woman grabbed her, and the man injected her with something. I screamed, and then they came after me, but I ran back into the school, and they didn't follow me. They've come back for me, Flo. They are going to kill us."

Flora cupped her face and said, "Listen to me, Isy. I'm going to fight them all the way, and your family is going to find us. No matter what happens, always try to stay behind me. I'm here, and we're going to get home, okay?"

Isla nodded and hugged Flora tightly. Flora was terrified, every anxiety-filled part of her teetering on the edge. If this had happened before she'd met Mack, or before she'd started her therapy and medication, there would be no hope. There might still be no hope, but Flora resolved to go down fighting.

❖

Mack was doing some admin on the computer at reception while Liam worked on a client. It had been a slow day, but that suited Mack just fine. She and Flora had made plans to pick up an Indian takeaway after dropping Isla back home.

She smiled when she thought about having two of her favourite people next door, waiting for her. In fact, it was hard to stop herself from going next door most days, just to hang out with Flora and generally gaze at her lovingly.

*I am so lucky.*

At that moment Sandra burst through the door. "Are Flora and Isla here?"

Mack immediately jumped up on high alert. "No, why?"

"I was on my break, and when I came back, there was no one there. The back fire doors are wide open, and bags of rubbish are all over the place."

Shit. "Show me."

Liam asked, "Mack? Do you want me to—"

"No, you hold the fort here, and watch Dexter."

"Anything."

Dexter barked in distress as she hurried out of the shop.

Mack ran as fast as she could into Flora's shop and out back. He heart sank when she saw the mess that was left. Flora would never have left this mess here.

Sandra came out and said, "What do you think happened?"

"Do you have security cameras out here?"

"No, nothing like that."

Mack looked over the ground and saw something glinting. She reached over and found the locket she had given Flora. The chain was broken at the back as if it had been pulled and snapped.

Cold rage started to fill her veins. She closed her hand tightly on the locket and said to Sandra, "Can you shut and lock up the shop, Sandra?"

"Of course, then what?" Sandra asked.

"Just head on home. I'll call you when I can."

Mack ran up to the end of the lane. She turned the corner and saw that some of The Deep's security cameras faced the end of the lane. She stuffed the necklace in her jeans pocket and pulled out her phone. She dialled Nikki's number.

"Mack?"

"I think someone has taken Isy and Flo. Meet me at the club."

They both hung up immediately and Mack ran across the road to the club. She pushed through the doors and saw Jay talking with one of the bar staff.

"Jay? With me."

Jay hurriedly followed her into the office. The security monitors were on the back wall.

"What's happened?" Jay asked.

"I think Kevin Drury or the McDades or both have Flo and Isy."

"Jesus Christ."

"Nikki is on her way. They were snatched from the back alley of the shop and there may be some footage on the cameras. Two of them on the corner look directly at the end of the alley."

"I know which ones you mean. Hang on, I'll get the footage."

Jay took a seat in front of the computer and started searching for the footage, while Mack paced backwards and forwards, flicking her cutthroat razor open and closed.

"If it is that fucking little prick, I'm going to gut him."

Mack's anger was like no other rage. She felt sick, and a cold sweat erupted over her body.

"How long ago would this be?"

"It couldn't have been more than an hour ago. Sandra was on her break, and when she got back, they were gone."

Jay searched for about five minutes before she said, "Mack, look at this."

Mack looked over Jay's shoulder, and she played the tape. Mack saw a white van zooming out of the alley behind Sweet Surprise and almost causing an accident as it went into oncoming traffic.

Suddenly Nikki burst into the room. "What the fuck is going on?"

"I think Kevin Drury or McDade has taken Isy and Flo from the back of the shop. Jay's found some footage of a van leaving the alley."

"Show me."

As they watched, Nikki almost growled, "I'm going to kill him, and I don't care if I go to jail for the rest of my life."

"We'll get them. Can you zoom and get a licence plate number, Jay?" Mack said.

"Yeah, got it."

"Write it down for me," Nikki said. "I can get it traced."

Nikki started dialling a number, and Jay handed her a notepad.

Mack flicked open her cutthroat razor. After a long break, it was time to be the Sharkey enforcer yet again. It was time to be Mack the Knife.

## CHAPTER SEVENTEEN

Flora held a crying Isla in her arms and was trying to comfort her, but it was hard when she was shaking herself.

"I want my mum," Isla cried.

"I know. Your mum and Mack will be looking for us. Promise. In the meantime, no matter what happens, stay behind me. Okay?"

In her own mind she tried to believe Mack would find them, but in reality, how would she have any clue where they had been taken? That same reality wanted her to shut down, to protect herself from all fear and stimulation.

Her compulsion to do her OCD ritual was sky-high. Every minute or so, Flora was tapping as best she could, while holding Isla tight.

The van came to a halt, and Flora's fear was increasing exponentially. She felt sick but couldn't let Isla see that.

The doors opened and she was faced with a dishevelled thin man and the woman who Isla remembered.

"Get the girl," the man said to his female partner.

"That's his voice," Isla said.

"Whose voice?"

"The man in the mask who killed my friend."

Kevin Drury.

As the woman went for Isla, Flora launched herself at her. "Don't touch her."

Catching her by surprise, Flora knocked the woman backward. She landed on the concrete floor badly, and Flora landed on her. Flora heard the crack of the woman's head hitting the floor, and then she went limp.

The man grabbed her by the hair and pulled her off. "You fucking bitch."

Flora felt a hard blow to her face, which made her drop to the ground. She tasted blood in her mouth and felt kicks to her stomach and ribs. Her vision went blurry, but she could hear Isla scream.

She couldn't pass out. Isy needed her.

She was dragged over to a wall and propped up against it. The man got some insulation tape and wrapped it around her wrists.

"Please let Isla go. Please, you can do what you want with me."

Kevin held her by the throat. "Your girlfriend and Nikki put me in hospital for a month. You think I'm going to let either of the two of you go, without you paying for that? Besides, your fate isn't mine—it's Mr. McDade's."

McDade. Mack had told her all about them and how dangerous they were.

He pulled out a cutthroat razor, similar to Mack's. "Stay here and don't move, or I'll finish that fucking screaming lassie off."

Flora kept silent. She was shaking with fear as millions of terrifying thoughts ran around her head. Then one stopped her in her tracks—Mack walking in here and finding their two dead bodies.

She could feel the hurt, the pain, and the violence that would erupt in Glasgow because of it. Flora had to keep Isla alive at least. She looked around the space and saw it was an old warehouse building. The main doors facing her were closed and looked locked, but at the far end, the door the van came through was still open, and Kevin's helper was still out cold on the floor.

Isla was dragged over to Flora. Kevin placed a length of tape across her mouth.

"Maybe that'll shut you up, stupid bitch. Be quiet. I need to make a call, but you won't move because you would pay for it."

Kevin ran the knife down Isla's chest.

"Don't, you're scaring her."

Kevin grabbed her by the hair again. "I'm scared every second of every day."

"Mack will find you," Flora said.

"She'll find two dead bodies." Then Kevin walked away.

Isla was screaming through the tape on her mouth, and Flora's hands were shaking. She didn't even like to use a telephone, and now she had to try to save them both. Flora thought about Mack. Mack would believe in her. She could do it. Out of the corner of her eye, she saw a thick plank of wood lying on the floor, with nails sticking out of it. Could be a great weapon.

First Flora had to get Isla to calm down. "Isy? Isy? Nod if you're listening," Flora whispered.

Isla turned her head, and she nodded. Tears were rolling down her face.

"Okay. Do you see that open door at the far end?" Again, Isla nodded. "When Kevin comes back, I'm going to throw myself at him and knock him down. When I do that, I want you to run and don't look back."

Isla shook her head vigorously.

"Yes, Isy. You have the best chance. Keep running until you find someone, or get to a shop and ask them to phone the police. It's the only way. Okay?"

Isla nodded this time.

Flora looked up at Kevin and listened in to the conversation. He was pacing while tapping her knife against his leg. He was clearly stressed.

"I got them for you, Mr. McDade. You said you'd send someone to finish them off, and my debt would be paid."

He listened for a second and replied, "I know I messed up getting her daughter the last time, but Nikki and Mack will hunt me, and I'll be dead by tomorrow morning."

Kevin hung up and kicked the van. He paced around, probably considering the risks of what he was about to do. Then he began to walk over to them.

"Promise you'll run and not look back, Isy," Flora said in the quietest voice she could.

Isla nodded, still with tears in her eyes.

"Get ready."

Kevin approached and said to Flora, "Get up."

When he grabbed her, she used his momentum together with every ounce of muscle in her legs to briefly stand and throw herself into him. He was taken by surprise and knocked off his feet. She landed on him, and he brought up the knife to try to cut her, but Flora rolled to the side to dodge and get nearer to the plank of wood.

He came again for her. "You're fucking dead."

Flora was severely restricted by the tape on her wrist, but in her struggle, it had loosened slightly, giving her more room to play with. Flora reached over her head and got a grip on the wood. The pain in her ribs as she did that made her feel sick. He must have broken her ribs.

When Kevin was about to bring his razor down on her, Flora used as much force as she could and whacked the wood into the side of his face. He looked shocked as blood from the impaled nails ran down his face.

He then dropped the razor and fell on Flora. She cried out in agony as he fell on her broken ribs. Kevin was a dead weight, but she managed to turn to the side and vomit, and then everything went black.

❖

"I wish Kevin Drury was alive every time I look at her," Mack said as she paced around the hospital room.

Nikki, who was sitting by Flora's bed, said, "I know, but he's not coming back. He can't hurt our family any more, but the McDades are going to pay for this."

Isla had told them the whole story. She had run just like Flora told her to, and found help, who had phoned the police. While Flora and Mack were trying to find them, Nikki got a call from the police to tell her they had been found.

"I can't believe he took them to the same place we kicked the fuck out of him, to kill them," Mack said.

"He thought it would hurt us more, but he didn't realize who this amazing girlfriend of yours was," Nikki said.

Mack came back over to the hospital bed and sat next to Nikki. She took Flora's hand and kissed it tenderly.

"Do you know what she must have gone through, not just physically? And she still protected Isy."

"She's as brave as a lioness, Mack. I'll never be able to repay her for saving Isy."

"I'm so proud of her, but looking at her beautiful face covered in bruises makes me sick," Mack said.

Nikki patted her on the back. "She'll be looked after for the rest of her life. Flo is one of us now. Mum and Aunt Mary are just waiting for her to get home to fuss around after her."

Mack nodded. Uncle Thomas, Aunt Chrissy, and her mum were beyond grateful for what Flora had done and were making preparations to welcome her home to the Sharkey homes when she was ready.

Flora started to stir, and her eyes flickered open. Mack was up in a second, sitting on the bed and stroking her hair.

"Hiya, wee mouse."

"Oww," Flora said as she wriggled in bed.

"Try not to move. You've got broken ribs and a lot of bruising."

"Isy? She okay?" Flora asked.

"She's absolutely fine. Isn't she, Nik?"

Nikki stood up so Flora wouldn't have move to see her. "Yes, perfect. She found help. I can't begin to thank you for protecting her. You were prepared to sacrifice yourself for my girl."

"And I would again," Flora croaked.

"Mack told me you had no family left after your grandpa died. I want you to know, you do now. You're a Sharkey officially." Nikki looked at Mack and grinned. "Or unofficially. You'll always have us."

"Thank you." Tears started to fall from Flora's eyes.

Nikki bent down and kissed her forehead. "I'll let you two be alone now."

"Tell Isy I can't wait to see her."

"I will do. See you at home, Mack."

"Thanks, Nik."

After she left, Flora asked, "What about the woman?"

"The one that helped abduct you both?"

"Yes."

"She's in hospital too. Bad concussion, they said."

"Isla was scared. She said that woman helped with the attack on her friend. She tried to grab Isla, so I had to jump on her, and she hit her head on the ground. And what about him?"

Mack hesitated. She didn't know how Flora would cope mentally with this news. "He isn't a problem any more."

"You?" Flora asked, clearly thinking they had dealt with him, which they would have done if the police hadn't gotten there first, and if he hadn't already been dead.

"No, he was dead when the police arrived."

Tears started to fall down Flora's face. "All I wanted to do was cover my ears and hide."

"But you didn't." Mack wiped Flora's tears. "How you found the mental and physical strength to hit him with that piece of wood, while you had broken ribs, I'll never know."

"I'm not strong. You are, and I love that about you."

"To live the life you have, coping with your difficulties on your own? You are the strongest woman I know, and I love you, Flo."

"I love you, Mack."

They clasped hands, and Mack softly kissed her lips. "I'm going to love you forever and make sure you are always safe."

"My guardian angel, right from the start." Flora smiled.

"Always."

# CHAPTER EIGHTEEN

Flora ended up staying in hospital for five days. But today was her leaving day. She had a visit by the police for questioning about Kevin Drury, but with the lawyer Nikki provided for her there as well, it went smoothly, and she was reassured she wouldn't face any charges.

The nurse talked Flora through her medications, while Mack packed up Flora's last bits and pieces in a holdall.

She was still very sore, and the bruising on her face didn't look too good, but she was desperate to get out of hospital. They were going to Mack's mum's house straight after leaving. She felt worried about not staying in her flat or Mack's, but Mary and Chrissy insisted they'd take care of her.

They had been up to visit every day, so she had gotten to know them much better, and to be honest, despite her difficulties with talking to most people, she had enjoyed their motherly care. It had been such a long time since she had felt it. And, like Mack, they didn't make an issue out of her quietness or OCD.

The nurse left them, and Flora handed the medication to Mack to put in her bag.

"You ready?" Mack asked.

"Yes. You'll maybe have to leave me at the door and go and get the car. I don't think I can walk very far."

"No need." Mack put the bag on her shoulder and her other arm around Flora's waist for support.

"Why?"

"Because Uncle Thomas has sent two of his best people, Jamsey and Murdo, to take us back home."

"That's nice of him." Flora was immediately nervous. She had seen them from afar, when they'd picked up Isla, but had not talked to them.

"Don't worry," Mack said. "I'll be your voice if you need it. Let's go."

They made slow, painful progress down the corridor to the lift.

"Are you sure you don't want me to get a wheelchair?" Mack asked.

"No, I'll be okay."

They got inside the lift, and thankfully it was empty. Flora hated the close confined space of a lift with strangers. Mack turned to her and said, "You know I'm never going to let you go, don't you?"

Flora smiled. "That would make me happy."

"Will you live with me? I mean, can we live together?"

"I'd love that." Flora felt so happy. She would never have to feel unsafe and alone again. "But where will we live? Yours, mine, or somewhere new?"

The lift stopped and someone got on. Mack rolled her eyes, but after one stop they left.

Mack put her hands on Flora's hips. "I was thinking yours and mine."

Flora was lost. "What do you mean?"

Mack pulled a set of keys from her pocket. "I'm your new neighbour."

"The upstairs flat?" Flora said excitedly.

"Aye, I thought we could put the flats back together into the house it was years ago."

Flora forgot about her rib pain and made a move to hug Mack. "Oww, that's sore."

Instead Mack put her arms around her and gently kissed her. "I'm going to do everything to make sure you have a happy life."

The lift opened, and Mack helped her out. But Flora felt she had to say one thing. "Wait a minute before we go outside."

"What?"

Flora was nervous to say this. She rubbed her nose and tapped her chest discreetly.

"You know that with the new medication for my OCD and my therapy with Dr. Carrson my symptoms will become easier to manage, but I'll always be autistic and have anxiety issues. I won't just get better."

"I know that. Why would you even say that?"

"I—I wanted you to be clear before your tied yourself down to me," Flora said.

"I won't be tied down to you—we'll be tied together, hopefully for the rest of time. I love everything about you, wee mouse. Everything. Okay?"

Flora smiled. "Okay. I just had to say it."

"Before we go, I wanted to give you this." Mack took out Flora's heart-shaped locket.

"You found it?"

"I found it and had it repaired. I'll put it on, and we can get going."

Mack led her out front, and the blacked-out car was waiting for them. Jamsey and Murdo got out and stood by the car with big smiles on their faces. There were a few steps to go down, and Murdo hurried forward to take Flora's other arm.

"Take your time, Ms. Buchanan."

Jamsey had the back door open when they got to the car. Mack handed Jamsey Flora's bag, and before she got in, they both asked to shake her hand.

"Thanks for saving Isla," Murdo said.

Then Jamsey said, "You are a hero."

Flora didn't know how to react to that. She looked at Mack, who said, "She is. Thanks, boys."

"Yes, thank you," Flora managed to say.

Mack helped her into the back seat, kissed her, and then said with a smile, "You're my hero too."

❖

They pulled through the gates of the Sharkey property, and her mum's and her aunt's houses were both covered in balloons and *Welcome to the Family* banners at the front.

"What's that for?" Flora asked.

"For you. Who else?" Mack smiled.

Then right on cue, Uncle Thomas, Aunt Chrissy, her mum, and Isla with Dexter up in her arms came out to welcome them.

"Wow."

"I know this might be a lot for you, especially today of all days, but they just want to show how much they love and appreciate you."

"It's okay. I appreciate it. I have a family now," Flora said, "My guardian angel rescued me and gave me life and hope. Thank you, Mack, I love you."

"I love you, wee mouse."

## Epilogue

Flora walked arm in arm with Mack through Glasgow's arty west end. She still had pain in her ribs but was getting much better.

"Do you think Dexter is okay?" Mack asked.

"For the twentieth time, yes, he'll be fine." Isy had gotten her dream Christmas present from her mum, a fully trained service dog for anxiety and PTSD. Daisy the labradoodle was making Isy's life calmer.

At first Dexter wasn't too sure of another dog, but he soon found out he had a great playmate. But Mack was nervous because this was the first time leaving the two dogs alone without her there.

They arrived at their destination, an upmarket tattoo parlour where Mack and the other Sharkeys had gotten work done. Mack opened the door and held it open.

"Are you sure you want to do this?" Mack asked.

"As sure as I've ever been about anything."

Mack kissed her cheek and walked in. Mack spoke first, being Flora's voice. "Ms. Buchanan has an appointment in ten minutes."

"Okay, that's fine. Can you show me what you are wanting today?"

Mack pulled up her sleeve and said, "She wants this."

"A shark's tooth, yes."

Flora looked up at Mac and smiled. "Yes. I'm a Sharkey now."

❖

"Ah, that nips."

"I told you it would for a bit. You still think you did the right thing?" Mack held her arm and carefully kissed her way up to the tattoo site. It was wrapped in a bandage with cling film over the top to protect it.

"I would do it every day if I needed to. It means the world to me. I'm part of the Sharkeys now."

"You are, and you're never getting rid of us."

They lay in bed, in their newly decorated bedroom. While Flora recovered at Mack's mum's house, Nikki's building contractors set about making the upstairs flat part of Flora's home and redecorated. It was Nikki's gift to both Mack and Flora.

In the meantime, Flora was looked after hand and foot by Mack's mum and auntie. They loved fussing around her, not just because of what she had done, but because they couldn't have imagined a more perfect woman for Mack to bring in to the family.

They didn't push her for conversation or anything like that. It was all taken at Flora's pace.

Another thing that was taken at Flora's pace was this, intimacy. They hadn't made love since before the attack, and Mack was being as careful as she could with her partner.

But Flora had taken her by surprise. After coming home from getting her Sharkey tattoo, she jumped on her, literally, just after they got through the door. Mack carried her upstairs to their new bedroom, and it was as they undressed each other that Flora felt the pain of her freshly inked tattoo.

Mack pulled her into her arms as they lay in bed. "Are you sure this is the right thing to do? Your arm is going to hurt."

Flora's face fell. "Do you think it's a bad idea? Do you not want me?"

"Did I say that?" Mack said.

This was one of the facets of Flora's mind that Mack was learning about. She didn't always get the intention behind how or why Mack had said something.

"I just don't want you to think you have to do this for me."

“For you? No way.” Flora giggled.

This was another new thing Mack had to get used to. Conversations could go from sadness and misunderstanding to laughter in seconds. It kept Mack on her toes.

Flora rolled on top of Mack and kissed her. “I’d only started to explore this, sex with you, before I was injured. I’d waited a long time to have this kind of relationship, and then in you walked, my dream butch.”

Flora saw the edges of Mack’s mouth rise up into a smile. It was lovely to see.

“As much as I love your mum and Auntie Chrissy, all I could think about while I was recovering was touching you again.”

Mack had a full-on grin now, and she didn’t hold back any more. Flora groaned as Mack grasped her breasts. Flora leaned over and placed small kisses on Mack’s lips and face.

“I don’t know why, but after I got the tattoo, I just had this huge burst of energy, and I wanted to kiss and touch you everywhere.” Flora whispered in her ear, “Let me.”

She kissed her way down Mack’s body until she got to her sex. She could tell Mack was so ready for this, and as soon as her tongue hit her clit, Mack tensed and thrust her head back.

When Flora began to suck her, Mack grasped her hair and said, “Fuck, I missed this so much with you.”

Flora was turned on all the more by Mack’s reaction and undulated her hips, but frustratingly there was nothing to give her relief. She stopped sucking and teasingly ran her tongue around Mack’s clit.

She heard Mack give a deep moan and allowed herself to look up for a second. Mack had her arm thrown across her face, and then she felt the other hand grasp her hair. “Don’t slow down. Faster, darlin’.”

Flora resumed her attentions and felt Mack’s grip on her hair get tighter as she thrust her hips against Flora’s mouth and tongue. A few seconds later, Mack went stiff and gave a long groan as her hips thrust in orgasm.

"Fuck," Mack shouted.

Flora heard Mack try to get her breathing to slow down, while Flora climbed back up to Mack.

Mack pulled her into a deep kiss, then breathed heavily as she said, "I love you, Flo."

"I love you."

Mack brushed Flora's hair from her eyes. "This is what you've been thinking about while you've been getting better at Mum's?"

Flora smiled. "This and so much more that I want to explore with you."

Mack dragged her hand down teasingly between Flora's breasts. "You've got so much more to explore." Mack pulled up her knees, so that Flora could lean back against her legs. She touched her between her legs and felt how ready Flora was. "You're so wet."

When Mack slipped her fingers inside Flora, Flora grasped her own breasts and squeezed. "That's it, squeeze them."

The feeling inside Flora was growing by the second, and every time she rocked her hips, she got closer to the need that had been growing and growing since her recovery. Her breathing became heavier and heavier, and her hips started to shake. The feeling was too big, but she couldn't turn back. "Love you, love you."

Flora cried as her orgasm exploded inside her. She tensed and fell forward onto Mack.

Mack stroked her hair until she could control herself again.

Flora rose up on her elbows and said, "Thank you for coming into my life. I love you."

"It was fate, darlin'. You were always meant to be a Sharkey." Mack pointed to her tattoo, then kissed her.

Life wouldn't always be easy for them. Flora knew she would have ups and downs, but one thing was for certain—she would get through those low times with Mack's love and because Flora was now a Sharkey.

## About the Author

Jenny Frame is from the small town of Motherwell in Scotland, where she lives with her partner, Lou, and their well-loved and very spoiled dog.

She has a diverse range of qualifications, including a BA in public management and a diploma in acting and performance. Nowadays, she likes to put her creative energies into writing rather than treading the boards.

When not writing or reading, Jenny loves cheering on her local football team, cooking, and spending time with her family.

Jenny can be contacted at www.jennyframe.com.

# Books Available From Bold Strokes Books

**A Convenient Arrangement** by Aurora Rey and Jaime Clevenger. Cuffing season has come for lesbians, and for Jess Archer and Cody Dawson, their convenient arrangement becomes anything but. (978-1-63555-818-0)

**An Alaskan Wedding** by Nance Sparks. The last thing either Andrea or Riley expects is to bump into the one who broke her heart fifteen years ago, but when they meet at the welcome party, their feelings come rushing back. (978-1-63679-053-4)

**Beulah Lodge** by Cathy Dunnell. It's 1874, and newly betrothed Ruth Mallowes is set on marriage and life as a missionary…until she falls in love with the housemaid at Beulah Lodge. (978-1-63679-007-7)

**Gia's Gems** by Toni Logan. When Lindsey Speyer discovers that popular travel columnist Gia Williams is a complete fake and threatens to expose her, blackmail has never been so sexy. (978-1-63555-917-0)

**Holiday Wishes & Mistletoe Kisses** by M. Ullrich. Four holidays, four couples, four chances to make their wishes come true. (978-1-63555-760-2)

**Love By Proxy** by Dena Blake. Tess has a secret crush on her best friend, Sophie, so the last thing she wants is to help Sophie fall in love with someone else, but how can she stand in the way of her happiness? (978-1-63555-973-6)

**Marry Me** by Melissa Brayden. Allison Hale attempts to plan the wedding of the century to a man who could save her family's business, if only she wasn't falling for her wedding planner, Megan Kinkaid. (978-1-63555-932-3)

**Pathway to Love** by Radclyffe. Courtney Valentine is looking for a woman exactly like Ben—smart, sexy, and not in the market for anything serious. All she has to do is convince Ben that sex-without-strings is the perfect pathway to pleasure. (978-1-63679-110-4)

**Sweet Surprise** by Jenny Frame. Flora and Mac never thought they'd ever see each other again, but when Mac opens up her barber shop right next to Flora's sweet shop, their connection comes roaring back. (978-1-63679-001-5)

**The Edge of Yesterday** by CJ Birch. Easton Gray is sent from the future to save humanity from technological disaster. When she's forced to target the woman she's falling in love with, can Easton do what's needed to save humanity? (978-1-63679-025-1)

**The Scout and the Scoundrel** by Barbara Ann Wright. With unexpected danger surrounding them, Zara and Roni are stuck between duty and survival, with little room for exploring their feelings, especially love. (978-1-63555-978-1)

**Can't Leave Love** by Kimberly Cooper Griffin. Sophia and Pru have no intention of falling in love, but sometimes love happens when and where you least expect it. (978-1-636790041-1)

**Free Fall at Angel Creek** by Julie Tizard. Detective Dee Rawlings and aircraft accident investigator Dr. River Dawson use conflicting methods to find answers when a plane goes missing, while overcoming surprising threats and discovering an unlikely chance at love. (978-1-63555-884-5)

**Love's Compromise** by Cass Sellars. For Piper Holthaus and Brook Myers, will professional dreams and past baggage stop two hearts from realizing they are meant for each other? (978-1-63555-942-2)

**Not All a Dream** by Sophia Kell Hagin. Hester has lost the woman she loved, and the world has descended into relentless dark and cold. But giving up will have to wait when she stumbles upon people who help her survive. (978-1-63679-067-1)

**The Secrets of Willowra** by Kadyan. A family saga of three women, their homestead called Willowra in the Australian outback, and the secrets that link them all. (978-1-63679-064-0)

**Turbulent Waves** by Ali Vali. Kai Merlin and Vivien Palmer plan their future together as hostile forces make their own plans to destroy what they have, as well as all those they love. (978-1-63679-011-4)